TH3 BRAV5

TH3 BRAV5

JAMES BIRD

SQUARE
FISH

Feiwel and Friends

New York

SQUARE
FISH

An imprint of Macmillan Publishing Group, LLC
120 Broadway, New York, NY 10271
mackids.com

Our books may be purchased in bulk for promotional, educational, or business use. Please contact your local bookseller or the Macmillan Corporate and Premium Sales Department at (800) 221-7945 ext. 5442 or by email at MacmillanSpecialMarkets@macmillan.com.

Library of Congress Control Number: 2019948848

Originally published in the United States by Feiwel and Friends
First Square Fish edition, 2022
Book designed by Mallory Grigg
Square Fish logo designed by Filomena Tuosto

ISBN 978-1-250-79174-0 (paperback)

P1

AR: 4.2 / LEXILE: 620L

This book is for the four chambers of my heart . . .

First chamber: My son, Wolf, who is the bravest person I know. I love you.

Second chamber: Adriana Mather, who gave me her heart when I gave her mine. I love you.

Third chamber: Mama, who gave me my heart and taught me how to use it. I love you.

And lastly, the fourth chamber of my heart is reserved for whoever my son one day falls in love with. I gave him his heart and he gave it to you. I love you.

BRAVE

/brāv/
a. (noun) a Native American warrior
b. (adjective) ready to face and endure
danger or pain; showing courage

CHAPTER ONE

-《◆》-《◆》-

CATERPILLAR

"How's your nose, Collin?" Principal Harris asks from under his thick tobacco-stained mustache.

"Eighteen," I say, and wipe the small stream of blood escaping out of my right nostril.

Principal Harris and my dad, who sits beside me, both stare at me like I'm a stain that won't come out of an expensive carpet.

"Can you not do that right now?" Principal Harris asks, with irritation aimed at me.

Again, each letter invades my skull, separating itself into a countable sequence. First, they appear as puffy white clouds, but then morph into smoky white numbers, similar to those planes you see in the sky that leave messages for people: "50% off sale!" or "Will You Marry Me?"

But mine aren't cute. My letters are stubborn and invasive. And I can't ignore them. They are in my head, pressing hard against the backs of my eyes until I give in and give them my attention.

"Twenty-three. And like I've told you a million times before, I'm not trying to do it, it just happens."

Principal Harris shifts his eyes toward my father. "Oh, I see. It just happens, huh? Well, maybe it does, but you know what doesn't just happen? Fighting. In my school. So, tell me why you decided to fight," he says, like a lawyer trying to convince a judge that I'm guilty of something. Anything. Everything.

I watch his letters crawl into numbers at the same drawn-out pace in which he speaks. As much as I don't like him, his letters are slow and easy to count, which is sometimes refreshing. Most people's letters move fast like bees, stinging my mind until I release them, but this guy's letters slink across my brain like a caterpillar.

"One hundred and thirteen. I didn't decide to fight. He and all his friends were doing what they always do to me at lunch," I say, hoping I don't have to explain further and reveal to my dad what a wuss I usually am at school.

"Which is what?" my dad asks.

Great. I lost a fight, and now I'm going to have to inform my dad that I'm the kid who gets picked on every day. How much of a disappointment can one son be?

"Eleven. Tease me. Get right in my face and talk. All at once. And they never shut up," I say.

"Collin. You can't start a fight with people just because they want to talk to you," Principal Harris says, even though he very well knows that no one wanted to simply chat with me. They wanted to say as many big words to me for as long as they could and laugh at me as I struggled to count them. It's a sick and twisted game the other students play on me on a daily basis.

His words bounce around inside my head. From ear to ear, behind my face, ricocheting off the back of my head, finally turning into numbers as they reach the exit: my mouth.

"Sixty-four. It wasn't my fault. I didn't start it. This happens every day, and no one blinks an eye. The one time I stand up and fight back, I'm the one that gets in trouble? That's bullcrap!" I say.

"Language!" he snaps back at me, and through my peripheral I see my dad bury his face into his hands. Looks like I haven't reached the bottom of disappointing him just yet. I'm still digging.

"Eight. Sorry. I didn't want to fight. Obviously. Look at my face," I say.

Principal Harris leans back in his leather chair, like a king on his throne about to deliver my punishment. But he doesn't look like royalty at all. He resembles Mr. Potato Head. That's why he's referred to as Mr. Potato-Harris by most of the students, and even some teachers. "Witnesses said that it was you who threw the first punch. Is that not true?"

"Fifty-nine. He spilled my lunch all over me," I say as I show him my stained shirt.

My dad glances at my shirt. But it's not a look of support. It's more disappointment. I not only lost a fight, but I also managed to ruin my clothing. At least blood hides better in black fabric.

"How did he do that?" Harris asks.

"Fourteen. Like I said, I was minding my own business, just drawing. When they started talking over each other, reciting a bunch of tongue twisters to watch me struggle counting, I tried to leave, but he shoved my food tray into my chest and tripped me. I got up and hit him. He hit me back. I hit the ground. That's what happened," I say.

"He said that was an accident," Principal Harris says.

"Twenty-three. And you believe him?"

"I do."

"Three. Then you're an idiot," I say before thinking.

"That's it. Cover them up! Now!" orders my dad.

"Twenty-one. Fine," I say, and pull the gray fuzzy earmuffs up from my neck and place them over my ears. One positive thing about having no friends is I have a lot of time to experiment with gadgets in my room. Like these earmuffs. To this day, the only time I have ever seen my dad truly impressed with me was last year when I showed him how I connected my headphones to my earmuffs. I can listen to music as people talk. For someone with my condition, this invention of mine is a lifesaver.

Why? Because for some unexplainable reason, I can listen to music all day long and not even count one lyric. It's my heaven. My number-free heaven. Naturally, I'm obsessed with all kinds of music. But my favorite is rap. Hands down. I think it's because there are so many words, spoken so quickly. An army of words that invade my head but never attack. So I guess they're not an army at all, more like a parade. How many are there? I don't know. I don't count them— and I love it.

I take a deep breath and try to make my last words as clear as possible. "Believe me, if I could just turn it off like a light switch, I would have done it years ago."

My dad clears his throat, so I trace the cord down to my phone, which is in my pocket, and hit PLAY. A song begins. Normally, this is where my dad tells me that bullies only pick on weak people, and if I don't want to get bullied, then I shouldn't be so weak. Of course, that wouldn't make sense this time, since I finally fought back. But with these things over my ears, I hear lyrics and music, not grown-up words saying how much of a problem I am.

I just watch Principal Harris and my dad smack their lips back and forth like old friends. In fact, they are. They played football together in high school. I wonder if Harris ever teases my dad for having such a wimpy kid. His son is an athlete. His son doesn't sit alone at recess under a tree and draw pictures. And even better than that, his son doesn't count the letters of whoever speaks to him. Nope. Unlike me, his son is normal.

About five minutes later, my dad taps my leg and signals me to remove my earmuffs. Great. More talking. More counting. Can't we just go home now? I press STOP, ending the song, and remove them, give these men my best attempt at a smile.

"Collin . . . what I think Mr. Harris is trying to say is, we think your condition might be too difficult for other students to adapt to."

I close my eyes and clench my jaw. I'm counting and trying with everything I have to not relay the total. But the cloud won't dissipate until I release it. It will linger inside me forever, driving me crazy. I hate this.

"One hundred and three," I say.

Principal Harris sighs in frustration.

"Difficult for everyone else? Seriously?" I ask my dad.

Principal Harris sets his elbows on his desk and leans forward. "It's just not working out for you here, Collin. I suggested to your father that homeschooling could be beneficial for someone like you."

That was a mouthful. They watch me squint my eyes up toward the ceiling as I count the invisible letters like someone trying to count the stars during the day.

"One hundred and nine. Are you guys kicking me out of school?" I ask.

My dad puts his hand on my arm, which he never does, and shifts his position to face me. "He suggested homeschooling, which we simply can't do."

"Forty-three. So, what exactly are you saying?" I ask.

"I can't have you at home. We can't afford a teacher to come every day," he says.

"Fifty-two." So I ask again, "Well then, what are you saying?"

My dad goes silent, and Principal Harris delivers the death blow. "We think it's best if you transferred schools."

I should've seen this coming. This is a familiar road between schools and me. I show up, quickly become that "weird" kid, and before I have a chance to let the jokes settle with the dust, I'm hauled off to another campus and it all starts over. And over. And over. Forever being the freak.

But this time feels different. This time my mind's legs are too tired of running. I'm exhausted. Maybe that's why today was the first time I actually stood up for myself and fought back. Never mind the fact that I lost and got a bloody nose to show for it, but the point is I didn't curl up like a frightened caterpillar and wait for the bully bugs to stop picking on me. I didn't hide. I didn't run. Now that's exactly what my dad wants me to do: switch schools and run.

"Thirty-seven. What school, Dad? I've been to almost all of them by now. And how is it going to be any different? It's not like the counting is going to stop," I say.

My dad rubs his hand across his unshaved face. Not because he's thinking. It's to hide his shaking. When he doesn't drink for a few days, he shakes. Everyone knows he drinks, but he still comes up with these little tricks to hide the effects from everyone.

"I've been thinking about this for a long time and . . ." He stops talking and just presses his lips together. He doesn't know what to say, or worse, he does. He just doesn't quite know how to say it.

He's at thirty-nine letters right now, but I don't think he's done. I need him to end his sentence. The clouds are filling up my sky. *Come on, Dad! Blurt it out!*

"And what?" I impatiently ask.

"And I contacted your mother," he says.

Wait. *What?*

The clouds in my head burst into a million fluffy white question marks. I'm momentarily speechless. My mother? Who is she? It's a pretty strict rule in our house to never ask questions about her. Did he throw all of that away and track her down? What does that even mean? To me, mothers are just roles that actresses play on TV. They're movie stars. They're not real. They live off in some fantasy land with Santa, Bigfoot, and the tooth fairy.

Sure, I suppose some kids believe they're real; some even claim to have a mother, but having is not believing. Seeing is believing. And I haven't seen a mother near our house ever.

"Collin?" my dad asks.

And the numbers rush back into my skull full force.

"Thirty-nine. Twenty-three. Six."

Principal Harris hands my dad my most up-to-date report card. "Who knows, maybe this move will be good for him," he says, and my dad nods like he's heard that line before. Many times. Too many times.

"Thirty-seven," I say, under my breath.

"It's only October," my dad says. "School just started. It's the perfect time to hit the reset button." My dad slaps his thighs like our time is up.

"Sixty-seven. But . . . I don't know her," I say as I stand up and try to shake this foreign feeling off my body. "At all."

My dad stands, shoves his hand into my hair, and ruffles it into a messy bird's nest. I guess he wants to look like a caring dad in front of his buddy. He even fakes a smile. "Change is good, kid," Dad says.

He's lying. Change has never been good. Change hasn't changed anything for me. "Fifteen. I'll be in the car," I say, and walk out of the office.

I march down the hall and stop in front of the deep blue sea of lockers. The thought of punching a locker fills me, but there's been enough punching today. The last thing I need is a broken hand to match my bloody nose.

I bend down to my locker and twist it right. Seven. Then left. Twenty. Then right again. Eighteen. It clicks, and I swing it open. I pull out my backpack and slam my locker shut for the last time at this school. I put it on and tighten the straps to begin my final walk through these halls.

I put my earmuffs on again and hit PLAY. Eminem begins to spit into my ears. I bob my head as I head toward the parking lot. This is when I appear normal to the outside world. Just a kid listening to music.

As I turn the corner, a teacher passes me by and points to my ears, gesturing for me to remove my earmuffs, but I ignore him. I know headwear is prohibited for students at school, but I'm not a student here anymore.

CHAPTER TWO

- ‹‹◆›› · ‹‹◆›› -

A BOY'S BEST FRIEND

We're almost home, and my dad hasn't said one word to me. That's not too strange, though. We hardly ever talk. Sometimes we try, but neither of us has the patience it takes. And it's not only because he gets super annoyed by hearing me tally up his letters. It's mainly because we are so different from each other. He was an all-star athlete his entire life, but as he grew older and had a kid without planning to, reality kicked him in the head. He never married the head cheerleader. He never signed a multimillion-dollar deal to get drafted to the pros. He was never the smiling face on the box of cereal. He was just good enough to play in high school. A dreamer. That's all. But dreams don't pay the bills. And adults have to wake up and deal with things like that, or so I'm reminded every other day by him whenever I leave a light on or take a shower for too long. Reality is, he never made it.

But if you fail, you try again, so after he failed, he tried to reach stardom again, this time through me. His plan was to pass down his unfulfilled athletic dreams to his only son. So he enrolled me into as many junior football leagues as possible. I was supposed to be his shining star athlete. But sadly for him, I never quite caught on to sports. I tried to, for my dad, but I was awful. After football, we tried baseball, then basketball. He even signed me up for soccer once, but no matter the sport, I was like a fish out of water. He was forced to watch his dreams shatter all over again.

There's another reason we don't talk much. My dad drinks a lot. I guess that's what happens when you have to work a nine-to-five job you hate just to put food on the table for a son you don't necessarily like. And as hard as I tried to make him like me, it's pretty hard making an alcoholic happy.

Nowadays, our only quality time is when we watch a football game on TV together. It's a win-win for both of us. We don't have to say a word to each other. He's on the couch, rooting for his team, getting wasted . . . and I sit there smiling, just waiting for the game to end or for him to pass out. That's our relationship in a nutshell.

Still, deep down, I suppose we both love each other, even if we don't really know each other. Without him, I'd have nowhere to live and nothing to eat. And without me, he'd have no one to put a blanket over him when he's snoring on the couch. I guess that's love. Or at least, that's our version of it.

"It won't be so bad," he says, but keeps his eyes fixed to the road as he turns the old pickup truck onto our street.

"Thirteen . . . How would you know?" I ask.

"I'm being optimistic. Look at this as a fresh start. Somewhere new. You might even make some friends in Duluth."

"Eighty-seven!"

He glares at me.

"Where the hell is Duluth?" I ask.

"Minnesota. It's where your mother lives."

"Thirty-two. I have to move to Minnesota because people can't deal with me here? Am I that much of a problem? I'm being exiled from Huntington Beach? They're just numbers, Dad!"

"I know it looks that way to you, but that's not the whole story," he says as he pulls the pickup into our driveway.

"Forty-eight. It looks like the school wants me to stay home, but you don't want me there either. So you're shipping me off to live with someone I don't even know."

"She's your mother," he repeats.

"Fourteen. But I don't know anything about her. You refuse to even mention her, and now you want me to *live* with her?"

He stops the truck inches before colliding with our garage door and puts the gear in park. I reach for the handle, but my dad grabs my arm. He never touches me. This is twice in one day. This is serious. "I lost my job, kiddo."

"Fifteen. What? I mean how?" I ask. "When? Why?"

"A month and a half ago."

"Seventeen. But you've been getting dressed and . . . Where have you been going every day?"

"You have enough problems to deal with. I didn't want to pile more onto your plate. And I've been searching for something new, but things aren't looking so good . . . I'm selling the house. Like I said, a fresh start wouldn't be so bad."

I hold the young numbers in my head and try to kill them before they bloom. I know they won't die, but I promised myself I would never stop trying.

"One hundred and seventy-six."

"That many, huh?" he asks.

"Eleven. Yeah. That many. You know I'm not going anywhere without Seven, right?"

"Don't worry. Your dog's going with you," he says, knowing it would be a deal-breaker if she weren't.

"Twenty-nine."

I'm not sure what else to say, so I pull my arm away from him and get out of the truck. I head toward the side of our house and pull the string that unlatches the wooden door on the fence. As soon as it swings open, the only soul who loves me as I am jumps up and nearly knocks me off my feet.

"Hey, Seven!" I shout, and run deeper into the backyard.

She gives chase. One of my many childhood doctors suggested to my dad that I needed a companion who would never judge me. So he bought me a black Labrador puppy. Apparently, animals are far more understanding than we humans are.

Her real name is Numbers. I gave her that name so that word would no longer have a negative effect on me, but every time my dad called for Numbers, I would blurt out "Seven," for obvious reasons. So now she answers to both names.

Seven and I do everything together. We are inseparable. I would die for her, and she would die for me. She's not only my "therapeutic companion," or my pet, or even my best friend. She is my solid. She is the only solid in my ever-changing life right now.

I pick up one of her slobbered-on tennis balls and toss it across the yard.

"Good girl!" I shout as she chases it down.

She returns and drops the ball at my feet. So I pick it up again and hold it above my head. She barks and bobbles her head, waiting for me to launch it into the air. I wish I got this excited about something.

For selfish reasons, I hold the ball longer than I should. I don't count the letters in each of her barks. I like to think even if I somehow could count them, I wouldn't. I'm just a normal boy with a normal dog doing normal things whenever she's around.

But . . . all that changed today. I wish my life were more like hers. She sees something, and she goes and gets it. She keeps it simple. I don't judge her by how fast she runs or by the way she picks it up. As long as she's happy, I'm happy. So why do people care about what I do after they talk? I count. So what?

I throw the ball again and focus on the distance it travels. I'll be traveling a huge distance soon. But unlike the tennis ball, I won't be coming back.

Duluth, Minnesota . . . It sounds like a whole new planet. California is my earth. It's the only world I've ever known. I need to find out about this new place I'm about to live in. All I know about Minnesota is what everyone knows about it: that it gets really cold there. So cold that when it rains, the water actually freezes on the way down.

I've never actually seen snow before. I mean, I've seen it plenty of times in movies, but everybody knows that movies make everything ten times bigger and more exciting than they actually are. Maybe snow is boring. Still, I'll need a warmer jacket for Duluth. And besides the town, you know what else I need to find out about? My mom.

Is she nice? For as long as I can remember, my dad refused to speak about her. He said, "Let the past be the past." It's kind of his mantra for everything in life. All I was able to get out of him was that my mom was a twenty-five-year-old Native American girl he met at a rock concert thirteen years ago. And after he knocked her up and I was born, his parents agreed to raise me. He told me it was because my mom already had enough on her plate. This made me feel wary around every plate of food growing up. Like the side of mashed potatoes was more important than me.

That would make her thirty-eight now. As much as I hate numbers, this condition does make me rather good at math. At the time they met, my dad was twenty-six. Which makes him thirty-nine, although he looks much older. Maybe it's the stress of having me for a son, but his face looks like he's pushing fifty. Or maybe it's the drinking. His nose is constantly red, and his cheeks are always swollen. Once, a few years back when he was asleep on the couch, I took a marker and tried to blend in the rest of his face, making every inch of him red. He didn't notice until the next morning. I was not allowed to draw for two weeks after that . . . And it took a whole month for him to give me my red marker back.

Not all his nights of drinking were bad, though. One time, he actually let a few details about my mom slip out. He mentioned that my mom was very pretty and very funny, but back then, their worlds were just too different to merge their hearts together. My dad came from a wealthy family. They weren't too pleased to hear about their only son getting mixed up with a girl from the other side of the tracks. They nearly cut him off financially when they found out he got her pregnant. But their tune changed when they found out the baby was going to be a boy. I was the only way to keep their last name alive. So they made my dad a deal he couldn't refuse. He was to have a son and bring him back to California so they could raise me, completely shutting out my mom's side. They argued that he was too young to be a father and that she was way too poor to raise a child. They told her they could give me a better life. A life full of opportunities and promise. I guess my mom agreed, because that's exactly what happened. Little did they know I'd come with so much baggage. And that's pretty much all I got out of him that night before he passed out.

But when I asked him about it the next day, he didn't know what I was talking about and refused to admit saying all of that. Truth is, I don't think they were in love. And if love didn't make me, how could either of them actually love me? My dad kept me so he could keep his parents happy, and my mom, well, I don't know why she gave me up. I guess I'll find out soon enough.

My grandparents kept their word about raising me for the first six years of my life, but after a dozen failed attempts by a bunch of speech therapists and doctors, they handed me back to my dad and told him it was high time he grew up and faced reality. They thought raising a kid might steer him away from the bottle. They were wrong. I think they just wanted to retire, far away from the responsibility of a kid like me and an adult like my dad. So they moved to the Florida coast. I haven't stayed in contact with them too much beyond post-cards sent on my birthday and Christmas.

I can't believe my dad tracked down my mother just to hand me off. I'm like a hot potato: No one keeps me for too long. I wonder how he asked her to take me? Did he beg? I bet she regrets answering the phone. Did he even tell her about my counting problem?

Seven barks, reminding me to live in the moment. She's right. She's always right. I wrestle the ball out of her mouth and throw it again.

"Collin!" my dad shouts from the sliding glass door at the side of our house.

"Six. What?"

"Come inside. We need to . . . go over the plan."

Before I can respond, he shuts the door, so he doesn't hear how many letters were in his last sentence. This is a technique he adopted early on. I guess it makes him feel a little better. Out of sight, out of mind.

"Thirty-one," I say anyway.

CHAPTER THREE

-《◆》-·《◆》-

THE PROMISE

Dear Reader,

I know we haven't personally met, but hopefully one day we will. Believe it or not, I love meeting new people now. After you read the rest of this story, you'll understand why. But before you read on, I want to thank you for getting here. Most people would have left me by now. In fact, the time you've spent with me thus far would've been one of my longer friendships . . . well, besides with Seven, of course.

The truth is, I know how annoying this counting thing of mine is. And if I could turn it off for you, I would. But at this point in the story, you're just going to have to bear with me a little bit longer.

I know, I know, you're only two chapters in and want to tear your hair out and tell me to SHUT UP, right? I get it. Don't feel bad; it happens to everyone I speak to. But before you throw this book across the room, I would like to make you a deal.

Here it is . . . From this page on, I will give you the numbers in new situations. But for people we've already met and spoken to, I will mostly keep the numbers in my head except . . . when I can't. This way, you don't have to be as annoyed as whoever I am talking to. How does that sound?

But every deal has two sides. I just told you my part of the deal. Now you've got to live up to your end. If I do this for you, you have to also make me a promise. You must promise to do what I ask you to do when you reach the very last page of this book. Do we have a deal?

All right, I'll let you get back to reading now. Thanks again for taking the time to hear my story. I hope you enjoy reading it as much as I enjoyed telling it. And who knows, maybe one day I'll be lucky enough to know your story.

Your friend,
Collin

PS. There are 1,250 letters in the body of this letter, just in case you're curious.

CHAPTER FOUR

-《◆》-·《◆》-

MY LAST NIGHT
ON EARTH

Even for us, I'd hardly call that a conversation. He did all the talking—three thousand four hundred and seventeen letters total, to be exact. I sat there and listened as the numbers piled up in my head. After all, how could I respond? I have no say in the matter. The arrangements have been made, apparently before I even knew this was happening. Seven and I will leave tomorrow morning.

I fit all my drawings into a small box and tape it shut. As I do, my stomach drops. This feels like I'm packing away me. My drawings are my life. I've spent so much time alone that my drawings have become my closest friends. I first learned to draw as an exercise to deal with my counting condition. It was intended to pull all my focus into one area and allow my brain to slowly relax as my fingers did the work. It's like how some people doodle when they want to relieve stress. And if my counting problem was somehow stress related, then drawing should help. Well, it did nothing for my numbers, but I did fall in love with making something with my own hands, all while being silent. So I kept drawing. Most of my drawings are of silent things. Like trees, flowers, buildings, rocks, and the moon. I guess I like them because they are able to be themselves in complete silence. I wish I could be silent after someone talks to me.

My walls look so naked with only the marks from tacks left. Just a hundred tiny black stars in a four-cornered white sky staring back at me. It looks like the opposite of outer space. I'm like an astronaut leaving my only home planet to discover some distant nine-lettered world called Minnesota.

I open my closet and stuff all my clothes into my black suitcase. Anyone seeing all the black clothes that I own might assume I attend many funerals. But out of all the colors there are, black speaks to me the most . . . by not speaking to me at all. Black fabric feels like outer space. And outer space, even though I've never been, feels quiet to me. All the other colors are so loud. So I started wearing black all the time, and it was the best decision I've ever made because hardly anyone in school walks up and starts a convo with the kid that wears all black. They pretty much stay as far away from me as possible. Which is good, because the last thing I want to do is let them talk just to see that look on their face when I start tallying up their letters. The downside of it is that it keeps me from making any friends. Which sucks, but even if I dressed in every color and made a million friends in one day, by nightfall they'd all be sick of my numbers, and I'd be right back where I started. Wearing black saves me from the pain of being ignored for who I am as opposed to for what I look like. Mostly.

I wonder if my mom will be shocked when she sees me. Most

people are. I look like a vampire and sound like a calculator. I bet it's pretty confusing for people.

I hope she doesn't do what my dad has done, which is insist on taking me shopping for a new wardrobe to snap me out of this gothic look. Sometimes an oversized football jersey of his favorite team finds its way into our shopping cart. To avoid a fight, I appease him and allow a few to hang in my closet for a while, until eventually I dye them all black. Which causes an even bigger fight. But then again, he says my mom is poor, so I doubt we'll be shopping for a new wardrobe. Good.

I bet my dad even wishes Seven was another color. He can't stand seeing his black-haired boy, dressed in all black, playing with his black dog, and listening to what he calls "black music." But that's not his problem anymore. Now it's my mom's.

I walk up to my globe near my window and spin it. It revolves half a dozen times before I close my eyes and slam my finger down onto it. If I am meant to live in Minnesota, then it will be right under my finger. I open my eyes. It looks like I'm meant to live somewhere in the middle of the Indian Ocean. I turn it left half a day and place my finger on Minnesota. It looks like it's in between a bunch of lakes. I like lakes. They are fun to draw. And they're quiet. And usually surrounded by forests. Which are also really fun to draw. And also pretty quiet.

Maybe Minnesota won't be so bad? Or maybe my mom will get so tired of my mouth and send me off to wander into the forest armed with a notepad and markers, and I'll spend the rest of my days drawing every single tree there is before I die of starvation. Oh wait, it's super cold there, so maybe I'll die first from hypothermia. I'll need gloves if I'm going to draw in the cold. I wonder if my dad told her I draw? Didn't the Native Americans love drawing? I remember learning something about that in school. How they didn't write down their language or history. How they preferred to draw them, sing them, and tell their stories out loud. But maybe that was when they lived in teepees and hunted buffalo. They are probably like everyone else now. They go to a job they hate and eat TV dinners while watching football. If that's the case, I'll be fine in Minnesota . . . I have plenty of experience of that kinda life living with my dad . . . But if it's not, if they live differently, then I need to learn how to be a Native American.

One good thing did come out of the lopsided conversation with my dad, though. He said that when he told my mom about my condition, she blew it off like it was nothing. "Numbers never hurt anybody," she told him. I hope she remembers that.

I pat down my bed, and Seven excitedly flies up to me and nestles in for sleep. I take one last glance at the room I'll never see again before I turn off the light.

Night is my favorite part of the day. Total darkness meets total silence. This is when I lie in bed and imagine I'm normal. Where I can dream about a world without letters becoming numbers. In here, there's no one talking to me. There's no myriad of colors reminding me that I dress like a shadow. It's just me and my dog in the peace and quiet.

I close my eyes, but I don't count sheep. By this time, I'm too exhausted by counting. Instead I try to focus on Seven's heartbeat. I don't count the number of beats either. I just love having another heart next to mine. It's like music to me. And it's by far my favorite song. I play it on repeat every night. I know it by . . . well, heart.

She falls asleep much faster than I do, and within minutes, her heartbeat is drowned out by her loud snores . . . but I don't mind; I kind of like that song, too.

I listen to them compete with each other. But tonight, something is off. It doesn't quite sound right. Her heart is normal. Her snores are normal, but there's a third song playing.

It's a faint tapping. It's sporadic and desperate. I sit up. Seven doesn't notice it. She's probably off chasing a dream rabbit somewhere in an open field by now. But this third song is getting louder and more chaotic. I'll never be able to sleep to this music.

I reach over to my nightstand and turn on the light, but as soon as the light wraps around my room, the tapping stops. Was it my dad at the door? Did he change his mind? Has he realized he can't live without me?

"Dad?" I say, loud enough for him to hear, but he doesn't respond, because he's not there.

I turn off the light again and bury my head into my pillow. And as soon as my comfort sets in, the tapping returns. This time, I carefully get out of bed and walk through the dark toward the unidentified pitter-patter.

It's near my window. I push my curtains aside, letting the moonlight see me. The tapping stops again. And now I see why. Against the glass rests a butterfly. I don't remember ever seeing a butterfly at night, and definitely never in my room. I reach out and touch its yellow-framed brown wings, and as soon as my fingertip makes contact, it panics and tries to dig through the glass to escape.

"You trapped, butterfly?"

I open my window and guide the stranger out. It springs off the glass and lands on my hand. I don't know where a butterfly's eyes are exactly, but I can feel it looking at me.

I extend my hand out of my window and let the night air invite my little friend toward freedom. Its wings flutter, then it lifts off my skin and takes flight. It darts up and down like a surfer waiting to catch the perfect wave. And it finds one. A light breeze hits it, and the little butterfly rides the wind until it vanishes into the night.

I close my window and look over at Seven's face before I release the curtains. She's lit perfectly by the moon. So beautiful, like a sleeping wolf. I hope my mom has a backyard for her. I can't believe I forgot to ask my dad about that.

I crawl back into bed. If I wake up early enough tomorrow, maybe I'll do one last drawing before I leave . . . I've never drawn a butterfly before.

CHAPTER FIVE

- ‹‹◆›› · ‹‹◆›› ·

FLYING ON A SHEET OF PAPER

I sit somewhere between the wing and the back of the plane. Seat 26A, to be exact. And even though I'm kind of nervous, this being my first time in a plane, I'm happy I got a window seat. I mean, if we're going to crash, I want to at least see it coming. I want to see that mountain get closer. I don't want to be sitting there staring at some guy's bald head and then—*bam*—I'm extra crispy. I want to have time to draw it before we explode into a million pieces.

I guess Minnesota isn't a very popular place, because half of the plane is empty. I hope Seven is okay down below in the cargo area. But she's always been braver than me, so I bet she's already making friends with the other dogs. Even cats like her. It's weird.

We take off. I watch the land get smaller and smaller. What was once home is now a white clouded floor that looks thick enough to walk on. When you look up from the ground, the clouds are in the shapes of animals and pirate ships, but from up here, they're just an endless blank sheet of paper waiting for someone to draw on.

So that's what I do. I reach down and pull out my backpack.

Before I draw, I take notice of a few things. The plane doesn't sound quite how I imagined it would. I expected a cool whooshing sound as we barreled through the sky, but sadly, it's as smooth as a car, and it just sounds like we're inside an elevator: just a low buzz with the occasional hiccup.

It all happened so fast, but now that I have time to think about it, my dad looked kind of sad as he walked me through the airport. He even wore a button-down shirt for some reason, like this was an important event for him. And not one word about my all-black outfit. Maybe there's a part of him that will miss me. He didn't give me some important parting speech like they do in the movies. He just said, "Be good and be safe." To which I replied, "Fifteen."

A tall woman wearing a blue uniform approaches me. Her blond hair is pulled back, and her smile looks exactly like a billboard ad for a dentist. Her teeth are as white as the cloud sea we are flying on.

"Would you like a drink?" she asks.

"Eighteen," I say.

She laughs. "Let's just start with one, shall we?"

"Twenty-seven. Apple juice?"

Now she looks confused. Not knowing what to say, she pours me an apple juice and flashes me her smile again. I must look a bit nervous, because she kneels down and speaks in a whisper. I hope she doesn't have much to say.

"First time on a plane?" she asks.

"Seventeen. This is my seventeenth flight," I say, which makes her eyebrows lower.

Before she can respond, I speak. She looks too nice to interrupt someone, so as long as I keep talking, she won't be.

"I guess I am a bit nervous. How often do planes crash?" I ask.

She stands up and gives me a wink. "Just once," she says.

"Eight," I say, and laugh.

I like her. She's funny. She hands me a napkin for my apple juice. "Don't worry. This is my nine hundredth flight," she says and smiles.

"Thirty-six," I say, but she is already handing a tomato juice to the man behind me.

I down the apple juice in two huge gulps and pull out my notebook. I dig through the bottom of my bag to find a pencil. Got it. I lean back and flip through a few drawings and get to a fresh blank page. I stare at it and decide it's an already completed drawing. It's the sheet of cloud. It looks perfectly accurate, and I didn't even have to lift a finger to draw it. I flip to the next blank page.

I know exactly who to draw. The butterfly from last night. I put pencil to paper and begin. Once I have her wings fully outlined, I start to draw her body. But before the drawing is complete, a rather small brown-haired girl in a denim dress approaches me.

"A butterfly?" she asks.

"Ten. Yes."

"How did you know I was ten?"

"Twenty. A lucky guess."

"You're twenty?"

"Eleven."

"You're funny."

"Ten. You're funny too."

She laughs. Little kids are much better conversationalists for someone like me. They just laugh and get over it. Adults try to problem solve, which only creates a bigger problem. I hand her the drawing before she can say anything else.

"For me?

"Five. You like butterflies, don't you?"

"Yes. They're so pretty."

She takes the butterfly with a huge grin on her face.

"Thank you."

"Twenty-five. You're welcome. Make sure to color her wings brown and yellow."

Her mother swoops in and takes her daughter's hand.

"Sorry if she was bothering you."

"Twenty-five. She was no bother," I say.

Her mother tilts her head at my response but says nothing. She doesn't have to. I know that look all too well.

She escorts her daughter back to her seat. This reminds me to put on my earmuffs. No one will try to talk to me if I'm wearing those. I don't know why I gave her my drawing, but hopefully she'll hang it on her bedroom wall, and over time the butterfly will get to watch that little girl grow up and turn into a young woman.

I put on my earmuffs on, plug the cord into my phone, and hit PLAY. As a pop song begins, my eyes catch a fly buzzing by and landing on one of the seats. I lean closer to get a better look, but it sees my movement and takes off toward the front of the plane. If I was that fly, I'd go find a seat in first class. I'd be a fly that flies in style. Plus, the food looked way better than the crackers they give back here.

I wonder which state we are flying over? At thirty thousand feet in the air, it's hard to get a sense of the rest of America. This is my first time traveling, and to be honest, this feels more like sitting in a bus, near the window, parked at the top of a very tall building. I was hoping we'd be zigzagging through clouds as the captain would list off every city we flew over, but I guess he has better things to do, like fly a metal box carrying a hundred people through the air at hundreds of miles per hour.

I start drawing another animal. This time a stork. But this stork is in the shape of a plane. And this stork-plane is carrying a boy to Minnesota and is running twelve years behind schedule, to finally deliver him to his mother.

CHAPTER SIX

- ⟨⟨◆⟩⟩ - ⟨⟨◆⟩⟩ -

MINNESOTA GROWS YOU UP

I once heard that *it's not the destination that matters, but the journey getting there*, and I just slept through most of the journey. Shoot. Now we're here. Now I'm nervous.

How can it be that I am almost thirteen years old and about to see my mother for the first time? I wonder how much I look like her? The only thing I inherited from my dad was his pale skin and stubbornness. Once, when I was nine years old, he told me that I have my mother's cheekbones and her almond-shaped eyes. I never understood if he was saying that to be nice or to be mean. Comparing eye shape to a type of nut doesn't seem like a compliment, but I like almonds, so I'll take it.

Now I get to see for myself what a real Native American looks like, not just the ones you see on screen. I shake my head to wash out the stereotypes embedded in my mind from the countless Western flicks I watched growing up. My mother will not jump out from a bush armed with a tomahawk. She will not be covered in war paint with eagle feathers framing her head. She will not raise her hand to me and say, "How."

But I do have a question for her, and it isn't *how*. It's *why*. Why did you give me away so easily? In cartoons, Native Americans are always so tuned in to nature. Perhaps it's true, and the animals spoke to my mom and told her I'd be too much of a hassle to live with? Is it possible some messenger bird reported my condition to her? I know the Spartans threw away their defective babies, but did Native Americans, too?

I should have read more about my people. My people? My half people? I never had a people before. It's always just been Seven and me . . . and my dad passed out on the couch.

I step off the plane and instantly see the difference between California folk and Minnesotans. Everyone here is bundled up in scarves and coats like puffy birds. And to my surprise, there are even people walking around this airport with earmuffs. That's a plus. In California, I was the only person wearing earmuffs.

Wearing mine, I blend in with the people around me for the first time in my life. I know the Minnesotans are doing it to keep their ears warm, but I can't help imagining that perhaps I just landed onto a planet where everybody counts letters like I do.

What if this is where they send people like me?

I ask an airline attendant for directions to the gate where they release the animals. I can't wait to see Seven. I always feel better when she's by my side. Especially in new places, and this is the newest place I have ever been. This is my new life, and I need her with me more now than ever.

There's a small woman at the cargo gate handing over the pets to their owners. I watch her lift two cat carriers at once. Wow. She's stronger than she looks. When the cats' owner chats briefly with the cargo handler, I'm disappointed that I don't hear numbers, even though the cat lady has earmuffs hanging around her neck. I guess people here just wear them for the weather. Too bad.

I step forward and hand the airline woman the paper that joins Seven and me together. She accepts it and smiles. I pull down my earmuffs and smile back. Hopefully this will be the extent of our conversation . . . But instead . . .

"How was your flight?" she asks with an accent I can't quite place.

"Sixteen. It was good," I reply.

"Sixteen?"

"Seven. My dog's name is Seven. Wow, it's cold in here," I say, and put the earmuffs on, in hopes that she'll get the hint.

It works. She heads back behind the gate to find my girl. Even though I don't want to talk to this woman, she is very nice to look at. Her skin is much darker than mine, and her accent sounds like she came from somewhere far away, much farther than California. Her hair is covered in a floral fabric that wraps around her head, almost resembling an upside-down beehive.

I wonder if she had to take a plane to America, and maybe she loved the flight so much that she made sure to get a job that kept her close to planes. She looks happy. Way happier than my dad ever looked when he was working. He hated his jobs, and he had a lot of them. Maybe I'll tell him to apply at the airport. Maybe he could be as happy as this lady.

But there is one person who is happier than her right now. Me, because I can see Seven running toward me, dragging the small happy lady behind her. I squat down, and Seven barrels into my body, licking my entire face, knocking my earmuffs from my ears, bringing all the airport noise back to me. I'm not counting the licks, but the number is certainly high.

"You two have a nice day," the lady says as she hands me the leash.

I am close enough to read her name tag. SHIMAH. It's six letters.

"Eighteen. Thank you, Shimah," I say, and leave before she can respond.

Seven and I stand and wait for my suitcase at baggage claim. There are so many people here, but luckily for me, no one is talking. Everyone is either looking at their phones or eyeing the conveyer belt, searching for their stuff like it's a race to see who can get out of this airport the fastest.

After a few minutes, I pull my suitcase off the belt and head outside to the area where people get picked up.

I see boyfriends embracing girlfriends, wives embracing husbands, and parents scooping up their little traveling children. It's like one of those commercials on TV where everyone is paid to be overly happy. But I don't see anyone who could be my mother waiting to greet me.

I look at my watch and see that I'm right on time, to the exact minute.

It's much colder than what I'm used to. It kind of stings my nose, but I'm not sure if it's because of the temperature or the fact that I was punched the other day. Whatever the case, it hurts, so I lift up the collar of my shirt and cover my nose. I probably look like a bandit, but even bandits need to stay warm.

I wonder if Seven likes this new cold feeling. Her nose is much bigger than mine, so she must be feeling it more. But she looks excited as she sniffs the air. It smells much cleaner than in California. I guess I got so used to the smog that I started to believe all air is dirty, but the air here actually smells nice, like the first few seconds after a shower. It's crisp and fresh.

As the crowd dwindles, I see an empty bench and walk toward it. But on the way, Seven jolts me to a stop. I turn around to see what grabbed her attention.

Standing before me is the most beautiful woman I have ever seen. Is this my mom? Her skin is like what a fire would look like if it were perfectly still. It's the color of darkened flames, brown, orange, and red mixed together to make one color: fire-skin. I've seen many skin colors before, living in California, but never fire-skin.

And her long black hair is like the heavy smoke above the fire. It drapes down and crawls away from the sky as she walks toward me. I should probably say something, but I don't.

My dad was telling the truth when he said that her cheekbones look as if they were chiseled by an artist. But the most beautiful part about her is her eyes. They are every shade of brown, swirling around in circles. Speckled with tiny gold dots. I feel dizzy staring at them. But maybe that's because I'm so nervous. This woman gave birth to me. When you're born, the first way you greet your mom is with a loud cry, but what do you do twelve years later? I can't start wailing. That would be weird. So what do I say? What do I do?

My mouth is open; I can feel the chilly breeze hitting my tongue, but no words are coming out. I need to say something. But despite everything that has gone on for the last forty-eight hours, I failed to ask my dad one very important question . . . What is my mom's name? I can't believe I don't know it. That's horrible, but it's not all my fault. My dad did brush away every question I ever asked about her. Over time I gave up on asking.

"One thing you will enjoy about our family is we only speak when we have something to say," she says after she removes my earmuffs from my head, placing them around my neck.

Her words drift like boats from one end of my mind to the other. Oddly, I don't mind counting her letters. I'm sure I will later, but not right now.

"Seventy-one," I say.

She smiles. "That many?"

"Eight," I say.

Her voice is soft and soothing. The kind of voice that might make you smile for no reason. Which is probably why I'm smiling now. And she does have an accent, but not like one I've ever heard before. It's nothing like Shimah's or any of the Spanish accents I heard in school. It's more like she adds two spacebars after every word instead of one. They are more pronounced and meaningful. It's almost as if everyone else speaks in italics and she speaks in bold. She grabs the leash from my hand and kneels down to Seven.

"And you must be his best friend, which now makes you my best friend," she says, and cradles Seven's face in her fire-skin hands.

Seven's tail goes wild. My mother stands up and extends her hand to my cheek. By instinct, I back away. I'm not used to being touched, unless it was a fist from some jerk in school. But I instantly feel bad for dodging her attempt. I know she meant no harm. But now I'll feel stupid if I lean my face toward her. What do I do? Do I tell her to try again? Should I reach out and touch her face? Is this a Native American thing I don't know about? I hope I didn't insult her.

This is not a good start.

"Let's go home," she says.

"Ten," I say and follow her.

My mom leads Seven and me toward the parking lot. We enter the sea of cars, and like a bonehead, I can't help but be on the lookout for a horse. I know there won't be one, but a part of me wishes that this one stereotype was true. I mean, it would be so cool if we rode a horse to my new home.

She stops in front of an old, rusted red pickup truck.

"Here we are," she says.

"Nine," I respond.

That's one thing my parents have in common. They both drive pickups. I don't know if that connection warrants having a baby together, but here we are.

She opens the back and pats the side of the truck, sending puffs of dirt into the air. Seven hops up and sits.

"Were you expecting a horse?" she asks, smiling.

"Twenty-two. No," I lie.

Wow. Can my mom read minds? If so, all she'll see in my head is a bunch of numbers. I must be a boring subject for her.

"Toss your stuff in the back and sit up front with me."

"Forty-one. Can I ride in the back with Seven?" I ask.

"I don't bite. I promise," she says, showing her teeth behind her smile, and opens the passenger side door for me.

"Seventeen. It's just that I've never seen Minnesota before."

She shuts the door. "In that case, I'll go easy on the bumps," she says, and walks over to the driver's side and climbs into her red metal steed. "It's going to be cold, so hold on to that furry heater of yours."

I know I should sit up front and bombard her with the hundreds of questions I have for her, but the truth is, I don't want her to dislike me yet. I don't want her to second-guess her decision to take me in. Especially after leaving me twelve years ago.

I toss my luggage over the rail and climb into the bed of the truck. And after a few jolts, the old engine roars to life like a hungry lion. Music plays from the truck's radio. I can't hear it well enough yet to figure out what song it is, but I'm just happy that my mom likes music. Sounds simple, right? I mean, who doesn't like music? Well, my dad never listened to music, even though he met my mom at a rock concert. He listened to talk radio, obsessively.

As we turn, the breeze subsides, and the music takes the lead. It's country music. Now, I don't know much about country, but I haven't been impressed with what I have heard so far. But this move is all about second chances. So if I get one, then so does country music, and—to be honest—it doesn't sound half bad.

I lean back and watch the animal-shaped clouds above me come and go. It's beautiful. And the distant mountains look so close and so far away at the same time. Some of them look close enough to run to, and some look so far it would take a plane to get to. But the coolest things I take in are the trees. They line the road on both sides of us, pointing high up to the sky like they're all giving me a standing ovation. *Yes, I survived the flight and found my mama. Let's all celebrate.*

In Huntington Beach, you are lucky to see any trees that aren't palm trees. I have nothing against palm trees—in fact, I have drawn dozens of them—but it's nice to see trees with actual branches that are thick like elephant limbs and sprouting colorful leaves as green as grass, as brown as wood, and as orange as . . . an orange? So this is what fall looks like, huh? It's beautiful.

As the sun slowly dips into the earth, it lights up the tribal designs painted onto the bridges and overpasses as we drive beneath them. They resemble the logos that superheroes plaster on their costumes across their chests. They look like birds with jagged edges instead of feathers, kind of similar to those drawings we read about in school while studying Egypt and the pyramids. On the side of the highway, I see a small makeshift pop-up shop with a sign that reads AUTHENTIC NATIVE AMERICAN JEWELRY. If I were a tourist, I'd definitely stop in for a cool bracelet. But I'm no tourist. No, I'm a resident now.

I look into the truck's back window to see if my mom is wearing a bracelet, and she is. Hers is a thin red leather band wrapped around her wrist a few times. Maybe all Native Americans wear jewelry. Kind of like how lots of rappers wear gold chains and how my dad wears his favorite football jersey every Sunday. I wonder if she bought it at that stand? Maybe that's why she was late. If she got me one, I hope it's black.

Two hours later, we pass a sign that reads FOND DU LAC RESERVATION: 7 MILES with an arrowhead pointing left. As soon as we pass it, the truck veers left off the highway and continues down a long road that appears to run right through the middle of a forest.

Fond du Lac doesn't sound Native American at all. It sounds more like a French dessert. I thought Native American names were supposed to be how they are in movies, all about animals and thunder and start with things like "he who walks with" or "she who stands with," yadda yadda. But if learning French is something I have to do to be a Native American, then I'm screwed. My head is going to explode. And what is a Fond du Lac anyway?

We pass another sign that reads HOME OF THE OJIBWE. I wonder how that's pronounced. Are any of the letters silent? I freeze frame the word in my mind. Six letters. This is what I do every time I discover a new word. I must be able to count it if I ever hear it in a sentence. If I can't, my brain freaks out and sizzles, like when a pilot spills coffee on the flight control board. Okay, not really, but that's what it feels like.

My mother pulls back the sliding window behind her head.

"We're Ojibwe," she shouts to me without turning around.

Holy crap. My mom is a legit mind reader. Either that or she really grilled my dad for details about my counting issue. But it's more fun to believe in magic. I lean into the open window.

"Ten. It's pronounced O-jib-way?" I ask.

She nods and pulls the window shut again. That's the end of

our talk. That was perfect. A question asked, an answer with a nod, then boom we're done. If all people could be this easy to talk to, I'd actually have friends that stand on two legs. I lean back into Seven and pet her head.

I'm Ojibwe. That's so cool. Or at least I think it is. I know nothing about the Ojibwe people other than one is my mother and she drives a pickup truck. I remember in school reading how the Native Americans were fearless warriors that had many battles with the US government back in the day. But so many Westerns I've seen also showed me that the Native Americans are wrinkled-up old men who deliver a super-wise message just when our white American hero needs to hear it most. And if they weren't old and wise, they were portrayed as violent savages. Red-skinned villains who leaped out of bushes and attacked indiscriminately. I'm starting to think that Hollywood might have to travel to Minnesota and see my mom. She's beautiful, has a soothing voice, and she can read minds . . . She'd be an instant star. And she'd definitely make people see Native Americans differently, that's for sure.

The ride becomes uneven and rough as the paved road ends and a dirt road begins, so I pull Seven tightly into my arms. Together we watch the sun melt behind a snowcapped mountain. And just like that, day becomes night. And night is much darker here. Huntington Beach had light posts and headlights in all directions, but here, now, I can barely see Seven's face, which is just inches from mine. After a long stretch that seems like another hour, we pull into a pebbled driveway. It's too dark to make out the neighborhood, but from the truck's headlights, I can see that the house we are parking in front of is small and cream colored.

As soon as the engine stops, I grab my luggage and hop out of the truck. I don't see the ground I'm standing on. It's so dark it looks like I'm standing on the night sky. A black sheet. But not a smooth black cloud, one that feels like it's made of a million little rocks. The porch light flips on. I look over toward it and see a woman standing at the front door, staring at me. She looks like an older version of my mother.

"We are home," my mother says as she exits the truck and approaches me.

She slides her arm over my shoulder, which stills my body. I am not used to affection . . . at least not from a human. But this time, I let her touch me. And to be honest, it feels nice. Her arm is warm. It must be that fire-skin.

"Nine" exits my lips.

She pulls me in closer to her. Our bodies touch for the first time. She's so warm. Her ribs against mine. The feeling makes my heart beat faster.

"Breathe in the air. You need to fill your body with this place," she says.

"Forty-nine. Why?"

"So you two get to know each other."

"Twenty-six. That's weird."

"This place is very weird. You'll see," she says, and pats the side of the truck with her other hand, the way people pat their pets.

Seven hops out of the truck and rushes over to my mom. I've never seen Seven react this way to anyone besides me. Seven never really liked my dad. They just coexisted.

"Twenty-eight. She really likes you," I say to her, but I'm sure she can tell by the way Seven keeps licking her.

"Of course she does. I'm very likable," my mother says.

"Twenty-eight."

"Is she fixed?" she asks.

"Ten. She's not broken," I reply, which causes her to laugh.

"I mean, is she spayed? We have many strays around here that would fancy a good-looking gal like her."

"Seventy-eight. No. My dad was planning on taking her to the vet, but I guess he was always too busy," I say.

"Well, let me get a good look at him," the older woman shouts to my mother. "I need to make sure you picked up the right one."

Her voice is not as soft as my mother's. Hers is worn and raspy. But as someone who pays very close attention to words, I can tell that there is something special about her dialect that is unlike any way of speaking I have ever heard before. It's almost as if each word is its own sentence.

"Sixty-three," I say, loud enough for her to hear me.

I hope this doesn't turn into a conversation. I'm tired and hungry. The last thing I want to do right now is count.

"Sixty-three? You guessing my age now, kiddo? Not even close. Aim higher. Reach for the stars," she says while pointing up to the star-filled sky.

I count her letters. "Seventy-one," I say.

"Now you're making me sound like I'm old enough to be your grandmother," she says.

"You are his grandmother," my mom replies.

"Fifty-five," I say back to her. "And twenty to you," I say to my mom.

"Fine. Fifty-five it is," my grandmother says happily, like we just settled on her new age.

"Seventeen. You're my grandmother?" I ask her.

"I am. Three. I did that one for you," she says, and laughs at her own cleverness.

"Twenty-five. It doesn't work like that."

"Mother. Zip it," my mom says. "Let the boy taste before all this chewing."

My mom nudges me toward my grandmother. I approach her, and she immediately puts her hand on my face—just like my mom tried to do at the airport. This time I let it happen. The last thing I want to do is insult an old lady, but this face touching is all so new to me. Is it an Ojibwe thing, or do I come from a family of face touchers?

Up close, my grandmother wears more wrinkles than my mom but is just as beautiful. Her emerald-green dress flows to her feet. Her deep brown eyes move slowly across me, studying my face. I follow them from my forehead to my injured nose, my ears, my mouth, and finally my chin. She smiles. I guess she approves?

"You're our little red-blooded boy, all right," she says as her hand slips off my chin.

"Thirty-five. Isn't everyone red-blooded, technically?" I ask her.

"Maybe. But you're *our* red blood. That makes you special," she replies.

"Forty-three. I've been called <u>m</u>any things in my life, but never special."

She hugs me. It catches me off guard. And when she starts squeezing me, I immediately get embarrassed by the fact that my grandmother is much stronger than I am. She finally releases me and steps aside for me to enter the home.

"Gifts are wrapped so you don't see what's inside. You are special, you just have to tear away the wrapping paper to see what your gift is," she says as I pass her.

Her words roll in like a thick fog and begin to take shape. As I count the letters, I read them, and her words hit me even harder than her hug. Maybe I do have a gift and I just don't know what it is yet.

"One hundred and seven," I say, and enter my new home.

The scent of burning wood and ash fills my nose. I inhale deeply to take it all in. I remember this smell from the only time I ever went camping with my dad and his friends. He wanted to teach me how to be a man by showing me how to fish and start a fire and not get scared during campfire ghost stories. All three were disasters. I begged him to throw back every fish he caught. There was so much fear and pain in those beady little fish eyes that I couldn't bear being a part of their deaths.

Needless to say, I wasn't invited to go fishing with them the next day. And I guess someone like me takes all the fun and spookiness out of ghost stories when I recite numbers the entire time. I was looking forward to building a fire, but that was thwarted by the park ranger telling my dad that due to a heightened forest fire danger, campfires were prohibited. So really, camping was just me sitting under a tree and drawing all day while my dad and his friends did their thing. But I did like the smell of the fires they made anyway, when the forest ranger wasn't around.

The living room walls are decorated with all different kinds of art. Some are paintings, some are hanging fabrics, and others are drawings. As I scan the room, I notice all of the artwork is of animals. It immediately gives me a feeling of belonging. These are my people. I can actually be a productive addition to this house. I love drawing animals.

"There's always room for more, you know," my grandmother says, and hugs me again. It's almost overwhelming, all this affection. And I don't even know their names yet.

"Thirty. Thanks. I love to draw," I say.

"All red bloods do," she says, and points to the crackling fireplace. "Warm your bones."

"Twenty-seven," I say, and walk toward the fire.

At Dad's house in Huntington Beach, we didn't have a fireplace. We had a heater. We hardly even needed that. But this fire is real and alive and loud.

I sit down beside it and put my palms near the flames. The heat wraps around my hands like it is grabbing my skin. It moves up my arms and presses against my face. I close my eyes and listen to the flames crack like whips against the burning logs.

My mother speaks to my grandmother in a language I've never heard before. She and my grandmother go back and forth a bit, but I stay focused on the stream of heat flowing through my body. I didn't realize how cold I really was. I am actually thawing myself out like I was a bag of frozen vegetables.

I've read somewhere that there is always something positive to find in every situation. When it comes to my counting problem, there are not many positives; believe me, I've searched. But I did discover one. A loophole I found during one of my failed attempts at being an athlete. During soccer tryouts, a bunch of kids were speaking Spanish. And I guess since I didn't know what they were saying, my brain wasn't compelled to count. Of course, this led me to actually trying to play soccer. If I made the team, I'd be in a place where I could appear normal. But alas, when you suck, you suck. And I sucked.

As my mother and grandmother speak to each other, I wonder if they're talking about me. Maybe bringing me here was a huge mistake and they're fighting over which one of them has to drive me back to the airport.

"Are you hungry?" My mother breaks into English.

I open my eyes and see that she is on her knees beside me, warming her hands. Her skin is so close to the flames that they nearly touch. And the colors of the two are nearly identical. Fire-skin suits her perfectly.

"Twelve. I was, but I think I'm now too tired to eat," I say.

She rises from her knees and offers me her hand.

"Let's introduce you to your room, shall we?"

I love how she makes everything seem alive. Her truck, the cold

Minnesota air, our house, the fire, and now my room. Everything has a life.

"Thirty-three. Okay," I say, and take her hand.

I stand up and nearly trip over Seven, who is already warm and passed out directly behind me.

"Let her sleep. Her body needs the fire, too," my mother says.

I step over Seven and follow my mother into the hallway, which has even more artwork adorning the walls.

"We are a million moving paintings, all blending together to make one masterpiece called life," she says, and stops in front of a closed door at the end of the hall.

Okay, so maybe Hollywood did get one stereotype about Native Americans right. Maybe they are all wise, because my mom just said the wisest thing I've ever heard.

"Seventy-seven. I never really thought of life that way," I say, and take my first step into my new room as she opens the door.

But before I see inside, I turn to her.

"I know this sounds horrible, but I don't even know your name," I say.

She smiles. I can tell she wants to say more, but for me, she simply says, "Cecelia."

"Seven," I say, which prompts Seven to wake up and trot into the room. Cecelia and I share a laugh. "She has superhero hearing," I add.

"Just call me Mama," she says, and shuts the door behind her.

"Fourteen," I say under my breath. "Thanks, Mama."

A baby's first word is probably *mama*, and here I am, almost thirteen years old, saying it for the first time in my life. *Mama*. Two letters repeated one after the other. Like *yo-yo* and *tutu*. But I don't have a yo-yo and I don't wear tutus. I do, however, now have a mama.

I guess I'll learn my grandmother's name tomorrow. Right now, all I want to do is sleep. The room is smaller than my room in

California, but that's okay, because I don't own much. The walls are empty, but I'll fix that in no time. The bed is against the wall with a red-and-blue blanket covering it. Above the bed is a large dream catcher. The only other time I saw one of these was dangling from the rearview mirror in my neighbor's car. I wondered why people had them in their cars. I figured the last thing you'd want to do while driving was have a good dream.

I dig into my bag and pull out a drawing of Seven that I made a few years ago and my box of tacks. I walk over to the wall, pull out one red tack, and hang the drawing next to my bed. There, now it feels like home.

There's a wooden dresser on one side of the room, which looks homemade, but I'm too tired to unpack. Instead, I kick off my shoes, turn off the light, and make my way through the darkness to my new bed. I pull back the blanket and nestle in. Seven jumps up, and her body pins me down. Although this bed is smaller than my previous one, it feels more comfortable, more slept in. I wonder who slept here before me? I sink into the indentations of the mattress. Whoever it was, they were bigger than me.

"Good night, girl," I whisper to her . . . and she licks my cheek.

"Hi, room, I'm Collin. I guess you and I will be living together now," I say aloud, but the room doesn't respond because it's, well, a room.

"I'm quiet, too. You and I will get along well," I say.

I shift to my side so I can face the window. Before I sleep, I try to watch the dozens of tiny twinkling dancers perform on the black-night stage to the orchestra of the howling Minnesota wind, but I'm too tired to enjoy their performance. I close my eyes and sleep for the very first time in this strange and new place I'll now be calling home.

CHAPTER SEVEN

-《◆》-《◆》-

MY FIRST DAY AS A NATIVE AMERICAN

Under my eyelids, everything is orange and warm. I open them and let the sun hit my face. It's like my skin is walking on hot pavement. Not so hot it makes you run, but hot enough to wake you up and get you out of bed. I never noticed things like this in California. Maybe it was because everything over there moved so fast. My dad banged on my door for me to wake up, get going. He was always in a hurry. Feeling sunlight touch your cheeks wasn't an option then. But here, I can take in the morning. Maybe this is what it means to be Native American? To notice all the nature around you. Are the rays of the sun considered nature? Or maybe I'm just really exhausted and too tired to make sense right now.

I sit up, and as I do, a folded piece of paper falls from my chest. *Breakfast is ready*, it says. It even has *(16)* written above the note. That's cute. My mom is trying to make me feel comfortable. It won't last long—it never does—but still, I appreciate the effort. My dad never tried this hard. But he saw my situation as a problem to fix.

Maybe my mom doesn't see it that way. Maybe she just sees it as me being me. Only time will tell. And I'll give her time. I hope moms are more patient than dads.

Seven is still asleep, so I leave the door cracked open and make my way toward the kitchen. Halfway through the hallway, in the center of the animal kingdom of drawings, there is a photograph of a young man. He wears a military uniform, and his cheekbones match my mother's. The frame is surrounded by shells and beads. Who is he? And why is he so cool-looking? I slug my way into the kitchen. My mother is doing the dishes with her back to me.

"Good morning," I say through a yawn.

She turns around and hands me a dirty plate.

"You can help me," she says, and takes a step to the side, giving me room to share the sink with her.

I state the number (twelve) and accept the ketchup-stained plate.

"You just missed all the kids," she adds as she runs another plate under the sink.

"What kids?" I ask as I pick up the sponge and wipe down the plate.

"Where you live now, everyone is family."

"Everyone is related here?" I ask.

"Family doesn't always mean blood related."

Back in Huntington Beach, we rarely talked to the neighbors. Especially at our house. I had the dad that drank too much, and he had the son who had something wrong with his brain. And it wasn't just us. The family to our left was in the middle of a nasty divorce. They'd scream at each other until midnight sometimes. And the family to our right were super religious and routinely left Bible verses on all the cars in our neighborhood. His wife caught him with another woman, and after that, we all thought the notes would stop. They didn't. They doubled. Once, my dad got so pissed thinking there was a parking ticket on his truck, but it was just another note from good old Lord-loving Larry.

I have never heard of a place where everyone is considered family.

"Who's the guy in the hallway wearing the uniform?" I ask.

She smiles and pulls the plate out of the running water.

"That's your brother," she says.

"So he is a neighbor, too?" I ask.

"No, he *is* blood related. You have a brother."

Wait. What? Why didn't my dad tell me this? I thought I was in this world on my own. For all the beatings I took from bullies, having an older brother would have been helpful. Especially him. He looks super tough. Nobody would mess with me if they knew I was related to him.

"Where is he?"

She turns off the sink and sets the plate down.

"He's here. Would you like to meet him?" she asks.

"He's here? Yes."

I push my hair back, as though that will make me more presentable to meet my long-lost brother, and I try to clear the sleep debris from my eyes.

"Follow me," she says, and walks out of the kitchen and into the living room.

I wipe my hands on the towel next to the sink and follow her into the next room.

She stands near the corner. I'm confused. There's no one in here but my mother and me. I follow her eyes toward the top of the shelf. On it sits a clay-colored urn with a beautiful black design that looks like a tree with roots painted around it. It stares back at me, just as speechless as I am. It is set in the center of a dozen neatly placed flowers.

"Ajidamoo, this your brother, Collin," she says.

My brain doesn't count her letters because she isn't talking to me. In fact, she isn't talking to a person. She is speaking to the urn. I see the pain in her eyes as they finally drift from her other son to me.

It clicks. My brother is dead. And I just made my mother talk about him first thing in the morning. Again, this is not a great start.

"How did he . . . ?" I ask.

"He fought for this country," she says proudly.

"I'm sorry. That's horrible."

"I can't think of a greater way to go. Don't be sorry. Be thankful," she says as she reaches out and grabs something from the shelf.

"What's that?"

She pulls down a necklace made of bone and leather, and in the center is a turquoise stone. It the coolest-looking necklace I have ever seen.

"This was Aji's. I believe he would want you to have it," she says, and places it over my head, letting it fall around my neck.

The turquoise stone rests over my heart as I tally up her letters (forty-one). It feels heavy, or maybe that's the weight of the situation. I can't tell for sure.

"Are you sure?" I ask.

"I'm sure."

"It's beautiful. Thank you."

She kisses her fingertips and places them on the urn.

"Even from the next world, he's still giving to this one," she says.

"Tell him I said thank you."

She turns to me, tears on the curbs of her eyes. "Tell him yourself," she says, and walks back into the kitchen, leaving me alone with my brother.

I stare at the urn and try to picture the guy from the photo. I wonder if he knows what's going on right now. I haven't thought much about death before, and I don't believe in angels or anything like that, but maybe Native Americans are different. Perhaps death is just another part of life for them. I mean, my mom talks about it so easily. She just introduced me to my deceased brother and went right back to washing dishes. There's so much I have to learn if I'm ever going to be a real Native American.

"Thank you, Aji," I say to the urn.

He doesn't respond. Usually this is my favorite kind of conversation, but not this time. I would have loved to have a brother. I would have loved to know him, to see him, to count his letters. Early on, my dad pushed playdates on me. I think he made a deal with my classmates' parents. Maybe he even paid them. But one by one, they stopped coming by. What was cool and funny soon became annoying. But a brother would have been different. We'd have had a blood connection.

My thoughts are interrupted by a large grumble south of my heart. I nearly forgot how hungry I am. I skipped dinner last night, and now my body is in full protest. I take one last look at my brother and head back to the kitchen. A warm plate of eggs and hash browns awaits me. I take a seat and immediately dig in. My chewing is drowned out by Seven, who is near the corner, scarfing down whatever food my mother set out for her. I love that she thought to feed Seven. Back in California, if I didn't feed her, she didn't eat. My dad never took the time to make sure she was fed. Maybe it's a mother thing.

She hands me a large glass of freshly squeezed orange juice and takes a seat across from me.

"Thank you," I say, but she just smiles back at me.

Good. She's learning how to communicate with me. Already, she's better than my dad at this parenting thing. With me, less is more.

"How do you spell my brother's name?" I ask.

"*A-J-I*. It's short for Ajidamoo. That's *A-J-I-D-A-M-O-O*."

"Ajidamoo, that's eight. Aji for short, that's three. What does it mean?" I ask in between bites.

"Squirrel," she says.

"Also eight letters. Why squirrel?"

For as long as I can remember, I've always tried to avoid talking, and here I am, striking up the conversation.

"As a boy, he was always outside, climbing trees."

"But how did you know he would do that as a boy? I mean, didn't you name him when he was a baby?" I ask.

"Mothers just know. You're not a tree climber . . . You're more of a tree drawer, aren't you?" she asks.

How did she know that? Do mothers really know their kids, even before they do? Her letters fall into my head like someone shaking branches from an apple tree, but instead of apples, they only get inedible numbers.

"Yes. I have a notebook full of trees. An entire forest," I say.

"Well, we have beautiful trees here. You can climb them and draw them when you're ready."

"What do you mean when I'm ready?"

"I'll leave that between you and the trees," she says, and reaches for my empty plate.

I guess she means I have to get to know the trees here. Everything is alive here. I forgot. All the plants at my dad's house were fake. Even our Christmas tree. I never minded that, though—after all, California is constantly in a water crisis—but my dad had them be fake for other reasons . . . He didn't want to see them die. He said fake plants were less responsibility, and that was exactly what he strived for. Well, he has finally achieved it. I'm no longer his.

"Where'd you go?" my mom asked, snapping me out of my daze.

"I'm here. Sorry. I'll introduce myself to the trees pretty soon," I say.

"I have to go to work. You and Seven should get to know the house while I'm gone," she says, and washes my plate. "It's full of stories."

"Okay. On a Sunday? Where do you work?" I ask.

"On the rez. I'm a Mather," she says.

"What's a Mather?" I ask.

"It's what the kids call us. It's short for math teacher. We got Sciencers, Englishers, and Arters. I'm the Mather. Sundays are my prep days."

"I didn't know you were a teacher."

"You do now. And hey, we're looking for a PE teacher. You interested in being a PE'er?" she says, and laughs. "That joke's funny to a bunch of six-year-olds," she says as it finally clicks. A pee joke. I laugh.

"I already have that job. Every morning," I say, which makes my mom laugh again.

I'm smiling. I usually never smile in the morning. My dad was always in such a rush to do whatever he did that he'd practically toss me out the front door with a banana so I wouldn't miss the bus. Never did we have time for morning jokes. And look at me now: My mom and I have already shared a pee joke.

"Put the seat up. You ain't the first boy to live under this roof. I know how messy you animals get," she says as she starts to walk out of the kitchen.

"I will. Before you go, can I ask you something?"

"Of course."

"Who else lives here?" I ask.

"In this house?" she asks. "Including you?"

"Yes."

"That's hard to say. In time, you'll see why. Have a good day, son," she says, and walks out of the kitchen.

"Forty-six," I say under my breath, wondering what she meant by that. Another thing I really like about her is that I don't see any pity in her eyes, at least not yet. She treats me like there's nothing wrong. I hope it stays this way for a while longer. I know it won't last forever, but it feels good not being looked at like there's something deeply wrong with me.

I watch her from the kitchen window as she climbs into the pickup truck. It looks as if she's talking to the truck before the engine roars to life. Do all Native Americans have this kind of connection with everything around them, or is it just my family? Maybe it's just my mom. Maybe she's known in town as that lady who talks to cars and trees. If that's the case, then it would make sense that she wouldn't find my letter counting that strange.

I look down at the sink and give it a shot.

"Hi, sink," I say, and wait.

Nothing.

Seven barks and rushes out of the kitchen. It's playtime, and even though we are thousands of miles away from the only home we have ever known, that is not going to stop Seven's schedule. Not a chance.

I run with her through the living room and toward the sliding glass door that opens to the backyard. After I slide it open, Seven rushes out at a full gallop. The ground outside is shriveled up and brown, encased in a square fence about half the size of my previous backyard. Seven doesn't care. To her, outside is outside; she keeps it simple like that. And after a few minutes of sniffing the new area, she picks out the perfect spot to pee. She got the job. She's the new PE'er.

"You like it here, don't you, girl?" I say.

She runs toward me, but something catches her eye. She stops. Her ears rise. Her entire body perks up. I know that look. There's a squirrel running along the fence. It locks eyes with Seven and stops. It's a face-off. It's dog versus squirrel. *Dun dun dun.*

"Hi, squirrel," I say, just to give the connecting-with-nature thing one last go, and as soon as the word leaves my mouth, the squirrel bats its tail at me and takes off running.

Seven chases it along the fence until it disappears into the neighbor's yard, which shares the fence with our house.

"You'll catch it next time, girl," I shout, and slap my thighs, calling her back to me.

I repeat my brother's name in my head. Ajidamoo. Squirrel. Maybe that was him just now, reincarnated as a small furry animal that came to see who is now sleeping in his bed. The thought makes me happy and sad. If it was him, I hope he liked me. And if it wasn't him, well, I hope the squirrel liked me too, because why not?

It was so dark last night that I didn't even realize there was another house right next to ours. The fence between the houses is old and dirty, so I jump a few times to see over it, to catch a glimpse of my neighbor's house. But the fence is too tall. I imagine this height was nothing to my brother. If he climbed trees with ease, then he'd clear this fence no problem.

Whatever, I need to shower anyway, I may as well get a little dirty. I grab the top of the fence and hoist my body up. My head hovers inches above it, and I'm able to see the next yard, which has grass just as dead as ours. But past the dead weeds, toward the back of the yard, is a large tree, full of thick green-leafed branches sprouting in all directions. That's odd. How is the ground so dead, but the tree so green and full of life?

My hands begin to shake from the strain, but as I lower my head, I catch a glimpse of something in the tree. It looks like . . . a wooden tree house?

I lift my head a bit higher and see there's a window, and through the window, a pair of human eyes looking directly at me. Who is that?

Snap!

One of the wooden boards splits in half beneath me and sends me crashing to the ground, with my left leg now stuck halfway into the broken fence. I hit the ground on my back, hard, knocking the wind out of me. Seven leaps toward my face, covering me in a dozen licks to make sure I'm okay. I lie there and catch my breath for a few moments. My brother would not be impressed. I hope the squirrel didn't see that.

Great. I'm left alone for five minutes, and I'm already destroying the house. I look up and see the damage. I need to fix this before my mother gets home. I know nothing about woodwork, but how difficult can it be? I just need to find a new board and hammer it to the fence. Sounds simple enough. I get to my feet and peer through the break in the fence to take another look at the tree house. I can't see those eyes anymore. Whoever it was just saw me take an epic fall.

"Don't worry, I'll have it fixed."

I turn around and see my grandmother staring at me.

She's grinning, standing with one foot in the house and one foot in the backyard. Today she is wearing a brown dress, but it looks like the exact dress she was wearing last night, like it just changes colors depending on the day.

"I'm sorry," I shout back to her.

"Don't be. It used to happen all the time," she says.

"Really? With Aji?" I ask.

Her eyes focus in on mine. I can't tell if hearing his name out loud hurts her or soothes her. Her smile hasn't faded, so I don't think I've upset her.

"He was quite the little squirrel, that boy."

"I'm sure he wasn't as clumsy as I am."

She laughs. "No, he wasn't," she says, and steps back into the house.

"I'll fix it. I just need to find some wood and a hamm—"

I stop talking because she closes the sliding glass door. Oh no. Have I already annoyed her too much? I look back at the fence and realize this all happened because of that darn squirrel.

"That little guy bested us both, Seven," I say.

I pick up the split boards and carry them to the house. Halfway to the sliding glass door, I begin to limp. I look down and see a bit of blood soaking through my pants. Great. I don't mind the pain so much, but I definitely don't want to break my family's fence *and* track blood through the house.

This is a rough start to my new life.

I stop in front of the glass door, set the wooden pieces against the wall, and remove my black shirt. It's cold, but I'd rather be a little chilly than be the reason a trail of blood is streaked across the carpet. I wrap the shirt around my leg. Once it is fastened tightly, I reach for the door handle to slide it open . . . but it doesn't move.

My grandmother locked me out.

It would be funny if it weren't so darn confusing. She knows I am out here—we just talked. I peer through the glass but don't see her. I tap on it a few times, but she doesn't come.

"Hello?" I shout.

Nothing. Seven is more patient than I, so she lies down and

waits. I limp over to the side gate. Nope. That's locked too. The only way for me to reach the front door is to hop the gate, but after I just broke the fence, the last thing I need is to break a gate. I'm trapped in the backyard. This is ridiculous.

I limp back to the freshly made gap in the fence. I might be able to squeeze through it and get out through the neighbor's gate. My eyes shoot up to that strange tree house. Good, I'm not being watched. Coast is clear. I lift my injured leg and put it through the gap. I step down into the neighbor's yard. I'm halfway through.

Am I trespassing? Well, technically, yeah, but I'll be quick. I squeeze through, nearly getting stuck, but after my skin scrapes against the two wooden planks on both sides, I'm finally on the other side. Just then it hits me: What if their gate is locked too? Then I'm stuck in two backyards. And if I'm caught, I'll look like a shirtless burglar. But burglars try to break into houses. I'm trying to break out of one—well, two. What's the opposite of a burglar? I have no idea.

I hurry over to the gate, but halfway there, something slams into my head. The impact knocks me off my feet. I hit the ground for the second time today. My head throbs. I scan all four directions, but I don't see anyone. Then as I lie there, in the dead grass, I look up and see the tree house. And from the window, a girl is perched, leaning out, looking directly at me . . . wearing a guilty smirk.

It takes a few blinks for my double vision to merge her into one person. I focus in on her face. She looks like an angel . . . if angels had no wings and lived in tree houses. Her eyes reflect like diamonds, sparkling back at me, but I am not sure if it's her sparkle or the water built up in my eyes from the impact. Her skin is a different shade of flame than my mother's, like hers was dipped in gold before it was set ablaze. Her long black hair is straight and pulled into two braids, like two powerful black snakes protecting her neck, but what grabs my attention most is her mouth. Why? Because she's tightening her jaw, barely able to contain herself. And then it happens. She erupts into hysterical laughter.

I stand, keeping my eyes on her. Now that I have a better look, it is confirmed . . . She is by far the prettiest girl I have ever seen. Before this moment, Jenny in my sixth-grade class had that trophy. But this strange girl, whoever she is, just took gold. Sorry, Jenny.

"Did you just throw something at my head?" I shout up to her.

"Maybe," she replies.

"Five. Why?"

"Five nothing. It's for your dog," she says, and disappears back into her tree house.

"Twenty-four. Wait!" I shout even louder, but she doesn't reappear.

I look down and see a worn-out baseball near my feet. This girl hurled a baseball at my head. I mean . . . who does that?

"Hello?" I shout up to her.

Nothing. I could climb the tree, but that would just be creepy. After all, I am technically still trespassing. Plus, I don't climb trees very well. I couldn't even successfully hop a fence.

I rub the lump forming on my head. It stings. I can't believe she threw a ball at me. Who does she think she is? I mentally play back our conversation for clues. You'd be surprised by how often people's words reveal things about themselves without them knowing. I may not be much of a burglar, but I'm a pretty good word detective.

She said "maybe," but then admitted it was her who threw the ball, which tells me she's not a liar. That's good. Honesty is important. But when I asked why she threw it, she said it was for my dog. Maybe she accidentally hit me while she tried to do something nice like give Seven a ball to play with?

I turn around and see Seven sitting there staring at me, obviously waiting for me to throw her the ball. All I know about this girl now is she either has great aim or poor aim. Depending on which was her actual target, Seven or my head. Whichever is the case, she has a great arm.

I toss it over the fence, back into our yard. Seven darts toward the gap in the fence and easily jumps through. I take another look up to see if I can get one last glimpse of the girl in her tree house.

"Thank you," I shout.

I walk back toward the fence, laughing to myself because I just thanked a girl for firing a baseball at my head. As I step into my yard, Seven is waiting with her brand-new ball in her mouth. I'm still trapped outside and now doubly injured . . . but I guess it's still playtime. I launch the ball across the yard and watch Seven chase it. I wonder if she's imagining the ball as the furry ajidamoo that got away.

CHAPTER EIGHT

-《◆》-《◆》-

HOW TO BEAT
A BULLY

"I said get to know the house, not fight it."

I open my eyes to my mother standing over me. It takes me a second to realize where I am, and to count (twenty-one). It's nearly sundown, and I'm still lying in the backyard, using Seven as my pillow. The temperature has dropped, and my entire upper body feels like a Popsicle. I sit up.

"I must have fallen asleep," I say. "After I fell off the fence," I add as I follow her eyes toward my injured leg.

"Are you hurt?" she asks.

"No. But the fence is," I say.

She doesn't even look at the fence, almost as if she's been through this same scenario a hundred times before.

"And you just wanted to . . . take a nap? Out here? Shirtless in the cold?" she asks curiously.

"Grandma locked me out," I say, which causes my mother to laugh.

"Oh, that's funny?" I ask as I put my shirt on.

"Well, isn't it?"

"Not really. I was locked out all day."

"Well, I'm sure she had her reasons," she says, and walks back into the house.

"Twenty-six." I quicken my pace toward her as she pretends to slide the door shut and lock me out again. "Very funny."

Inside, a zoo of delicious flavors immediately races up my nostrils. "What's that smell?" I ask.

"Dinner."

"It smells amazing." I peek my head into the kitchen. "Where's Grandma?" I ask.

"She's around."

"I'm going to ask her why she locked me out."

"Good luck with that." My mother releases a giggle.

"Sixteen," I shout as I begin my search.

But after walking through the entire house, I come up empty-grandma'd. The only room left is my mother's bedroom. But her door is shut. I look back to make sure my mom is still in the kitchen before I grip the door handle and turn it. It's unlocked. I know I shouldn't go into her room without permission, but it's the one place left where my grandma could be hiding. So I push the door open and step inside.

The walls are decorated with dozens of photographs. I step farther in to get a better look at them. It is a time line of my brother's life, running from left to right. I see Aji as an infant, toddler, little boy, and then as a teenager. There are photos of him with friends, climbing trees, on a basketball team, and even one of him in a colorful costume, which I assume is traditional Ojibwe attire.

I wish I had his life. He looked so happy and confident, but the photo line ends abruptly with a picture of him as a young man in a military uniform. I can see how much my mom loved him, enough to line the walls in her bedroom with his life; his death must have been earth-shattering. This is the saddest room in the world, I think. He's dead, and my mom keeps a daily reminder of him. That must hurt her every single day. But it would probably hurt even more to take these photographs down and wake up every morning not seeing her boy.

On the next wall, another time line of photographs catches my eyes. I see a baby in a sink, getting washed by . . . Wait! I know that face. It can't be. But it is . . . That's my face! This time line is mine. How is this possible? My mom has been watching me grow up my entire life without me even knowing it.

I see a few more of my baby pictures, then two more of me as a toddler able to walk. Then another of me in a Ninja Turtles shirt. I remember that shirt. I wanted to be a Ninja Turtle so bad. I even painted my face green and wore a pillow in the back of my shirt to school once. No one thought it was a shell. They just thought I was a strange green kid with a pillow on my back.

Wow. What's going on?

I step farther down my life line. There are a few pictures of me drawing animals as a little boy, sprawled out on the carpet in my favorite dinosaur pajamas. I don't remember my dad ever taking pictures of me. And yet he's been sending pictures to her this entire time. What the hell?

My time line ends with my fifth-grade school photo. I remember this day. The photographer nearly had a conniption trying to direct me. "Say cheese," he'd say. "Nine," I'd reply. This went on for almost five minutes before he finally snapped the photo and told me to get lost. I was so embarrassed. Now it just seems pretty funny. And look at my bowl cut. I was such a nerd.

"You used to be so cute. What happened?"

My mom is standing right behind me. I can see underneath her smile a familiar look of pain—the same happy-sad smile she wore when she introduced me to my brother.

"I was just thinking the same thing," I say, and try to make her smile last a bit longer.

She steps up to one of my baby pictures, and I watch her finger trace my little infant mouth.

"I would go to sleep holding this photo against my chest so I'd dream of holding you."

I count her letters before her words sink in.

"Did it work?"

"Some nights."

"What was Aji like?"

Her smile blooms across her face as she looks up. Are her memories of her son floating near the ceiling?

"Did you ever see *The Godfather*?"

"The really old movie? Yeah, it was my dad's all-time favorite, right beside *Rocky*. Why?"

"He was like that."

"A fat old Italian man with a violent streak that liked to leave horse heads in people's beds?" I ask.

She laughs. "Excluding all of that, of course. Just the part where everyone in the neighborhood looked up to him. Kids would come to him for advice, sometimes for protection from bullies. And all the girls fawned over him," she says, sweeping a tear from her eye before it melts into her cheek.

"I could have used a brother like him growing up."

"He wasn't always Mr. Popular. He was picked on as a kid, too, you know?"

"Really?" I ask.

I stare at his picture and doubt her words. He had muscles

those Greek gods have in paintings. Who would ever mess with him?

"Sure. He would come home from school in tears. Sometimes it was because he wore glasses, sometimes it was because of the way he talked, and sometimes it was for nothing at all. Kids can be cruel. As you know," she says.

"So what did he do about it?" I ask.

She sighs. I can't decide if it's out of joy or sorrow. Maybe both. Her body turns toward the hallway. "I'll show you," she says, and walks out of her room.

I follow her through the house and into the garage. It's dark. I haven't explored this part of the house yet. Maybe Grandma is hiding in here?

She flips on the light and steps inside. It looks like the training room for *The Karate Kid*. There is an old rusty weight bench in the center of the room. Two sacks of stones hang from both sides of the bar to act as the weights. And farther down hangs a punching bag, the kind that Rocky Balboa used in the movie. It is covered in dust, but I can still see the silver bands of duct tape keeping it together. Aji must have packed quite a punch. The walls are lined with bookshelves, and each shelf is packed to the brim with books. This garage is half dojo and half library. Two places I wouldn't think of mixing.

"This is where he learned to fight back," my mother says.

I run my finger along the dirty weight bench, coating my fingertips with dust.

"I'm not much of a fighter," I say.

Her eyes shift to the bookshelves.

"There are many ways to fight. He used the weights to get his body in shape, but he used the books to get stronger. There is nothing more powerful than the mind," she says, and steps out of the garage, leaving me to explore it on my own.

I'm realizing my mother says what she needs to and then splits.

I approach the punching bag. Two red boxing gloves rest atop it. I pull them down and shake them loose, just in case there are spiders hiding inside of them. I slip them on and clench my fists, securing my grip.

I punch the bag with my left hand.

It sways only slightly. I push it to redeem myself, and it rocks back and forth a bit more. The chain creaks back to life. I don't think anyone has punched it since he last did. I punch it again, this time with my right. It hurts my hand more than it moves the bag. I can only imagine how my dad would react if he saw me now. I take off the gloves before I can visualize his glare of disappointment and turn toward what I'll have better luck with . . . the books.

Every single book I randomly pick up has my brother's thoughts scribbled onto the pages. Some passages are highlighted, some underlined. Wow. He read a lot. The books range from philosophy to romance novels. No wonder everyone loved him. He was smart, strong, and sensitive. If I'm going to survive in a new school, I need to learn how to be at least one of those three.

CHAPTER NINE

-《◆》--《◆》-

EXPERIENCE
WINS BATTLES

I volunteer to wash the dishes after dinner, and my mom stands next to me to make sure I scrub them to her standards.

"You start school tomorrow," she says over the running water.

I nearly drop the plate in my hand as I count (twenty-two). I picture it shattering into a million different pieces to match the million different reasons why I don't want to go.

"Do I have to?"

"Don't worry. I spoke to the principal. She knows about your numeric mind and has assured me that it wouldn't be a problem. Get it? Numbers. Problem. I'm such a math teacher. Plus, you can't stay around the house forever, Collin. You've got to get out there and, you know, learn stuff," she says.

"I should warn you. School and I don't have that great of a

history together. I mean, the actual school part is fine, but the people in it . . . not so much."

She turns off the water and leans against the sink.

"Your dad gave me the rundown, but that was then and there. This is here and now."

"I hope you're right."

"I'm a mother. I'm always right."

I place the last dish on the dry rack. But I don't leave the kitchen just yet. There's something I've been meaning to ask her.

She walks toward the living room, so I block her path, awkwardly.

"What is it?" she asks.

"What is what?"

"What you've wanted to ask me all dinner but chickened out every chance you had."

Wow. She's good.

"I keep forgetting you people read minds," I say.

Her eyes squint at my choice of words, almost like a dagger just jabbed into her ribs and she's trying to not show any pain.

"You people? Is that how you see me? Am I so different than you, Collin?"

"No. I didn't mean you people, I meant, you know, you Native Americans," I say, which out loud sounds even worse.

"Oh, so you think it's a Native American thing, do you? Well, if we all could read minds, you think history would have played out the way it did for us?"

"I guess not. I'm sorry. I don't know anything about Native Americans. Only what I've seen in the movies and read in school."

"Apology accepted. Lesson one: Never judge someone by what color is wrapped around their bones. You judge them by the way they treat people. And animals. You can tell a lot about someone by how they act around things that can't talk back to them. And lesson two . . . You are 'you people' too."

Wow. Who knew that "you people" would hurt someone so much? I need to choose my words more carefully. My dad used that term all the time. I guess I picked up some bad habits from him. Hopefully my mom will teach me how to drop them off.

"Sorry, I'm still learning how to be Native American," I say, which causes her to laugh. Well, good—at least she's not mad at me.

"You're already Native American, Collin," she says. "Just be yourself."

"I'll try."

"Now, what was it you wanted to ask me?" She snaps our earlier conversation back to the front of the line.

"Oh, it was nothing," I say.

"Bawk bawk bawk," she says, and even mimics a chicken walking.

I laugh, which causes her to laugh. I snap another mental photograph of us in the kitchen right now. This should have been my life. This moment right here and now. Laughing with my mom, like we're a normal family. I don't remember the last time I saw my dad laugh.

"Okay, okay—I was just going to ask you about school."

"Welcome to Fibville. Population, one. You!" she adds.

"Fine. I was just wondering . . . I was curious to know . . . I guess I was . . ." I'm not ready to ask *that* question yet.

"Holy moly guacamole, just ask already," she says, slapping her hands together.

She's right. If I ever want to get an answer, I need to ask the question. Here goes nothing . . .

"Do you know who she is or not?"

A smile stretches from one hanging feather earring to the other. She knew exactly what I was going to ask.

"Of course I know who she is. She's my neighbor."

Oh, she's milking this. She's going to make me spell it out for her. Fine. There's no point dangling my toes in the shallow end. I'll just dive in and get it over with.

"Well, what do you know about her?" I ask.

She sees how excitedly nervous I am. And she stretches this moment even further. "I know many things. I know she's smart. And very pretty. Did you notice that yet?"

"I didn't really get a good look at her because she was so high up in the tree," I say, and pick up the nearest plate from the sink.

"We never lie in this house," she says, folding her arms. "Well, we lie in bed at night, to sleep . . . But other than then, we don't lie. Got it?"

"Fine. Yes. I noticed she was pretty. So, what's her deal?" I ask, and turn the water back on to wash one of the already clean plates.

"I can't tell you her story. She has to tell it. Don't you know how stories work?"

I shake my head.

"If you want to know her story, you have to be ready to tell her *your* story. That's how they work. It's a trade, and our people are very big on trading."

"But I don't know my story."

"Sure you do. You're the main character. Everywhere you go is your stage. And everyone around you has a part in your play."

Her letters shuffle in and take their seats inside my head, like they are the audience to the play she's talking about. But they don't sit still and enjoy the performance. They are wild and unruly, and pop into numbers and float toward the stage, interrupting everything.

"Ninety-four. So, what do I do now?"

"It seems to me that you both have stories to share with each other."

"Okay. That's if I survive my first day of school," I say.

"You've survived many first days of school. What's one more?"

"All it takes is one more to be the final straw that breaks the camel's back."

"Well then, it's a good thing you're not a camel. And look at it this way . . . You have the advantage over all the other students."

"How so?" I ask.

"You have more first days of school than anyone there. That's called experience. And experience wins battles."

"You really think I can do it?"

"Yes. Now, how dry do you want that plate?" she asks.

I look down and see that I've been wiping the same plate this entire conversation. I put it down with the rest of the dishes.

"I should shower," I add.

She sighs in relief. But not just a normal relief. A very embellished sigh that is very much an overreaction, in my opinion.

"Phew, I wasn't going to say anything, but . . ."

"Seriously? I smell?"

She laughs and turns off the light. "There's the understatement of the century. And you wonder why Grandma hasn't come home yet," she says, holding her nose and exiting the kitchen.

I sniff my right armpit and kinda agree. Wow.

No wonder Seven has kept her distance this evening. Once I'm in the bathroom, I pull a towel down from the towel rack. What is with me forgetting to ask people's names around here? I completely forgot to ask my mom what that girl's name is.

I keep myself busy thinking about her to distract myself from the terrifying fact that tomorrow I'm the new kid in school again. Ugh.

I run the shower, undress, and fill my open palm with the shampoo sitting on the ledge of the tub. I lather it up in my hands and cover my greasy head with it, something I've always done to save time since Southern California was in a perpetual water drought. It smells like honey straight from the hive. I step in headfirst, but the water is way too cold—so I jump right back out. I turn the lever all the way to the right and stick my finger in the flowing stream. I wait. Will it ever get warm? The shampoo foams up from the brief encounter with the water and runs down into my face, stinging my eyes. Shoot. I quickly douse my entire head under the shower's mouth and shake, rinsing out my eyes.

There's a knock on the bathroom door. "Better hurry. It only stays hot for three minutes," she shouts.

"Forty," I shout back, and fully step into the water.

It's warmer now. That must mean I have about two minutes left. As if my life depends on it, I scrub my entire body as quickly as possible, but as I reach my ankle area, the water goes cold. I guess my feet will have to wait until tomorrow. I turn the water off and wrestle the towel over my body for another minute. The mirror above the sink is completely fogged up, so I open the small window beside the shower, releasing all the white heat.

Like trapped spirits, a long stream of steam floats out of the window and meets the cold air. And just past the steam, I see the tree house in the next yard.

It's lit by flickering candlelight, and I make out her silhouette. A faint trace of music floats toward me and she is slow dancing to it. I watch her until she moves out of view. I lean my head out of the window to get a better angle.

I still can't see her well enough—just her elbow, shoulder, and the side of her head from this position—so I climb onto the sink and lean the upper half of my body out of the window. I know I should respect her privacy and not sneak peeks, but I'm the one almost naked and fresh out of the shower, so if anyone needs privacy right now, it's me.

The sound of drums rings through the air as I stretch my body out of the window as much as I can. I must look silly, but right now, I don't care. I just want a better look at her. I lean out even farther and hear another sound competing with the rhythm. It's her voice. She's singing. They aren't words I recognize. They sound more like chants and mouth exercises I've participated in during my many sessions at speech therapy. Is this Native American music? It sounds beautiful, but as happy as my ears are, my eyes are still not satisfied. I need to get closer.

I hold on to the windowsill and stretch my wet body as far out as I can, but I'm clumsy, and so it happens—I lose my grip and completely fall out of the window.

"Ahhh!" I shout as I crash-land. Not do I just fall, but I literally face-plant into the dirt.

I launch back to my feet and shoot my eyes up to her, hoping she didn't hear my shriek, but she did. Her shadow stops dancing and slowly walks toward her open window. Oh man. She looks out toward my house. I quickly hide behind the nearest bush. Her eyes search my yard. I can't believe I screamed like that. Maybe she thinks it was a shrieking cat?

I follow her eyes toward my open bathroom window. Wait . . . why is she smiling? Oh no! What is my towel doing there? It must have gotten caught on the window frame as I fell out. Then it hits me . . . I'm outside, and I'm naked. And it's freezing out here.

After a few moments, she gives up and returns to her song. I watch her until I'm overtaken by the cold. I feel goose bumps crawling all over my body. I count to three and make a mad dash toward the window. I reach up, snatch my towel, and climb back into the house. That was a close one. In one day, I managed to break a fence, injure my leg and head, and fall out of a one-story window. Perhaps counting letters is the least of my problems.

I wrap the torn towel around my waist and open the bathroom door. My mother is standing in the hall, waiting for me. She must have heard my scream. But she doesn't look concerned at all. In fact, she looks like she is about to laugh. Then she does. And she doesn't stop for a good minute.

"What's so funny?" I ask.

"Do people not know how to shower in California?" she asks.

"What makes you say that?"

Her eyes squint, like I'm missing something blatantly obvious.

"Look in the mirror," she says.

I turn toward the mirror, rub a circle of steam away, and see my reflection. My face is covered in dirt.

CHAPTER TEN

-《◆》- -《◆》-

MY FIRST DAY OF SCHOOL. AGAIN.

I'm fully awake and prepared for battle. I'm in my signature black shirt, black pants, black shoes, and gray earmuffs. My mom wanted to do my hair, maybe for all the years of missing out on it, so I let her. She combed it all to the side and made it look "neat." That was her exact word, so as soon as she put down the comb, I shoved both my hands into my hair and moved my hands like I was trying to put out a fire.

After two bowls of cereal, I'm ready for school . . . or at least I'm as ready as I'll ever be. I kiss Seven goodbye and walk her to the backyard. When I let her out, I notice the fence I broke has already been fixed. I wonder who fixed it. My grandma? My mom? Great. Now they are going to think I can't even clean up my own messes.

A loud honk snaps me out of my daze. I slide the door shut, leaving Seven to explore the yard until I'm back. I rush out of the house, toward my mom's idling truck.

"You don't want to be late on your first day, do you?" my mom asks.

I climb into the passenger side and fasten my seat belt. "Better never than late."

She laughs and peels her truck out of the front yard.

"It will only be as bad as you make it," she says.

That's a weird way of convincing me *it won't be so bad*. But my dad always said that, and he was always wrong. So maybe my mom is onto something. Maybe it's up to me how today turns out. But I doubt it. It's not like I can control how people treat me.

"It's too early for Native wisdom, Mama."

"*Native wisdom*, where'd you hear that term? Another one of those cowboy movies?" she asks.

"I guess. Why? Aren't all Native people wise like you?"

She laughs, but her laugh isn't because I said something funny, it's more of an "I can't believe you just asked me such a foolish question" laugh.

"I've known plenty of Native Americans who were total bone-heads. And I've known plenty who were very kind and very wise. You're still thinking on the surface, where the skin lives. You need to dig deeper, into the bleed, and see that it's not because of what they are that makes someone wise, it's because of who they are."

Even though I count her letters, her words grab me. She makes perfect sense. I can apply everything she said to my life. People see me as a freak. A walking calculator. A human math problem. But that's because they're looking at the surface. But if someone got to know me, the real me, they'd see I'm more than that. What that is, I'm not sure yet, but other than my counting, maybe I'm not so different from all the other kids.

"So I just have to get to know everyone's story before I can judge them?" I ask.

She smirks. "Yes. Hear them out before you slap a label across their forehead."

I've learned more from my mom in the last five minutes about myself than I did from my dad all the years living with him. Maybe because with him, I was so busy trying to be someone else, someone he wanted me to be.

"Did Grandma teach you all of this?"

"She did. And now I'm teaching you, so pay attention. Your teacher happens to be an incredibly wise Native American," she says with a gloating grin.

She turns onto the unpaved road that leads to the main highway. This town looks like it hasn't been disrupted by America yet. Back in Huntington Beach, every year it seemed a new shopping mall or parking lot would spring up where there once was a park or field. By the time I left, our neighborhood had two new car dealerships and a Walmart. But here, there are people on the side of the road riding horses.

My mind drifts away from all the wisdom talk and floats up into a tree house. *Her* tree house. Great. I'm thinking about *her* again.

I might not get another chance to ask and I need to know, just in case I don't survive my first day, so I clear my throat and speak again.

"Do you know her name?"

She smiles. "Yes. I know her name."

Is this a motherly trait? Do all mothers want to embarrass their kids a little bit, more and more, each day?

"You can't just answer me, can you?"

"I answered your question. If you don't like the answer, ask a different question," she says.

I say and choose my words carefully . . . after I count her letters (sixty-four), "You're just as annoying as I am."

"Maybe it's in our blood," she says and shoots me some side-eye.

"You're seriously going to make me ask, aren't you? Fine. What's her name?"

"Orenda. If you want to know anything else about her, you have to ask her," she says.

"Fine," I say, and lean back into the seat.

"Can you—"

"O-r-e-n-d-a. Six letters, like yours," she cuts me off, smiling.

Orenda. I've never heard that name before. A fellow six-letter. We already have things in common. It's fate. And if it's not, it's at least a conversation starter, which I'll need next time I see her, along with a helmet. I try to hide my smile by staring out the window. But my mom still somehow senses it and lets out another laugh. I can't believe how happy my mom is. She's literally the opposite of my dad. Maybe that's why it didn't work between them. Sometimes opposites attract, but clearly not always.

There are a few cars on the road, but it's nothing like the jam-packed California traffic. My mom rolls down her window and cranks up the radio.

"My favorite station kicks in right around . . . here," she says through the static.

"How far is—"

I am cut off by the sudden burst of music. An old classic rock song rattles the speakers. Wow, I live somewhere where there is no radio reception. That's weird. She sings along at the top of her lungs, whipping her black hair left and right through the wind barreling into the truck. I watch her in awe. She is so full of life. So free.

"Sing along," she says, dancing wildly in her seat.

"No thanks," I say.

But she chooses not to hear me. Instead, she grabs my hand and swings it through the air to match the swaying drumbeat. I wonder if she and Aji did this every day on the way to school. My dad would never do this. He'd only listen to men shouting at each other about immigration or the economy. Then he'd get so upset, he'd turn it off.

But with my mom, there's no OFF button. She lives life like it's a song and invites the entire world to sing and dance with her.

After two more songs, we pull up to the North Duluth Middle School. The campus is two large brick buildings, and both are swarming with students. I've never seen so many flannel shirts and camouflage pants in my life.

The good thing is that many of the kids are wearing bundled up layers and hats, so my earmuffs won't stand out. The bad part is, I'm going to be stuck in a class with about thirty of these kids at a time and my earmuffs won't be able to save me during roll call.

I hate roll call.

"Why can't I just go to school where you teach? I mean, at least I'd know one person on campus won't think I'm a freak," I say.

"You can . . . But you'd have to go back to fifth grade. We teach grades K–5. At least that way you'd be the smartest kid in class . . . maybe," she says jokingly. "But definitely the tallest."

"One hundred and twenty-one. So, I'm on my own, huh?"

"Yep, just you and hundreds of other kids who don't feel like they fit in," she says.

We stop behind a yellow school bus and wait for our turn to pull up to the drop-off zone. It surprises me how no one is in a rush to get where they need to be. In California, everyone was in such a hurry, and they'd let you know by holding down the horn when they were behind you. But here, it's super chill. Not one honk.

"After school, you can take the big green horse back to the rez border. I will pick you up there," she says.

"Okay, big green horse bus. Got it," I say, and nervously open the door.

She turns down the radio and leans closer to me.

"Remember. Normal people are jealous of special people. It's been that way since the first day the sun shone down on us," she says.

"Thanks, Mama. But it's your job to say something like that to me, isn't it?"

"Oh, is someone paying me? I don't feel money being stuffed into my pocket. So I guess it's not my job after all. Maybe I'm telling you this because it's true. Now go be special by being you," she says.

I tally her number and send it back to her. "I don't want to be special. I want to be brave," I say.

She waves her hand above my head like a witch casting a spell. "There. You are now brave. Now get to class, and I'll see you later."

"Okay. See ya."

She turns her head and leans in, closer to me. Why did she do that? What is she waiting for?

"Kiss," she says.

"Four." She wants me to kiss her? No way. I'm not a kisser.

"Now," she says.

"Three."

"Hi," she adds with a smirk.

"Two," I say.

"I."

"One," I say, and it clicks.

Oh, my mom is clever. She just made me count down to our kiss.

Well played, Mama. I look around and make sure no one is watching and then I lean in and plant a kiss on her cheek.

I see the happiness dancing in her eyes. I can't help but think that she misses getting goodbye kisses from Aji. She lost a son and gained a son, and now I'm the one that will be giving her these goodbye kisses. It was probably as natural as breathing for Aji, but I have never kissed my dad. This is like learning a new language for me. I think a kiss on the cheek translates to "have a good day at school today" in Kissish. She smiles and revs the engine. I step out and shut the door. She drives off to another song.

As I step onto the curb, I realize that other than Seven, that was my first kiss. And it was with my mom. Most kids have probably been kissed by their moms so many times they hardly notice when it happens. It's like opening a door or tying your shoes. Just something that happens every day. But I've never been kissed before. Not even when I was sick and my dad had to bring me soup and tuck me into bed. He'd pat my head and turn out my light.

I'm way behind kids my age. They're so used to kissing that they've branched out and started kissing people they have crushes on. I'm nowhere near that stage. I just got my first kiss from my mama. I probably won't be kissed by someone who isn't related to me until I'm much older. Not that I'd want to be kissed or anything. I mean, someone's lips touching you is pretty weird if you think about it. We eat with those things. But my dad once told me that when I'm older I'll meet someone special and we'll be so busy kissing, I won't have to worry about us talking. It was his way of trying to find something positive about my future with this counting condition. Obviously, I haven't met anyone special yet. But to be fair, I haven't exactly had the opportunities most kids my age have. I'm never invited to parties. I've never asked anyone to be my valentine, and I've never played spin the bottle before. On the rare occasion a girl has found me cute enough to send a note to my desk—it was over as soon as we had our first conversation at recess. But that was the old me. This is the new me. Everything is about to change . . . I hope.

I put my earmuffs on but don't play music. I want to hear these new surroundings. I walk toward the larger of the two brick buildings, weaving through the crowd, trying to pick up on the differences between this school and every other one I've attended. Sadly, not much differs at all. Everyone is still separated into the cliques—jocks with jocks, nerds with nerds—and the hot popular girls all band together in the center of it all for all the above-mentioned groups to see. School is school, no matter where you are.

Halfway up the steps that lead to the main building, the bell rings. I realize that here the bell actually means something. Imagine that. Everyone disperses on cue. In California, the bell usually means it is time to start thinking about getting to class . . . soon. It would take two or three bells to actually get people in their seats.

Before I know it, I'm the only person out here. These students sure do take school seriously. I need to find the office and get my schedule. It's bad enough I am the new kid in school, but now it looks like I'm also going to be late, which doubles the attention. And I hate attention. All those eyes staring at me. Judging me. No thanks.

So I run. Right before the two large corridor doors close, I rush inside and enter the hall. This school is much fancier than my previous one, and cleaner. It's so pristine that I hear the squeaking of my sneakers as I walk over the marbled floors, which makes me almost tiptoe across the hall to avoid being noticed.

I swing open the office door and step inside. I am the only late student in sight. How is that possible? The only other person in here is an older woman at the desk. I approach her, but she's too busy jabbing at her keyboard to notice me. So I wait.

She resembles a frog. Not in a mean way, but in the way owners somehow resemble their dogs. Or cats. I'm pretty sure Seven and I look alike by now. Maybe this lady has a pet frog at home? She has large chubby cheeks, a pair of thick oversized reading glasses, which magnify her eyes, and a green scarf bound many times around her neck. All I'd need to do is paint her face green, and I'd be waiting to speak to a frog.

She looks up at me. I am pretty experienced at this point at keeping conversations with strangers short, so I remove my earmuffs and pull out my most effective tactic: operation info-dump.

"Hi. My name is Collin Couch. I just moved here from California. Today is my first day. I'm just here for my schedule. Thank you."

I half expect a "ribbit" from her. But instead she repeats my last name.

"Kooch with a *K*?" she asks.

"Eleven. No. With a *C*, spelled like *couch*."

"Collin Couch," she repeats, and quickly types my name into her computer.

"Here you are. Under recent transfer . . . I'm printing your schedule now."

This lady is talking way too much. Just print the thing. I'm going to be so late. "Sixty-five. I'm in a bit of a hurry," I say.

"Sixty-five what, dear?" she asks, and hands me my schedule.

"Seventeen. Never mind. Thanks," I say, and dart out of the office before she tries to give me directions, even though I have no idea how to get where I need to go.

I speed walk down the hall and try to read my schedule just as quickly as my feet are moving. It says my first class is US history in room 113. Now all I've got to do is find it. I look at the closest door to me. It is room 7C. Hmm? I guess I have quite a run ahead of me. I go farther down the hall and pass rooms 8 through 25. I'm getting warmer, both figuratively and physically. I continue down the hall and hit a dead end. Now what? I'm lost. And the thing I want to avoid most is the thing I have to do . . . Ask someone for directions.

I see a random straggler rushing toward her class. Good. Glad to know someone else here is human. She has dyed red hair, the color of a fire engine. She's taller than I am and just as pale as I am. She wears black-framed glasses and ripped-up jeans. Not the kind of ripped up like she was attacked by a mountain lion, but the kind that is a fashion statement. And her pink bomber jacket is covered in safety pins and patches. I guess she is trying to make everyone that sees her stare at her rebellious punk rock appearance, rather than notice the birthmark on her face, but I pay attention to silent details more than most, so I immediately spot it. It's under her cheek but above her chin. It looks like all the freckles on her body united and congregated there. Like a dark island on a sea of white skin. She probably hates it, the way I hate my counting, but I think it looks cool. Maybe I should offer her a trade. Her birthmark for my numbers.

"Excuse me?" I say before she reaches the classroom door.

She turns to me, but before she can talk, I beat her to it.

"Can you tell me where room one hundred thirteen is?"

"It's in the next building. That way," she says, and points toward the left double doors, back down the hall I just came from. Her accent reminds me of a teacher I had back in California. Mr. Orlov. I think he was Russian.

"Twenty-seven. Thanks."

"Room twenty-seven is right there." She points to a classroom behind her.

"Twenty-seven again, and thanks again," I blurt out, and begin my run.

I don't wait to see her confused expression, but I know it's there. It's always there. I tighten my backpack straps and run down the hall toward the next building. When I reach the double doors, I don't slow down. I barge into them like I am a battering ram invading a castle, and continue my run. The cold wind punches me, but I take it head-on and run across the neatly trimmed grass.

I pass a man holding a travel mug in one hand and a briefcase in the other.

"No running," he says as I race past him.

"Nine," I shout back.

I realize if he was German, I just told him "no." The thought always makes me laugh. You'd be surprised how many people say something that totals nine. And usually, "no" is the perfect answer. Like now. No, I will not stop running because I am super late to my first class on my first day of school in my new life.

I reach the next building and pull open the door. Room 113 is directly in front of me. I stop in front of it and run my fingers through my hair, attempting to look presentable. I take a deep breath, put my earmuffs over my ears, because sometimes people think twice before talking to me when I have them on. This helpful trick sometimes buys me enough time to find an empty seat before I need to speak. I grab the door handle. Here goes nothing.

I open the door, which is the loudest door to ever open, and walk into the classroom. The teacher, Mrs. Hagadorn, stands near her desk and addresses her students. She has long silver hair, not gray like most older teachers, but as silver as a superhero's hair, like it was dyed to look cool. I don't keep my eyes on her long enough to see if she's wearing a costume or not; instead, I focus on my own feet.

The entire class shifts their heads from her to me as I take another step inside. I don't need to see this happen, I feel it. This always happens. I look up, just a bit, to see where I'm walking. I hate this part. I do a quick scan to find the only empty seat and head toward it. Luckily, it's near the back, by the window. I keep my head down and try to get to the seat before—

"And you are?" Mrs. Hagadorn asks.

Shoot. See? Another example of a nine-lettered sitch.

Now, I have two options. I can either face the music and speak, or I can risk being rude and completely ignore her. I choose to ignore her. I don't want to be the topic of the class yet. I just want to sit down and sink deep into my chair. So deep that no one can see me. Nine. Nine. Nine. It keeps bouncing from one temple to the other, nearly giving me vertigo. But I must hold it in. Stay strong.

"Excuse me?" she asks with a tone that suggests I am being rude.

And she's right. So I lock eyes with her, look surprised, and remove my earmuffs, making it look like I simply didn't hear her. Another trick I picked up over the years.

"Nine. Eight. Oh, sorry. I didn't hear you. I'm Collin Couch," I say, hoping to talk enough to make everyone forget about the two random numbers I started my sentence with.

It works. She checks her roster and circles my name. She's not wearing a superhero costume at all. She's wearing a plaid skirt and a blue blazer over a white shirt. I focus on her silver hair instead of her eyes; eye contact invites conversation.

"Welcome, Collin. It says you're a transfer. Where are you transferring from?" she asks.

This is exactly what I feared would happen. I've got to be clever here. I can't just plop my earmuffs back onto my head and smile. I've got to make these numbers make sense.

"Sixty . . . Ummm . . . Public School Sixty. It's a small middle school in California."

Her eyebrows rise. This is not a good sign.

"PS Sixty? I never heard of it. Whereabouts in California is it located?"

Shut up, silver-haired lady. Please! I know she's only being nice, but I don't need nice right now. I need silence. I need her to not care about where I'm from at all.

"Fifty-six. I mean, Fifty-Sixth Avenue. In Huntington Beach."

She smiles. I smile back. Please let this conversation be over.

"How exciting. Is this your first time to Minnesota?"

She won't give up. I guess people really can be *too* nice.

"Forty-one . . . times. I've been here forty-one times."

On cue, a dozen heads turn to me. Why are they all looking at me like I'm crazy? I think I'm covering up pretty well so far.

"Well, welcome back, then," she says.

"Nineteen . . . I plan on moving back there when I'm nineteen, but for now, I'm here. To learn . . . so . . . please, teach me US history," I say.

A few students laugh. I'm not sure why, because this is in no way funny.

Mrs. Hagadorn snaps her fingers, which turns everyone's attention back to her. She begins to jot down some words on the board. Whew. That was close. I look down at my desk to avoid any lingering eyes of students trying to already figure out what's wrong with me. Attention spans are low, and after a few seconds, they'll go right back to being bored and secretly texting their friends.

Perhaps Minnesota won't be so bad after all. Mrs. Hagadorn opens her history book and has the student closest to her begin reading aloud. I look out the window and see a fuzzy little squirrel dart across the grass and leap onto a tree. I can't help but think of my brother again. I try to picture him running across the grass and jumping onto the tree. I wonder if he attended this school—and if he did, did he climb this exact tree? Were people super impressed by him? Or was he also strange like me and my mom? Maybe he beat up whoever dared make fun of him. He was a buff squirrel, my brother.

As soon as the bell rings, Mrs. Hagadorn shuts her book. I snap out of my daze and realize I have no idea what today's lesson was about. If we were taking a quiz on whatever we learned, I'd have nothing but a squirrel dangling from a tree drawn on my sheet of paper. I need to focus. I want my mom to think I'm smart.

I keep my head down and file in line with the rest of the students escaping class.

"Collin?" Mrs. Hagadorn says as I reach the door.

I hope she doesn't ask anything about what was read aloud today. And if she does, I hope she loves squirrels.

"Six. Yeah?" I say as I approach her desk.

She holds up a note, but sets it down before I can examine it.

"I've been informed of your situation. I want you to know that you will get no special attention from me. You will be treated as fairly as everyone else."

"One hundred and twenty. Thanks, that's all I want."

Her head perks up from the total. She's impressed. They always are at first. Especially teachers.

"That's remarkable," she says.

"Fifteen. That's one way to put it. Another would be infuriatingly annoying," I say, and walk toward the door.

Good. I left her speechless. I pull out my schedule and search for my next class.

Science wasn't so bad either. The teacher was my favorite kind, the type who loves to hear himself speak. He went on and on about what he did before winding up as a science teacher. What those details were, I couldn't say, because again, I sat near the window and searched for furry versions of my brother hopping from one tree to the next.

I have no clue what to do about lunch. I'm hungry, but I want to avoid the sea of people lining up for food in the cafeteria. It's usually the nice students with excellent grades who try to talk to the new kid. Ideally, that would be awesome. I'd love to make new friends here, especially smart ones, but as good as making friends sounds, I quickly remind myself that losing friends is too painful. And I always lose friends. At first, the separations are subtle. They stop inviting me to their house. Or I'm not invited to the beach on weekends, or whenever there's a birthday party, I am "accidentally" left off the invitation list. And then it's just me again, in my room drawing. It's easier to avoid everybody.

My stomach barks. Maybe I will just keep my head down and play it safe for today. I'll eat when I get home. I walk across the grass and head toward the closest tree. I know the perfect way to kill time. I find a good shaded area, pull my sketchpad from my backpack, and begin drawing. Today, I'll draw a squirrel. That seems to be today's theme.

A few strokes in, I realize I'm not drawing a squirrel. I am drawing a girl. And not just any girl; it's Orenda. I must have snapped a mental photograph of her the moment we met. She is looking down at me, the same way as I looked up at her from the ground. She is peeking out of her tree house, smiling. This is after she launched the baseball at my head, of course.

I rub the bump on my head. It's still there. I push down on it to remind myself that she's real. Ouch. Yep, she's real. I think this drawing will go up on the wall, but not in the living room. It will be in my room, placed right next to Seven. Pretty things need to be put together.

The bell rings, and the students shuffle to their next class at a pace I never saw in California. There, everyone lollygagged and took their time to get from point A to point B. It was as if the later you were, the cooler you were. But here, people go where they need to go. It's simple and straightforward.

When I get to my next class, I head toward the back before all the seats fill up. The window seat is taken, so I grab the seat farthest from the front of the class, which is somewhere near the middle. Hopefully I'll blend in and go unnoticed. The teacher, Mr. Renaldi, is a bald, heavyset man wearing a denim shirt tucked into his jeans and a bolo tie.

In California, anyone who wears a denim top with denim jeans was referred to as wearing a Canadian tuxedo. I never really understood what that meant, but I'm not too far from Canada now, so maybe this teacher is just a really fancy guy.

He spots me easily and right away, like I'm an elephant in a room full of hyenas. And I know those hyenas will soon be laughing. He gestures for me to remove my earmuffs, so I do. I hope, hope, hope that's all the attention he'll pay to me, but something tells me the "all eyes on the weirdo kid" has just begun.

"Hello, class. Before we get started, I'd like to introduce a new student added to our mathematic family," Mr. Renaldi says.

Oh no. He's a Mather. I'm in math class. I should have ditched this class and asked my mom to teach me algebra. I hope he won't parade me in front of everybody as his new math problem to solve.

Clearly, he didn't get the same note Mrs. Hagadorn got. Or maybe he did, and maybe he just wants to see what the fuss is all about. He holds up his roll sheet and looks out toward his class like it's the guest list for his fancy denim party.

"Collin Couch?" he says, pronouncing my last name like a long comfortable sofa.

The room chuckles at my last name. Everyone assumes I'm a piece of furniture. I keep my head down and repeat "eleven" through my teeth at the lowest possible volume.

"Collin? Are you here?" he repeats, knowing very well I am.

Now heads are beginning to search for me. I may as well get this over with. Sixteen slams into the eleven that is waiting to be fired out of my mouth at any moment, nearly shoving it through my lips. But still, I keep my head down, trying to buy a few more seconds of freedom before my cannon fires.

"There you are," Mr. Renaldi says, and I look up.

He's staring directly at me. In fact, so is everyone else in the room.

"Eleven, sixteen, eleven," I blurt out.

Quick! Think! I need to salvage this. "That's my locker combination. Yes, I'm Collin."

A few students laugh. Mr. Renaldi's face twists.

"We don't need to know your locker combination, buddy, but thank you," he says, causing the class to laugh again.

"Fifty-three," I say. Dang it. I give up trying to mask it. There's no way I'm going to start telling the class I had fifty-three donuts this morning or it took fifty-three steps from my last class to this one. It's hopeless. I've lost this battle. I'm already weird, and class has been in session for only fifty-three seconds, maybe?

He looks at me like I'm one of his math problems.

"Excuse me?" he asks.

"Eight. Sorry. I'm Collin Couch, it's pronounced like *pooch*, but spelled like *couch*," I say.

The room laughs yet again. But not with me . . . at me.

"Quiet!" Mr. Renaldi hushes his class. "Welcome to math class, Collin Couch. What we like to do here is get to know each other before we get down to work, so if you wouldn't mind, can you stand and tell us a little bit about yourself?"

It's a violent pileup of letters smashing into each other inside my head. They burst from the impact, splintering off into shards of numbers. It's so loud I want to scream. Every single student is looking at me. My heart beats out of my chest. I feel the blood in my body begin to heat up and boil. I forget to breathe, which makes me gasp for air. I can feel my face turning redder by the second.

I push back my chair, sending a loud screech echoing through the room. Ugh. I didn't just lose this battle, I was slaughtered. It was a massacre. Or in this case, a mathacre.

I slowly put my backpack on and stand up. My hands are shaking. My legs feel wobbly, but they still work, so I use them before they have a chance to quit on me. I try to breathe as calmly as I can, but anxiety grabs my throat and squeezes. There are too many eyes watching. I hope I don't faint. It's too early to add "the kid who faints" to the list of why no one likes me. I need to survive this. I need to live to fight another day. I face Mr. Renaldi, who looks quite smug in his victory—although I'm sure he has no idea we just went to battle.

"One hundred and fifty-four," I say.

And before he has a chance to respond, I run out of the classroom. The trail of laughter fades as I get farther away from the class. I feel dizzy. Halfway through the hall, I see the bathroom door and dive in. It's completely empty. Good.

I stumble to the sink and even with my shaky hands, I manage to turn the nozzle. First one, then two, now three splashes onto my face, slowly bringing my heart rate back to normal. I take a deep breath and stare at my reflection. I need to accept my defeat. And why not? Losing is what I do best.

I spend the remainder of the time hiding in a bathroom stall until I hear the bell. As guys start piling into the bathroom, I make my way out and head toward the exit of the building. I still have two more classes, but I quickly decide I've had enough school for today. I'm done.

I push the double doors open and march toward the bus stop.

I'll wait it out right here. My watch says 1:25, which gives me two hours to kill. I sit down on the curb and put my headphones in. I hit random, and . . . and nothing. What the hell? Just my luck; my battery is dead. I lose again. Earmuffs it is.

I'll keep these on until I reach home. Just in case someone walks by and asks if I heard about the new kid that completely flipped out in class today. I know how gossip works. By this time tomorrow, I'll already have a nickname. Let's see how clever these Minnesota students can be.

CHAPTER ELEVEN

-«◆»-·-«◆»-·

THE LONG WALK HOME

The bus drops me off right where my mom said it would, but I don't see her waiting for me. And it's really cold out. I look around me. There are no buildings, no cars, no people. Just a sprawling forest of dancing trees in every direction.

The wind howls through the branches, swaying them back and forth like windshield wipers on my dad's pickup during Southern California's one rainy day a year. Oh no. I hope it doesn't rain. I look up and scan the sky for gray clouds, but they're all white and fluffy as cotton balls spread out across the light blue sky.

It's strange not to hear anything besides the wind. I'm so used to constant traffic and city buzz. Maybe I should start walking? But I'm not exactly sure how to even get home. Every direction looks the same. The thought of my mom having regrets creeps into my head again. What if she's not running late, but has no intention of picking me up at all? Maybe she already called my dad and begged him to take me back?

I shake my head to erase my thoughts, and as I turn toward the reservation, I see someone walking toward me. With the cold air stinging my eyes, the figure looks blurry. Is that my mom? Did her truck break down? Everything seems to break when I'm near, so the chances aren't too unlikely. So I start walking toward her. And as I get close enough, I see it's not my mom . . . It's my grandma.

She's wearing a dress that is the same cut and length as her two previous dresses, which convinces me that I was right; it's one color-changing dress. Today it's red. It flows across her body, seemingly not affected by the wind at all. Her long black and silver hair hangs down too, covering her shoulders. Her head must be used to this weather. Mine is not, and it whips back and forth like the leaves surrounding me.

You'd think at her age, she'd have a limp or slow walk, but she looks healthy as a horse. And as she gets closer, I see she's smiling. I've noticed that my grandma always seems to be in good spirits.

"Hi, Grandma," I shout through the cold gusts as she approaches me.

She takes a few moments, then lifts her fingers into the air, like a conductor. "Nine, I think." She laughs.

"Ten," I say.

"Oh, I was close," she says.

"Eleven. No, you were right. 'Nine, I think,' is ten. 'Oh, I was close' is eleven. This will go on forever," I warn her.

"We got nine, ten, and eleven . . . We need a twelve."

"Thirty-four. Sorry, but you said too much."

"I always say too much."

"Seventeen. We should stop this banter soon," I say.

"Stop? But we haven't even started," she says, and signals me to walk back toward home with her.

"Twenty-six. After you," I say.

We begin walking together. The only sound I can hear is our feet crunching the fallen leaves as we enter the reservation grounds.

"All these numbers are making me hungry," she says.

"Thirty-two. I'm pretty hungry, too. I skipped lunch today," I say.

"Hunger isn't always about food, kiddo. I'm hungry for an adventure."

"Fifty-two. What do you have in mind?" I ask.

"Let's see where our feet take us," she replies, and picks up her pace.

How does this old lady have so much energy? I'm already getting tired, and she's kicking up leaves and practically skipping.

"Twenty-five. Does my mom know you're here?"

"I told her I'd get you. Let's let the adventure begin, shall we?" She heads off the main road and into the pathless forest. "Feet! Take us somewhere special!"

"Seventy-three. Okay," I say, and follow her. Did she just talk to her feet?

About twenty steps in, she bends down and picks up a large stick. She shows it to me with wide open eyes as if it were made of gold.

"Do you know what this is?" she asks.

"Nineteen. A stick?"

She laughs as if I said something downright foolish. I don't get it. It's a freaking stick. She holds it up to my face, making me examine it more closely.

"Is that what you see?"

"Sixteen. That's exactly what I see. Do you see something different?" I ask.

She points it to the ground and carves three letters into the dirt. *Y-E-S*.

Clever. Now I get it. "I see a stick, and you see a very large pencil. Interesting."

She laughs and breaks the stick in half with her thigh. So she's as strong as a horse, too.

"Want one?" She hands me one of the oversized pencils.

"Seven, thanks. What was once a stick is now two pencils. Cool."

But she's not done yet.

"Yes, you can give it to Seven, and she won't see a stick or a pencil, will she?"

"Fifty-seven. Nope. She'll see a toy," I say.

She spins in joy, like I just solved some riddle.

"See . . . we all see the same thing differently, don't we?"

And here I thought grandmas were just mean old ladies who complained when you trod mud onto the carpet or when you didn't eat all your vegetables. But this lady is pretty cool. She probably loves mud.

"Forty. I guess we do."

She lets me ponder that as she continues to walk down the dirt road. I stick my large pencil into my pocket and catch up to her. I even kick up a few leaves on my way just to see why she enjoyed it so much.

We saunter back home in silence. Not because we don't want to talk anymore, but more because she said all she had to say and I heard all I had to hear, or at least I think that's why. I hope that's why.

When we reach the house, she points to the backyard gate.

"You go through that way. I'll let you in from the back," she says.

"Forty-one. Why?" I ask.

"Why not?"

Fair enough. Maybe she does care about dirty shoes on the carpet after all.

"Six," I say, and walk toward the back gate. It's unlocked. I step inside and see Seven sleeping in the shaded corner against the house.

"Hey, girl," I shout, and she springs to her feet, breaking into a full gallop.

She reaches me by the time I approach the sliding glass door. I try to pull it open, but it's locked. I wait for a few moments and press my hands to the glass to peer in, but I don't see my grandma. Oh, great. Not again.

I rush toward the back gate, but as I near it, I hear it click from the other side. I pull at it, but now it too is locked.

"Not funny, Grandma," I shout.

I look through the narrow wooden gaps, but I don't see her. Why is she always locking me out here? Is this another lesson? Being trapped in a backyard all day? That's ridiculous. But as I think it, I also arrive to the conclusion that if it is a test, I'm not doing so well at it. Last time I ended up with a bloody leg and a bump on my head.

Is my mom home? I didn't see the truck out front. I'm hungry and thirsty. How can I pass this test on an empty stomach? I look at Seven's water bowl and consider drinking from it, but I'm not that desperate . . . yet. I walk back toward the sliding glass door and try again. Nope. It's still locked. But then, in the reflection of the glass, something catches my eye. The fence. The hole I made in the fence is back. How is that possible? I saw that it was repaired last night. I rub my eyes to see if I'm hallucinating, either from the cold or my hunger. But it's as clear as the blue sky above my head; the two broken pieces of wood are leaning against the fence, right next to the opening.

Did Grandma seriously repair it last night only to break it again today? That doesn't seem likely. Maybe it never was fixed? Maybe I *thought* I saw it repaired? I mean, honestly, how could an old lady fix a fence all by herself? I know she's strong, but still. And I did tell her I would fix it. Great. Now I not only look clumsy, but also unreliable. Maybe this is why she locked me out here again, to do what I said I'd do.

I approach the fence and peek my head through the opening and can't believe my eyes. The neighbor's yard, which was as dead as ours was, is now covered in healthy green grass. How can an entire yard just completely bloom into life overnight? I feel like I'm a character in a fantasy novel. What is going on? What is with this strange place called Minnesota?

Then it hits me. Maybe I'm dehydrated. That's it. I just need to get into my house and drink a gallon of water.

So, just like yesterday, I step through the fence and squeeze my entire body through. I reach back and place the two wooden boards over the opening so Seven can't follow me through this time. And speaking of this time . . . this time, I'll be ready for any projectile being launched down toward my head.

I creep through the fresh grassy yard as quietly as possible. I notice many random orange pieces of fruit scattered throughout the yard. Are those peaches? In October? What's that about? As I get near a peach that has been cut in half, I see a butterfly on it, eating. In fact, as I look closer, most of the peaches have butterflies feasting on them. I didn't even know butterflies ate fruit. Seeing a peach at this time of year is odd enough, but isn't it way too cold for butterflies to still be around? It's fall. I should be staring at pumpkins and, I don't know, crows?

As I pass each peach, the butterflies take flight and dance around the yard. It feels like a fairy tale. In every direction I look, there are happy little butterflies with peach-filled bellies dancing to a song only they can hear.

I keep my eyes upward, to avoid any baseballs being hurled down, and reach the back gate. Just my luck; hers is locked too. Now I need her to let me out. I'm pathetic. I don't even know how to successfully sneak through a yard without asking for help. I walk over to the thick trunk of the tree. There aren't any wooden blocks nailed into the tree, or even a ladder propped against it. So how does she get up to her tree house?

"Orenda?" I shout.

I wait for a few moments, but there's no movement from above. I shout her name again. Just as I'm about to give up, a thick white rope drops down and nearly lands on my head.

I jump out of the way and look up to a square opening in the floor of her tree house, but from where I am, it's too dark to see inside. I grab the rope and tug on it. It feels secure enough. I hoist my body onto the rope and wobble a bit as I try to balance my weight on it.

I begin my climb, and halfway up, I realize two things. One, I have no idea what I'm getting into. And two, I really need to start working out.

The last time I interacted with this girl, she threw a baseball at my head. I hope she doesn't have the baseball bat up there. I go nice and slow. Easy does it.

I finally reach the top. I'm not really afraid of heights, but if I were to fall from this height, I'll definitely break a bone or two, so I don't look down. I grab the wooden floor opening of the tree house, lift my body up, and crawl inside.

It's like a large bedroom in here, much bigger than it looks from the outside. The wooden walls are all plastered with colorful paint-ings and hanging figurines of butterflies. Her bed is against the wall, covered in a large red blanket with a huge yellow and brown butterfly knitted onto it.

"Hi," she says from behind me.

I turn around and see her sitting in a shadow near the corner, wearing a white hooded sweatshirt and black jeans. It looks like her hoodie is splattered with every color of paint, either that or she just recently hugged a rainbow. Her long black hair flows out from a white knitted beanie. It's still a little too dark to see if she's holding a weapon in her hands, but it's safe to say that if she were holding a large baseball bat, I'd be able to see it.

"Two. Hi," I say, and shift the rest of my body to face her. She leans forward, revealing a thin red line of paint running from under her right eye to her right ear.

We stare at each other for a good twenty seconds. I guess this is what an awkward silence must be. It's hard to tell, because I'm always awkward.

"Is that war paint on your face?"

She raises her hand and touches her face, smearing the line under her finger. After examining it, she smiles, revealing her teeth, which are as white as snow.

"Are you and I at war?" she asks.

"Fifteen. No. Of course not."

"Then it's not war paint. I'm just a messy painter," she says, and points to an unfinished painting leaning against the wall.

Red paint is splattered against a white canvas. It doesn't yet resemble a butterfly, but I'm pretty sure that's exactly what it will soon be.

"It's pretty," I say.

"You really like numbers, don't you?" she asks.

"Twenty-seven. They're kinda my thing. You really like butter-flies, don't you?"

"They're kinda my thing," she replies.

"Eighteen."

We stare at each other, like animals waiting for one to pounce so the other can run. I need to stop looking at her face. She's so pretty, and I'm afraid I'll start drooling soon or my eyes will bug out like they do in cartoons. And why is my heart beating so fast? I tell my eyes to turn away, but they don't obey me.

"You're weird," she says.

"Ten. At least I don't throw balls at people," I say.

She laughs. "No, you throw numbers at people," she fires back.

"Twenty-five. I guess I do."

I finally pull my eyes off of her face. I see a wheelchair in the corner, splattered with paint and adorned with glitter, beads, shells, and colorful rocks glued on to it.

"Isn't it dangerous to have a wheelchair in a tree house?" I ask.

"Dangerous? How so?" she asks.

"Fourteen. Well, for one, wheelchairs have wheels, and we are pretty high up. It could roll right out of the hole in the floor. Then boom! You'd need the wheelchair for the rest of your life," I say.

She laughs, grabs a cane from the shaded corner, and lifts her body to a standing position. The cane wobbles before going stiff, and she slowly walks toward me. I mean, really slowly.

"I already need it for the rest of this life," she says as she passes me and reaches the wheelchair. I watch her position her body just right, before sinking into the seat. I'm such an ass. I feel horrible. I need to say something nice to fix this. Quick! Think!

"Thirty-four. Oh."

No, I can do better than that. I need to apologize without apologizing.

"Sorry." Ugh. I just apologized with one meaningless word.

She's smiling, though, somehow finding this all very amusing.

"Don't be sorry. This is all part of my metamorphosis," she says.

"Forty-one. What do you mean?" I ask.

"I'm changing. What else could I mean?" she says.

It dawns on me that I am right now talking, actually talking to a girl. And to top it off, she doesn't look annoyed in the slightest. And to top off the top off, I'm picking up absolutely zero pity from her.

What were we talking about? Oh yes. She's changing.

"Twenty-eight. How . . . are you changing?" I ask.

"That's a long story. To tell it to you, I first gotta know yours," she says.

"That's exactly what my mom said," I say, laughing after I count her letters.

"Your mom's a smart cookie. Now, spill the paint," she says.

I count her letters and look at her strangely, then I shift my eyes over to her tubs of red paint lining the wooden shelves nailed into the wooden walls.

"Thirty-six. You want me to spill some of your paint?" I ask.

Her eyebrows rise. "I meant, spill the beans," she corrects herself.

Wait (nineteen). So, the prettiest girl on earth has just asked me to tell her something about myself. This has never happened before. What do I say? What do people in tree houses talk about? I look down and notice that I'm repeatedly rubbing my hands together. They'll start a fire soon. I'm so nervous. I grab both of my knees and hold on tight.

"Nineteen. Well, what do you want to know?"

"Well, for starters, who are you?" she asks.

Her letters parade through my head like a marching band. I've never really enjoyed this counting thing, but her words, I don't know, I'd count them all day if it meant I could look at her all day. Maybe because they exited her lips. Oh yes. Look at them. They are so beautiful. I should probably stop staring at them. This is tough.

"Twenty-four. My name is Collin. I just moved in next door. I just met my mom. I had my first day of school today, and that didn't go too well. What else? Oh, I have a dog named Seven. And my grandma likes to lock me out of the house. That's me," I say.

"Oh yes, I heard about you," she says.

Great. Word travels fast around here. One day at school, and I'm already the talk of the town. How gossip found its way up into a tree house, I don't know.

"Nineteen. Don't believe everything you hear. I mean, maybe you heard I was weird or a freak or whatever, but did you also hear I was kicked out of my old school for fighting? I bet you didn't hear that," I say, trying for the less of a freak and more of a rebel angle.

Wow. Was that my attempt of trying to sound cool? Please don't ask me if I won the fight or not. Saying I lost will immediately make me uncool.

She clasps her hands together and smiles like I just said something interesting.

"A rebel! And I thought I was the only one left around here," she says.

"Forty-five. Yep. That's me. I'm a rebel. I fight. I trespass through people's backyards, I even break into tree houses, but technically, this time, you invited me in by dropping down the rope, so I'm a guest right now, not a bandit," I say.

She laughs. "Who still uses the word *bandit*?" she asks.

"Twenty-five. Rebels do."

"Twenty-five rebels?" she says and laughs again.

"Sixteen. No. All rebels say bandit. I think," I say, watching this conversation potentially flush down the toilet.

"I see. So I take it you won?" she asks.

"Nineteen. Won the fight? Sadly, no. But you can't win them all, right?"

"I can help you, you know."

"Eighteen. You can teach me how to fight?"

"Yes. I can help you with your number thing. I can train you to fight it, if you're not too scared, that is."

I've heard this from so many doctors that I've lost count. Imagine that. Me, losing count. But it's cute coming from a girl in a tree house that I just met. Naive, but cute.

I count her letters and offer her some friendly advice. "I think you'd have an easier time teaching me how to fight people instead," I say.

Her eyes widen like she was just offered a challenge and happily accepts it. "You don't think we can defeat it?" she asks.

"Twenty-five. You know how many doctors have tried?" I respond.

"Doctors try to fix whatever breaks. But as far as I can see, you're not broken. Look at me. They tried to fix me, but I'm not broken either," she says, and slaps her lap, all matter-of-fact-like.

She watches my eyes shoot up into her wooden sky above us and count the invisible letters.

"And how do you plan on beating it exactly?"

"Well, all we need to do is teach you how to be as brave as a brave. How we do that, I have no idea yet, but it will come to me. Don't you worry. I win all my fights. Even when I'm outnumbered," she says with a grin.

"So . . . what about you?" I ask.

"What about me what?"

"What's your story?"

She takes a deep breath and cracks her knuckles the way people do right before fistfights begin. I should know.

"One story at a time, buster. We aren't done with yours yet," she says.

"I'm really not that interesting."

"Well, that's because your story isn't finished yet."

"Well . . . I'm new here, so maybe my story has just started."

She claps three times. For no apparent reason.

"Stories need exciting titles. And Collin doesn't seem to fit you. I think the main character in your story needs a better name."

"One hundred and one."

"'One Hundred and One' is a horrible title," she says with a smirk.

"So what's my title?"

"Let's see . . . In my mind, I was referring to you as the wingless bird boy, but now that you're here, up close, you don't really resemble a bird," she says, and puts her hand over her chin, massaging it while she thinks. Tracking more red paint onto her face.

"Why wingless bird boy?" I ask.

"Well, the way you tried to fly out the window last night . . . Splat! Like a wingless bird," she says, mashing her palms together the way my face met the dirt.

She saw that. Did she see everything? *Everything?* I was naked. I'm so embarrassed. I need to brush this thought away. I need to focus on something else and not my nakedness tumbling out of the window. I stare at her hands.

They are covered in paint, and each second that passes, I oddly find myself growing more and more jealous of her hands. They get to touch this girl's face whenever they want to. What lucky hands. I want to hold them. They look so soft and, at the same time, so strong. I want to trace her fingers like a kid making a paper plate turkey with crayons in kindergarten.

Oh my God. I'm literally staring at her with a huge grin. And she sees it.

"I wasn't just thinking about your hands, or a turkey," I say.

She laughs. "Good to know, because that would be super weird," she says.

"Orenda!" a man shouts. "Dinner is ready." Nineteen.

She wheels herself over to the window and pokes her head out.

"Coming, Papa!" she shouts back.

She rolls toward the open hole in her floor and slowly climbs out of her wheelchair. I step back to give her room as she attaches the rope to the steel bar of the wheelchair's frame.

"Like a bucket sent down a well," she says, and tosses the rope over a wooden beam above her head.

"You need help?" I ask.

"Nope. I do it every day," she says, and pushes the wheelchair toward the opening. It rolls out of the floor hole and suspends in the air. She gently guides it down the tree, foot by foot, with the rope.

Her face tightens as she lowers the wheelchair until it hits the grass below. She's super strong. I hope she doesn't notice how weak I am. I hope she doesn't watch me try to get down.

"See you tomorrow. Oh, and don't try to fly out of here. Use the rope," she says with a wink, and grabs hold of both sides of the rope.

She uses her arms to climb down, as natural as can be, like a monkey down a vine. Her legs interlock as she descends, but they keep losing grip and dangling, like they aren't fully obeying her commands. I see her get a bit flustered about it, but she doesn't say anything.

I tally up her letters and step forward, watching her reach the ground, but right before she does, she swings her body forward and lands directly into the seat of the wheelchair waiting for her. There should be applause for that acrobatic stunt, but nope, there's just me smiling down at her like a goof. She takes one last look up at me, smiles back, and pushes the giant wheels through the green grass of her yard toward her house.

Now I'm alone in her tree house. I walk from corner to corner, examining her butterfly art. I wonder why she loves butterflies so much? Even more so, I wonder why she can't walk like a normal person. But who am I to know anything about normal people?

CHAPTER TWELVE

-《◆》-《◆》-

LEARNING
FROM WOLVES

I must have drunk two gallons of water after I was finally let back into the house by my mom. I want to find my grandma even more now. Not to ask her why she locked me out, but to thank her for doing so. If it weren't for her, I would have never spent time with Orenda.

But again, I couldn't find her. She's like a ninja in this house.

"Collin," my mother calls from the kitchen.

"Six," I yell back, and go see what she wants.

As I round the hall, I hear kids laughing. When I turn the corner, there are two little kids sitting at the table.

"Collin, I'd like to introduce you to two wonderful souls, Boy Who Runs Fast and Girl with Eyes Like Eagle," my mother says proudly.

They both look at me with equally proud faces, lips pursed

together like they're holding secrets in their mouths. I count the letters as quickly as I can to not look too strange in front of these little people.

"Eighty-three. Hello, Boy Who Runs Fast and Girl with Eyes Like Eagle. My name is Collin."

The boy looks at the girl, and the girl looks at the boy, then both look at Mama. Am I missing something here? Why is everyone smiling? And all at once, the three of them erupt into a deep and heavy laughter. The boy nearly falls off his seat. I look at Seven, and even she is grinning.

"What's so funny?"

"Those aren't our names!" the little boy barks out, while still laughing.

"Eighteen," I say, and end up laughing from all their laughing.

It grabs ahold of me in a way I'm not used to. I put both arms around my stomach to hold it in, but I can't. I let it out. Could it be? Am I becoming . . . Am I happy?

"You're so gullible," the little girl says, and punches me in the arm.

Wow. Even this little girl packs a punch. I really need to hit those weights soon.

"Fifteen. Well, you look like an eagle, so . . ."

They laugh again.

"I'm Anna, and this is my brother, Nando," she says.

"They are clever little foxes," my mother says, and ruffles both of their black-haired heads at once.

"Twenty-nine. Twenty-four. Well, I know of a beast that eats clever little foxes."

They both sit up straight with wide, curious eyes. Seven used to love chasing me around the house. All she needs to see is feet shuffling away from her and she'll tackle whoever owns them. It was one of our favorite games growing up.

"Seven!" I say.

Seven jumps up, and the kids scream and catapult out of their seats. Seven gives chase. My mother growls to help the effect, then laughs as the kids make a mad dash out of the room.

"You know how long it took them to get into those seats?" she asks me.

"Forty-three. Don't worry. Seven will drag them both back any minute now."

We hear Nando shout from the other side of the house. Seven caught him. Good girl.

"One down," I say.

My mother laughs and wraps her arms around me.

"It's good to finally have you home," she says, and squeezes me tightly.

I count her letters, and before thinking, I ask her something that has been on my mind since the moment I arrived here.

"Why didn't you ever come see me?" I ask.

She pulls away to face me. I know this just took a serious turn, but serious is sometimes needed. I mean, if we laughed all day, we'd be split at the seams within a week.

"I wanted to. But your father wanted the past to remain in the past."

I hear my dad's voice as she says that. It's something he has always said to me.

"But you're my mom. I should've known you," I say.

"He felt life would be easier for you out there, in a big house with nice schools. Growing up on a reservation isn't exactly easy," she says.

Seriously?

"Life wasn't easy for me there."

"He said things were always going well. He sent me the pictures to prove it."

I know why my dad told her that. He refused to fail as a father. That's why he kept me for so long. It's in his competitive blood. Like I was a sport he had to win. I guess I should give him some credit. I may not have been the son he wanted, but he never threw in the towel . . . well, until he did.

"He tried his best, I guess," I say.

"And now it's my turn to try my best. And I will start by making sure your dog didn't eat the neighbor's children," she says as she starts to leave the kitchen.

"Eighty-six. Wait. Mama?" I say before she leaves the room.

She stops and turns to face me.

"What?"

"Four. Did you tell those kids to ignore the numbers when I talk?"

She smiles. "Why don't you ask them?"

"They haven't even reacted to it. Everyone reacts to it."

"Maybe it's not as big a deal as you think it is," she says, and walks out.

"Finally. I'm boring," I happily say under my breath, once I count her letters.

That's it. It's my turn to try my best. I'm not going to hide anymore. Maybe people here are different. Maybe my dad wasn't lying when he said people here are more open-minded. From now on, I will make an effort. I am going to make friends and not sit alone in my room all day drawing pictures of animals. I am going to live my new life. And if people get annoyed with my numbers, so be it. If worse comes to worst, I can hang out with these two kids all day. But if better comes to best, then I'll be spending all my time with Orenda, up in her tree house. Getting to know her story.

The kids run back into the kitchen and take their seats. Seven follows and lies down at my feet. My mom hasn't returned yet, but that's okay. For the first time in my life, I want to get to know my neighbors. This is an amazing feeling. I just hope it lasts.

"So, Anna, what do you like to do?" I ask.

"Eat."

"Three. Is that all?" I ask.

"That's all right now. After I eat, I like to play. After I play, I like to dream," she says, like each activity is better than the last.

"Fifty-eight. You take your likes one step at a time. That's smart. What about you, Nando?"

He sits up proudly, back straight, and clears his throat. Like his hobbies are worth shouting from rooftops.

"I like to play basketball and football and wrestle. I like eating, too."

"Fifty-six . . . Do you wonder why I said fifty-six?" I ask them both.

They both look at each other like they are keeping a secret.

"It's okay. You can tell me," I add.

Anna places her elbows on the table like a miniature business-person addressing the boardroom.

"It's weird, but I think everyone is weird," she says.

If people thought like this back in California, I might have had an awesome childhood.

"Thirty-two. That's a good way to look at it. What about you, Nando?"

"How do you know it was thirty-two?" he asks.

"Twenty-six. I just do. I see it. In my head."

"But what if you're wrong?" he asks.

"Nineteen. If I'm wrong, then that means something is wrong with the calculator inside me."

He laughs and looks at my head, as if he expects to see an actual calculator protruding from under my hair.

"Can I try?" he asks.

"Seven. Yeah. Give it a try," I tell him.

He tries to count my sentence by sealing his eyes shut as hard as he can.

"You're not even counting. You're just closing your eyes," Anna says.

"I'm waiting for it to come to me," he replies.

I laugh.

"So if you think everyone is weird, how are you weird?" I ask her.

"I need a night-light to sleep," she answers.

"Twenty-three. I think that's pretty normal."

"It makes no sense," she says.

"Fourteen. Explain."

"I know there's no monster under my bed, but at night I think there is, so I turn on a night-light, and it keeps the monster away," she says.

"Ninety-seven. Okay, I get that."

"My mom is different, too," Nando says.

"Nineteen. She is?" I ask.

"Yeah. Her hands shake a lot."

"Twenty-one," I say.

"Her whole body shakes," Anna says.

"Eighteen."

"But she doesn't like being called Lady Earthquake," Nando adds.

"Forty-one. No. I bet she doesn't."

"That's why I like wrestling. If anyone calls her Earthquake again, I'm gonna beat them up," Nando says like a fearless warrior.

"Seventy."

"No one is beating up anybody," my mother says as she reenters the kitchen.

"Twenty-three. I thought you disappeared like Grandma," I say.

She ruffles my hair as she passes me. "I wouldn't leave you alone with these two wolves," she says.

"Thirty-nine. I thought they were clever little foxes?"

"A wolf can change into whatever it wants, right, kids?"

They both point their faces toward the ceiling and howl to an unseen moon.

Between these kids, my mom, and my grandma, I've already learned a lot about life. I've learned that I take it way too seriously. I shouldn't be worried about what other people think when I count their letters. I should be howling at the moon and seeing sticks as pencils and singing along to all the songs on the radio.

Man, I wish more people looked at life through the eyes of wolves and foxes.

"You never told me how your first day of school was," my mom says.

"Forty. It didn't go as well as I hoped."

"Well, starting is the hard part. Everything that follows is easier," she says as she walks the little wolves out of the kitchen.

CHAPTER THIRTEEN

-«◆»-«◀

A FEARLESS WARRIOR, NOT SO MUCH

Yesterday doesn't count. Even though it was technically my first day of school, that was before I had this revelation about not caring what people think. So I should get a do-over. Today counts. Today is my second first day of school. Second day, second chance. I'm a different person now. I'm a confident Collin. I'm ready to make friends and not hide out in bathrooms until the bell rings.

I check myself in the mirror. I'm still in all black, but this time I'm slicking my hair back. No more hiding my face. I'm almost surprised by my reflection. I'm smiling at me.

I eat my breakfast and even wash my plate before my mom finishes her eggs. She can see the difference in me. I'm smiling way too much. I hope it's not freaking her out.

"Someone's in a good mood this morning," she says.

"What can I say? I'm excited to go to school."

She tosses her last egg off of her plate straight to Seven, who catches it and eats it in one bite. But I don't have time to be impressed, because my mom launches out of her seat and grabs her keys.

"Well, let's get you there now," she says, and rushes toward the door.

I can't tell if she's joking or not. I rush Seven out the sliding glass door and try to beat my mom to her truck. She wins.

We get in and drive off so fast that I don't even remember if I shut the door or not. But maybe Grandma's home. I haven't seen her since she locked me out.

"Where's Grandma?" I ask, before her radio picks up reception.

"Around," my mom says, before a song kicks in.

And as we leave the reservation's main road, a classic rock song begins to play.

"I love this song!" Mom shouts, and jumps in, singing midverse.

"Thirteen," I say, but she doesn't hear me.

I watch her dance in her seat with so much passion, I start to think she actually believes she's front row at the concert. Or maybe even closer. She's on stage with the band. Singing along with them . . . as she drives.

I stare at her face. I can almost see what she looked like when she was my age. Music does that to people. It reverses aging. She looked the same as she does now, just less mileage around her eyes and mouth. But I bet her eyes haven't changed. I bet wild eyes never change.

My mom has wild eyes. My grandma has wilder eyes. But only one person has the wildest eyes. Orenda.

My mind fills with Orenda.

I want to ask my mom why she doesn't walk the way everybody

else does, but I know how she'll answer. *That's part of her story, and only she can tell it . . .* So I don't bother asking. My mom's right. It's Orenda's story. I've got a counting thing, and her legs are funky. I'll ask her about it after school. I hope she's there. My fingers begin to slip and slide on each other, like slippery fish trying to cuddle. Why am I so nervous to see Orenda? Or am I excited? I can't tell which one I am . . . Maybe both.

We pull up to the drop-off zone, and my mom turns the radio down.

"Same as yesterday," she says.

I wonder if she means she won't be there after school and I'll have to walk back with Grandma again. I wonder how many things Grandma will give new purposes to today? It is not a leaf, it's an umbrella for the snails. It's not a rock, it's a weight to stick into your pocket in case the wind tries to blow you away.

I leap out of the truck after I plant a quick goodbye kiss on my mom's cheek again. I did it so fast, that I'm sure no one saw it. I'm a new confident Collin, but I still can't have gossip going around about how I need to kiss my mom goodbye each morning.

It's time to turn over a new leaf. Time to be a normal student. Well, as normal as I can be. I walk up the main steps, into the sea of students, and notice everyone's face this time. Not just their shoes. My head is up, and I'm not afraid to talk.

But as I get closer to the building, doubt starts to set in. Am I setting myself up for more humiliation? What would Aji do? Well, I know exactly what he'd do. If someone made fun of him, he'd just throw a left cross and lay them out. Bad example. What would Orenda do? Probably the same thing.

I'm on my own. So the burning question is, what would I do? The bell rings. I guess we're about to find out.

I make my way to my first class and take my seat. The same seat as yesterday. But this time I'm not late. I pull my notebook out of my backpack and grab a pen. I'm officially ready to learn. Before Mrs. Hagadorn starts the class, someone taps me on the shoulder. I turn around. It's a guy wearing a blue flannel and a peace symbol dangling from his necklace. That's a good sign. I like peace. Peace is good.

"Hey," I say.

But he doesn't say anything. He's just looking at me like I'm a magician on a stage and he's waiting for me to perform my trick. By this time, a few of his friends are staring at me too. This is not good. He licks his lips like he is about to say something. Oh crap. I know this look. He's showing off. New me, meet bully. Bully, meet the new me.

I look to the teacher to save me but—just my luck—she informs the class she'll be right back and steps out of the room. I'm on my own, like always.

I focus on his short blond military buzz cut and take a deep breath. I know I'm not supposed to care what people think about me today, but this is literally the first two minutes of class. I was hoping to ease into this newfound confidence. I need to be smart and strong. I will not run away this time.

"What do you want?" I say.

"I want a double bacon cheeseburger, two large fries, one large Coke, three sets of chicken wings, a side of onion rings, and a tuna sandwich . . . to go," he says.

That didn't take long.

His friends erupt in laughter, but he doesn't laugh. He just stares at me, eyebrows raised, waiting to see if the rumors are true. I should have known this school would be no different. Bullies are bullies, wherever you go. Their names may change, their haircuts may change, but they're always definitely jerks.

And as hard as I try to turn around and ignore him . . . I can't. The letters flood in like an oil pipeline that burst. There's so many of them, gallons and gallons of letters. If I don't count them now, I might drown to death like one of those oil-covered birds, right in the middle of this classroom. I look up, take a deep breath, and count them before they kill me.

"One hundred and fourteen."

As the number leaves my mouth, I exhale, and I'm finally able to breathe again.

"That's amazing!" he says, and looks at his friends to make sure they're all watching.

"Twelve," I say, and hope he stops. But I know he won't, his kind never do.

"Hey, Josh, how do you know if he's right?" his friend asks.

"I don't," Josh says. "Either way, he's a freak."

I turn around, hoping Mrs. Hagadorn will return and interrupt this torment, but she's still out. Ugh. I've never wanted a teacher to start teaching her class so badly before.

"Hey, freak!" Josh says again.

But I don't turn around. I just hold the number eight inside my head, twirling it around for as long as possible. It spins, making the infinity sign, which is exactly how long this torture feels.

"I'm talking to you!" he says, and shoves me in the back.

I want to whip around and punch him square in the nose, but the last thing I need is to be kicked out of this school, too, so I shove my hands in my pockets, making sure they stay put. He shoves me in the back again. I turn around calmly and imagine myself cursing him at the top of my lungs to leave me alone, but instead, all that comes out of my mouth is a gentle "twenty-two."

They laugh again.

"I wanna try," his friend says.

I quickly slap my earmuffs on, covering my ears, and turn around. I hate this class. I hate this school. I hate every school that ever was. I hate these students, and I hate my stupid, damaged brain.

Josh rips my earmuffs off and tosses them to his buddy, a zit-faced kid that looks exactly like a meerkat, and not a cute one.

No. I need those. As he tosses them back even farther to another buddy of theirs, my stomach drops. Those earmuffs were my paddle. Now I'm up crap river and have no way to steer this boat. And I can feel the waterfall coming. It's close.

"Give them back!" I shout, watching the cord dangle above his desk as he waves the earmuffs around like a cheerleader with pom-poms.

"Nope."

"Four. Please."

"First tell me . . . How much wood could a woodchuck chuck if a woodchuck could chuck wood? Well, freak, the answer is, a woodchuck could chuck as much as a woodchuck if a woodchuck could chuck wood," he says, which now has the entire class laughing with him.

My mind nearly explodes by the plethora of letters battle-ramming my head, trying to enter like invading Vikings. There's so many that my vision starts to blur.

I try to stand, but I feel dizzy. I grab both sides of my desk and try to hold the door closed in my mind for as long as possible. But it's no use. The letters burst in and storm my brain. It has begun. *How* . . . is three. *Much* . . . is four. *Wood* . . . is four . . . I launch out of my seat. I hear my chair fly back and hit another desk, but I'm too busy counting to care.

The door opens and Mrs. Hagadorn enters her class. Too late, Mrs. H.

They stare at me like I'm not even human. I count, count, count.

My eyes move back and forth as the numbers line up, ready to depart through my lips. I count them all, hating every second of it. I need to breathe. I need to breathe now. I'm almost done counting, just a couple more.

"One hundred and fifty-two. Now just stop, dammit!" I shout. I'm gasping for air, like I just swam 152 miles.

The entire classroom goes silent. Mrs. Hagadorn drops the papers in her hands in shock. As my vision clears, I notice I am not just standing up, but I am standing on top of my desk. A complete silence rolls through the room like gray clouds quietly eating a blue sky.

Even Mrs. Hagadorn is speechless. This is my only chance to get out of here. I leap off of my desk, grab my earmuffs from the now open-mouthed kid, slap on my backpack, and rush toward the door.

Mrs. Hagadorn takes a step toward me. I hold up my hand, stretching out all five of my sweaty fingers to her.

"Not a word. *Please*," I say and I run out of the classroom.

How did this happen? My second first day of school is even worse than my first. Confidence sucks. Turning over new leaves sucks. The new me sucks. He's just like the old me. Damaged. Defective. Broken. What was I thinking?

I skip the bathroom and head toward the exit. My brain is freaking out, and I find myself counting my steps. No. I'm done with numbers. I hate numbers. I hate every single number from one to a zillion. I'm going home. And I'm never coming back.

I should have punched that guy in the face. I wish my brother was still around. He would have stepped in and mopped the floor with those jerks. But my brother is dead. And just like every other school I have ever attended, I'm on my own and will forever be the freak.

My heart is still beating a mile a minute. I'm not even sure how to get home. So I choose to go left and keep running. Once I'm past the campus grounds, I slow down to a walk. I'm exhausted. My breath plumes with each step I take. The coldness was kind enough to not bug me while I ran, but now it's buzzing around me, stinging my exposed hands, neck, and face like invisible frozen bees.

It seems like hours before I finally reach the sign to the reservation. A few minutes in, at the exact same spot as yesterday, there she is. My grandma is walking toward me.

But wait . . . How did she know I left school already? Did the school call our house and tell her?

I hurry toward her wearing a cheap smile, trying to hide how upset I am about what happened in school. I don't want her to know I was laughed at. I don't want her to know that I'm weak. I want her to keep thinking I'm special, even though I know I'm not.

"Hey, Grandma," I say, when she's close enough to hear me.

"Your school called," she says.

Well, there you go. (Sixteen.) But the thought of being grounded for ditching school doesn't seem so bad when you don't have any friends. In fact, punishing me would be forcing me to go to school and try to get along with people. Actually, that would be punishing them, too.

"Yeah, sorry about that," I say.

But she doesn't look mad. She looks pretty happy, actually. Then again, she always looks happy.

"Want to talk about it?" she asks.

"Seventeen. Not really," I reply.

"Good. Because we got more adventures to go on, you and me," she says, and turns off of the path and into the forest.

"Forty-four," I say, and follow her.

We walk. My grandmother steps with such determination, weaving among the tall trees like we are walking toward nothing and everything at once. I stare at the ground to see what she plans on picking up this time, but her eyes are fixed toward the sky. After a few minutes, I break our silence.

"Where are we going?" I ask.

"Beats me. I'm following the clouds. They're so indecisive today," she says.

"Fifty," I say, look up to the sky, and laugh.

The clouds are almost covered by the outstretched branches above us, but I see that they are moving fast. "Why are we following clouds?" I ask.

"Why not? Wait. Maybe they are following us. Let's head this way," she says, and turns again, in the direction of our home, I think. I'm getting kind of dizzy from looking up while walking.

"Forty-eight. Does my mom know I ditched school today?"

My grandma licks her fingertip and holds it up to the air. What is she doing?

"She knows," she says while holding her finger still, analyzing the wind to the touch.

"Eight. Is she mad?" I ask.

"No. Disappointed, maybe, but not mad," Grandma replies.

Ugh. There's nothing worse than disappointing someone. I should know. I'm an expert at it. And the thought of my mom being disappointed in me makes my stomach churn.

"Twenty-eight. Are you mad?" I ask.

She squints her eyes up at the sky and lets her finger linger there a bit longer.

"Me? No way. I like rebels," she says.

Eighteen. Yeah, my grandma is pretty badass.

She hears something my ears don't pick up. Her eyes widen, she smiles and stomps her feet in joy.

"Grandma, what are you doing?" I finally ask.

"Listening."

"Nine. Listening to what?" I ask.

"The clouds. I was right. They're lost."

When people get old, they lose their minds a bit, or at least that's what we're led to believe, but I can't help but think this incredibly strange cloud conversation must have a point.

"Twenty-eight. I'm not sure what you mean," I say.

She drops her finger, walks up to me, and whispers, "Lean closer."

"Ten," I whisper, and lean down to her face, within inches.

My grandma lifts her wet finger and sticks it in my ear. I jump back and shake my head.

"Grandma! That's so gross!" I yelp.

But she doesn't care. She's too busy laughing.

"Why did you do that?" I ask, holding back my grin, even though, let's be honest, it was funny.

"Wet fingers attract air. Air attracts clouds. Clouds jump on finger. Finger goes in ear. Clouds are now in your head." She explains like it's all so obvious.

"And why would I want clouds in my head?" I ask.

HOLY CRAP!!!! My eyes widen, and I jump up and down in pure excitement. And so does she! "That's why!" she shouts up to the sky.

I can't believe it. This is the first time I have ever started a sentence without using numbers. I didn't count her letters at all. How is this possible?

And just like that, she stops jumping.

"Why did you stop? I'm talking like a normal person, Grandma!" I say.

"Clouds never last too long. After a few moments of puffy happiness, they just . . . *poof.* Disappear," she says.

And she's right. Her letters pour into my head this time, making little white clouds of their own. My brain falls right back into line and counts them.

"Seventy-five. But how did it work? You need to do it again. Grandma, you can fix me," I say.

She shakes her head. "You're not broken, son," she says.

"Seventeen. But you did something to me. You planted clouds inside my head. You sent them to take away all the numbers."

I realize how crazy I sound, and so does she.

"Don't be silly. I just gave you a wet willy," she says with a smile.

"Thirty-two. Then how did I not count your sentence?" I ask.

"Maybe you got distracted. Clouds can be distracting," she replies.

"Forty-three. Teach me how to do it again, please."

"Okay. Lick your finger and stick it in your ear," she says.

So I do it. I stick my index finger into my mouth and collect a fair amount of spit on it. Then I stick my finger in my ear. She awaits my response.

"Thirty-seven. It didn't work."

She laughs. "Not enough clouds out, I guess. Come on, we're home," she says.

"Thirty-eight," I say, and follow her toward our house.

I'm not sure what the lesson was today, but there definitely was one. I mean, this is a huge breakthrough for me. I now know it's possible to not count. I have no idea what a wet willy has to do with it, but all I have to do now is figure it out. And the only clue I have to go on is clouds.

We reach the house, and my grandma stops and delivers a kiss onto my cheek.

"Go around back, and I'll let you in," she says.

"Twenty-six. No, you won't. You're just gonna lock me out again," I say.

"I know. But that's what you want, isn't it?"

"Thirty. What makes you say that?" I ask.

"Because I'm not the only one who likes rebels," she says, and gives me a wink.

My mind immediately shoots to Orenda. My grandma is helping me out. I may not have a lot, but who gets to say that their grandma helps them with girls?

"Thirty-six. Thanks, Grandma," I say as she walks toward the front of the house.

CHAPTER FOURTEEN

-《◆》-《◆》-

FIRESTARTER

I squeeze through the broken part of the fence and approach her tree.

"Orenda," I shout up to her, and after a few moments, the rope drops from the hole in her tree house. I smile. Has she been waiting to see me the same way I've been waiting to see her? I climb up as fast as I can, which is not very fast at all—but better than last time.

Once I'm inside, I see her painting near the corner. She's on her knees. The red paint splatter definitely looks like a butterfly now. Her black hair is twisted into one long braid today, slithering down her back.

"You don't go to school, do you?" I ask.

"Not anymore."

"Is it because you're sick?" I ask.

"Do I look sick to you?" she says, and sets her paintbrush down.

"No. To me you look perfect."

She smiles, crawls over to her wheelchair, and climbs into it. Her legs are working a bit less today. They kind of drag behind her. I want to ask her about it, but not yet.

"I was just about to feed my family. Would you like to help?" she asks.

Is she inviting me to dinner? This is a first. I might as well do it, since I'm pretty sure the next time I see my mom, she'll inform me that I am grounded for the rest of my life. I wonder if she'll use the word *grounded* literally. If that's the case, there's no way she'd let me be up in a tree, far off the ground. I better spend as much time with Orenda as I can.

"Hello?" she asks, which snaps me out of my thoughts.

"Fifty, total. Yes, I'd love to help you feed your family. What exactly does that mean?"

She rolls her wheelchair toward her open window.

"There's a bag of fruit over there. Bring it here," she says, and points toward the opposite side of the room.

I walk over and pick it up. It's not too heavy, but there must be a dozen or so peaches in here. I hand it to her. From under her seat, she pulls out a large knife with a blade made of bone and the handle wrapped in dark brown leather.

"You carry a knife in your wheelchair?" I ask.

"I do. Are you afraid of knives?"

"Nope. I'm a rebel. Rebels aren't afraid of many things."

She laughs and slices one of the peaches in half. She hands me one from the bag.

"Pass me the knife," I say.

"No. This one is for you to eat. You look hungry."

"I am hungry. I skipped lunch again today. In fact, I skipped school."

"Why'd you skip school?"

"Like I said, I'm a rebel."

She takes one half of the peach she just cut and tosses it out the window. She bites into the other half. It's juicy. I try not to stare at the peach juice running down the sides of her mouth.

"Well?" she says.

"Four," I say, and bite into my peach.

It's delicious. I think this is the best peach I have ever tasted.

"It's pretty good," I say, and wipe the dribbling juice off my chin.

"I know. I plucked them from the tree myself."

"The rest are for all the butterflies outside?" I ask.

"Yes," she says, and proceeds to cut each peach in half and toss it out her window. "We love peaches."

"Sixteen," I say, and watch her toss peaches until the entire bag is empty.

I could do this all day. Who would have known that watching a girl throwing peaches out a window could be so fun? I look at her legs, which look perfect to me, but I wonder why they don't work like mine. Was she in an accident?

She catches me staring and points the knife at me, which drips peach blood.

"Were you just checking out my legs?" she asks.

"Twenty-eight."

"Don't hide behind twenty-eight. Come clean, buster," she says, raising the knife a bit higher.

"I was just wondering why your legs don't work."

Maybe I shouldn't have asked her that. I don't want to sound creepy; plus, she is holding a knife.

"I came up with a name for you. It's a noble name," she says, completely changing the subject.

"What is it? I hope not Buster," I ask.

She puts the knife away and sets both hands on her lap, milking my anticipation.

"Well?" I ask.

"The Count!" she says, and stretches her smile, almost from ear to ear.

I smile too. You'd think I'd hate being referred to by anything that has to do with numbers, but this name is clever. And she's right, it sounds kind of noble and kind of like a vampire, which I do resemble, being so pale and always dressed in black.

"Do you like it?" she asks.

"No. I don't like it," I say, and her smile immediately vanishes. "I love it!"

And like a wave crashing against the rocks, her smile returns to the shore of her face.

"Oh, and guess what?" I say excitedly.

"What?"

"Today, for the first time I can remember, I answered my grandma without counting her letters," I say.

Orenda claps excitedly. "How'd you do it?" she asks.

"Eleven. I don't know, but it happened today. She was talking to the clouds and invited them into my head, and for a few moments, I guess my head was too . . . clouded to count. Isn't that amazing?"

"It is. So the clouds did it?"

"Twenty. I think so, even though I know it sounds crazy."

"It's not crazy at all. The clouds are full of information," she says.

"Forty-five. Really?"

"Of course. Let's see what they are saying now," she says, and leans her head out of the window, looking through the branches toward the sky.

She spots a herd of clouds drifting west.

"Thirty-five. What are they saying?"

She doesn't answer right away. Maybe she's talking to them? I walk over to her, and as I lean toward the window, I smell her. The scent of fresh peaches fills my nostrils. I close my eyes and inhale deeper. This is heaven. Heaven isn't a place at all. We got it all wrong. Heaven is a peach. And angels bite into heaven and smell like Orenda.

I open my eyes and look out the window and up to the sky.

The clouds are no longer fluffy, fast, and white. They are now blotchy, slow, and dark.

"They say they are about to cry," she says.

"Twenty-four. Clouds can cry?"

Oh. She means it's about to rain. I immediately wonder if Seven is in the house. She hates the rain. Well, not the rain so much, but she hates being wet. Sometimes my dad would forget about her when I was at school on a rainy day, and I'd come home to a completely drenched dog waiting at the door. But to be fair, it hardly ever rains in Southern California, so I couldn't be too upset with my dad when it happened. We all make mistakes. I know I do.

I look into my backyard. I see Seven waiting patiently at the door. The clouds must have spoken to her too.

"I should go," I say, and head toward the opening in the floor.

"Until next time, Count!" she says, using a pronounced Romanian accent, sounding exactly how Dracula would.

"Eighteen. Do you need help down?"

She shakes her head no. "I'm staying up here tonight. I love the rain."

"Thirty-four. Well, if I'm not grounded, I'll come visit you tonight," I say, and descend the rope.

As soon as my feet touch ground, I run through her yard, dodging the peaches, and make it to the fence before the rain begins to fall. But as I squeeze through, a loud roar of thunder barrels through the sky. I look up and see the sky turning. It looks and sounds like the muzzle of a giant hound foaming at the mouth. And as I step into my yard, it starts pouring.

I meet Seven at the glass door. I slide it open, and we step inside. Phew. That was close. But I'm not out of danger yet. The rain is an easy bullet to dodge. My mom, on the other hand . . .

As I step farther inside the house, she is standing there, with her hands on her hips, staring at me. And she doesn't look happy.

"Am I grounded?" I ask.

"Start the fire," she says.

I don't know how to start fires. I know that's pretty lame, but where I grew up, people never taught their kids how to start fires. We just turned on the heater or put on a sweater.

"I don't know how," I say.

"Figure it out," she responds, and walks away.

This sucks. She is usually so full of joy. I ruined that. I disappointed her. The least I can do is try to start the fire for her. How difficult could it be? Even cavemen figured it out.

I stand in front of the empty fireplace. Shouldn't there be logs or something? I look around the room but don't see a pile of chopped wood anywhere. Does she expect me to take an axe to a tree? Do we even own an axe?

Another growl from the hound thunders above. It sounds like the sky was just bitten in half. Even the windows shake a bit. Seven lies down by my feet. She must not know what is happening. I don't think she's ever experienced thunder. And my only memory of it is in those scary movies where a killer is on the loose and a bunch of friends happened to rent a cabin in the woods in the same area. Cue the thunder.

Seven must think there's a war raging above our heads, being fought on the rooftops.

Thinking of fighting reminds me of where I saw a stack of firewood. In the garage near the punching bag. So I walk to the garage and turn on the light. There it is. I pick up as many logs as I can and return to the fireplace. I stack them and grab a newspaper from the coffee table.

After I roll it up and stuff it in between some of the logs, I light the newspaper with the candle that sits on the mantel. The sports section burns first. Eat that, Dad.

I must admit, although most of this stuff was laid out for me, I can't help but feel very Native American about this whole thing. I mean, sure, anyone can start a fire, but this was my first time. And it's on an Ojibwe reservation. And it was for my fire-skinned mother. I hope she's at least a tiny bit impressed. Her city-raised son just made fire. That's huge. Like a baby taking its first step. Whoa. I just compared myself to an infant. Maybe I'm not too impressive ... yet.

But who knows, maybe I'll get so good at this that people start referring to me as FireStarter, or the Boy Who Makes Fire, or something like that. Maybe bullies will be afraid of me if my name has Fire in it.

But I quickly remember that I already got a name at school. It's Freak. It's not very original and not too clever, but sadly, it fits me. No one but Orenda will know that I'm the Count.

As I think these thoughts, the flames begin to rise. Success! My mom comes in and sits in front of the fire. She doesn't look impressed. She still just looks disappointed. Darn it.

"Hello, fire," she says to the sprouting flames.

They don't respond in words so much, but they do crack and pop. She pats the floor next to her. This is where she'll either ground me, toss me into the fire, or forgive me. I sit beside her and await my fate.

Together, we stare into the flames and let the warmth grab hold of both of our bodies. I mimic everything she does. When she pulls back her hair, I pull back mine. When she puts her hands together, over her heart, I do the same. I even close my eyes when she closes hers. My dad would always deliver my punishment right away, usually a "go to your room." Not a terrible punishment. My room was my temple.

"Is this something our people do?" I ask, and crack open one eye to see her.

And with her eyes closed, face toward the fire, she replies, "This is something all people do."

"Are you angry with me?" I ask.

She opens her eyes to the fire.

"Why did you ditch school today?" she asks.

"They all made fun of me," I say.

She takes a deep breath and lifts her hands toward the fire, nearly touching the tips of the flames. But she doesn't say anything else. I guess she wants more details?

"No matter which school I go to, it's always the same. The moment I start counting, I'm labeled a freak. I don't belong anywhere, Mama. So I ran. I'm sorry," I say.

She waves her hands toward the fire, and somehow, it responds to her by moving the tops of each flame in the direction that her hand goes. I shake my head to see if this is all in my imagination, but it isn't. The flames follow her fingers back and forth, like they're slow dancing to a song I cannot hear.

"How are you doing that?" I ask.

"I'm just moving my hands. The fire is doing what it wants," she says.

"But the flames . . . they're following you," I say.

"Like how the clouds followed you and Grandma. You did your thing, and they did theirs. You didn't try to control the clouds, did you?"

"No. We just let them follow us. That's when I forgot to count her sentence. But I don't know how I did it."

"Maybe you didn't do it. Maybe you just gave up control and let it happen," she says, and rises to her feet.

"Fifty-six," I reply, but she's already gone.

Was that her punishment? A small talk about fire and clouds? I know there has to be some sort of lesson in there. I just need to decipher it. Okay. Think. I shouldn't try to control everything. I should let clouds do what clouds do and let fire do what fire does. All I need to worry about is what I do. Right? How do I apply this to my life? I don't try to control people's words, do I? I mean, they talk, I listen, I see the letters in my head, they morph into numbers, I add up those numbers, I say the numbers, and then I reply.

Wow. I do a lot of things when someone speaks to me. I never really broke it down like that before. I guess knowing is half the battle, right? But the other half is the hard part. How do I make it stop? I still have no idea how to control my own brain.

Thunder cracks the sky and rattles the house again, which reminds me of Orenda. She's out in her tree house, all alone. And technically, she's closer to the thunder. I wonder if the rain and wind are shaking her tree house back and forth like a boat being battered at sea. Is she trapped? I can feel it pounding at our walls, but she's just behind a few wooden boards and a bunch of leaves. I'd be terrified if I were her. But she seems fearless. Still, her legs . . . What if she needs my help? I need to know for sure.

I gather up enough courage and stand. My mom never actually said the words "You're grounded," so I wouldn't necessarily be disobeying her if I were to go outside, climb a tree, and check on Orenda.

I turn around, only to find my mom staring directly at me with her eyes fixed on mine. I feel like a kid with his hand halfway into a cookie jar.

"Sit down," she says.

"Seven," I reply. "I was just going to see if Orenda is all right."

She walks past me and kneels beside the fire. Again, it gravitates toward her.

"Fire, explain to Collin here his two options." My mother is actually speaking to the flames.

I don't count her letters because they weren't directed toward me. A clever move on her part.

"What two options?" I ask her, and yeah, okay, I ask the fire, too.

"Tell him he can either be grounded the white way or be grounded the Ojibwe way."

"Fire . . . what is she talking about?" I ask.

"Fire . . . tell him that the white way is you stay in your room for a week or two and do whatever you want, completely forgetting about why you're even in there, learning basically nothing in the end."

"And the Ojibwe way?" I ask. "Fire?"

"Tell him our people build a fire and sit with it. We reflect on our actions as the flames are given birth, live their life, serve their purpose, then slowly die. We think about why we did what we did and what we plan on doing differently the next time. We do this until the fire completely burns out. And as the last flame breathes in air, we are only then no longer punished."

So . . . let me get this straight, I can be grounded for two weeks or be grounded for what, a couple hours? Ummm. Easy choice. Ojibwe all the way.

"Tell my mom that I choose the Ojibwe way."

She gets up, kisses me on the cheek, and walks out of the room. I look down at the fire and think that I should have used fewer logs.

CHAPTER FIFTEEN

- ‹‹◆›› - ‹‹◆›› -

NATIVE WARRIOR
IN TRAINING

I fell asleep beside the fire last night, and when I woke up this morning, it was completely out. No flames, no logs, and no heat. There was just black and white ash lying under the cold air. Good news is, I'm not grounded anymore, but bad news, I also didn't get a chance to see Orenda last night. I wonder if she enjoyed the storm. I imagine she did. I bet she loved the sound of rain falling all around her. She probably had amazing dreams of riding lightning and swimming through the raining sea-sky.

I, on the other hand, don't remember my dreams. I hardly ever do. I just remember Seven licking my face as I woke up. My mom said that if I agreed to go back to school today, then she'd consider allowing me to go to Orenda's tree house after school. It's a deal I can't refuse. Stay in school, I see Orenda. Ditch school, I spend my days talking to fires.

School wasn't as bad today, mainly because I spent most of the day in the office explaining why I ran out of class yesterday. The principal tried her best to not get annoyed with my numbers, but after a while, she gave up and just let me sit in her office and "think about my actions" . . . So I drew a picture of a fire and stared at it for three hours.

Technically I attended school today, but I didn't have to suffer humiliation by going to any of my classes. Which is good, but it doesn't save me from tomorrow. I got a firm warning to not ditch again. And the principal assured me that all my teachers were personally made aware of my condition. Apparently, not all teachers read their emails, which is how she first sent out the notification to her teaching staff. Now every teacher is to address each one of my classes aloud in front of everyone, so no one can plead ignorance when I blurt out numbers. I know she thinks that's somehow going to help me, but I know better. It just paints a bigger target on my back.

The bus drops me off in front of the reservation sign. This is where I'd usually see Grandma. I was really looking forward to the opportunity to somehow speak without counting again. Also, I'd love me some of her wisdom right now. I need to stop being so terrified of school. And if anyone can help me with that, it's my cloud-tongued grandma. But she's not here, so I walk silently down the dirt road alone. I should take the forest route and seek an adventure, but if there's no one to share it with, what's the point?

I pass hundreds of sticks, rocks, and leaves, but my imagination doesn't dance. I just see sticks, rocks, and leaves. Am I so boring that I can't even enjoy a walk home by myself? I need an old lady to walk with me to appreciate the stroll?

About twenty yards away from my house, I pick up a stick and carry it with me. I'm not sure why, but I refuse to be boring. This is not a stick. It's a gun . . . But I don't really like guns. When I was nine, a kid in my class found a gun in his dad's dresser and accidentally shot his sister. She died. I've hated guns ever since. So I drop the gun and enter my front yard.

For the first time, I can actually walk into my house through the front door. That is, if I want to. But I don't. Instead, I take my usual route. I open the gate to the backyard. One step in, and I stop in awe.

Now our dried-up and dead backyard is now completely green and full of life, just like Orenda's yard. How is this possible? I do a double take to make sure I'm in the correct yard. Yep, I am home. I guess the rain last night revived the ground or something. The land sure is different here in Minnesota. I see why my grandmother treats it like it's alive, because it is. I'm a believer. I may not fully understand it, but seeing is believing, right?

Seven greets me in the grass, and we throw the ball around for a little bit. Yes, it's the same ball that smacked me in the head a few days ago. I think Seven notices that I'm not really in a playing mood, so after a few fetches, she lies down by the sliding glass door and leaves me to my thoughts, which are pulled up toward Orenda and her tree house.

I squeeze through the fence and walk through the minefield of half-eaten, soggy, storm-battled peaches. The smell of them causes me to hold my nose all the way to the tree. The rope is already there, waiting for me to climb it.

So I do.

I spent the entire day in an office, not talking to anyone, which usually is fine with me, but I'm different now. I want to talk. Maybe not to strangers yet, but to my grandma, my mom, those little kids, and yes, Orenda. I may have not had the best start being my new, strong, confident self, but just being around Orenda makes me feel like I am getting stronger. And not just mentally, physically too. Lifting your own body weight isn't exactly easy, even when you're on the thin side like me. But it already feels easier.

Orenda is sitting on her bed surrounded by pillows and blankets, listening to music through her earbuds. She's facing the wall of butterfly paintings, so I don't think she knows I'm here.

I should announce my presence, but instead I tiptoe as quietly as I can to get a better angle of her face. As I step, the floorboards creak, but not loud enough to draw attention. I settle on a profile view of her and remain perfectly still.

She's so beautiful that my heart skips a beat. I always thought that was just a silly thing people say to each other on Valentine's Day, but it's real. My heart is actually beating so fast it interrupts my breathing. And what's strange is, every day Orenda looks different. Always beautiful, but different. Today her hair is shorter and cut in an Egyptian-style bob, like Cleopatra.

The song in her ears ends. She removes the earbuds and wipes a few tears from her eyes. It must have been an emotional song. But she hasn't moved her body yet, so she still doesn't know I'm with her. Should I clear my throat? Or am I overstepping my bounds being here without her permission? I take a step closer toward the opening to make it look like I just got here, but the floorboard creaks and she turns to see me.

"How long have you been here?" she asks. She looks startled.

"I just got here. I swear."

She gets up, grabs her cane, and slowly walks to me. If she's mad that I snuck in here and watched her cry, she'll easily be able to beat me with it and toss me out the window like I was one of her peaches. Instead she places both earbuds into my ears and smiles.

"Close your eyes," she says.

I close my eyes. But it's not a song that plays. Instead it is a recording. A young man begins to speak.

All right, Orenda. You're much better than me at this, but I think you'll like this one. I haven't thought of a title yet, so maybe you can help me with that. Here it goes . . . One night, during one of the most violent storms the people of the forest had ever faced, a baby boy was swept away from his village by a heavy flood. His family and the rest of the tribe searched for days for the little one, but never found him. They figured he must have died. But he didn't die. And after being dragged for miles through the thick mud and heavy rain, he found himself at the other end of the forest. This area belonged to the wolves.

While out hunting for food, a mother wolf came upon this human baby covered in mud. Knowing that if she left him there alone, he would surely die, this mother wolf decided to take the baby back to her den.

Word got out that she'd brought a human baby home, so all the other wolves called a meeting to discuss what to do. Some wolves thought they should put the baby back where it was found; others suggested eating the baby. But the leader of the wolf pack let the mother wolf who found the baby decide.

"You brought him home, so he is now your responsibility. What shall you do?" the chief wolf asked.

"Clearly the humans didn't want him. And if we put him back, aren't we telling the baby that we also don't want him?" she replied.

"Never mind what the humans want. Never mind what we want. The question is . . . what do YOU want?" he asked her.

The mother wolf stared deep into the baby's eyes. She didn't see a human, or a wolf . . . She simply saw a baby. And every baby needs a mother. So she addressed the pack and said, "I will raise him as if he were one of my own."

The wolves laughed at her, for they knew a human would have no chance in the wild, living the life of a wolf.

"He'll be too slow," one wolf shouted.

"He'll be too weak," declared another.

But the mother wolf simply replied, "Then together, we shall teach him how to be fast and strong."

The story abruptly stops. I open my eyes to see Orenda removing the earbuds from my ears. Her hands are trembling.

"What happens next?" I ask.

"Soon," she says.

"I have to wait to hear the rest?"

"Yes. When you're ready, you'll hear more," she says, and with her cane, slowly walks over to her wheelchair and sits in it.

"How do I become ready?" I ask.

She smiles and wheels herself to the opening. And like clockwork, she fastens the rope to her chair and guides the wheelchair down toward the ground. Before she begins her descent, she says, "We teach you," and then lowers herself to the ground.

Even with the way her body moves, she's better at climbing down than I am. She's already in her wheelchair and halfway across her yard by the time my feet touch soil. But she's not heading toward her house. Instead, she pulls up to the broken part of the fence and stops.

"You're going to teach me how to be ready to hear more of a children's story at my house?" I ask.

"Yes. You will learn how to be strong and fast, the same way I taught Aji how to be strong and fast."

"Wait. You knew Aji?"

"Of course, I know Aji!" she says, grabbing hold of the fence and pulling herself out of the wheelchair. I see the strain in her face, but it's easily overshadowed by her strength. She tosses her cane over the fence, and as if she's done it a million times before, she squeezes through the opening with ease.

On the other side, in my backyard, I see Seven grab her cane from the grass and run off with it. Orenda laughs.

"She's got a new toy," she shouts, while trying to keep her balance by holding the fence with one hand.

"Fourteen," I say through the fence.

Orenda knew Aji. That makes sense. They lived right next door to each other. I wonder how close they were. There are so many things I'd like to ask about him, but I haven't even really gotten to know her yet.

"What should I do with your wheelchair?" I ask.

"Leave it there," she says.

She snaps her fingers and howls, which causes Seven to rush back with her cane. She snaps her fingers again and gives a grunt. Seven gives the cane back to Orenda's open palm. I've never taught Seven that. Orenda must speak dog. How impressive.

"Twelve," I say, and slip through the fence.

She presses her wooden cane into the ground and slowly walks through my yard toward the sliding glass door. I follow her, and Seven follows me.

"We got grass now," I say to her, like my name is Captain Obvious.

"Yes. This home is happy again," she says, and slides the door open.

"Twenty-three."

I follow her inside, and she heads through the living room, but stops at Aji's urn. I can't understand what she's saying—she is practically whispering, and she's speaking in another language. But whatever she says must be quite personal. She intermittently wipes escaping tears from her cheeks as she talks to him.

Is this Ojibwe? I need to learn Ojibwe.

Even Seven feels the moment, because she leaves us and heads into the kitchen to finish whatever food is left in her bowl from lunch. Orenda turns around, forcing a smile, and gives me a thumbs-up.

"Thumbs-up for what?" I ask.

"Aji fully supports my decision to train you," she says.

"Thirty-six. Train me to be strong and fast so I'll be ready to listen to stories?"

She takes a few steps toward the garage door and turns to face me. "Exactly. You want to be a fearless Native American warrior—well, this is how."

"Sixty-one. Teach me."

She continues into the garage, and I follow her. There must be something about being in this room that brings back memories, because her eyes well up as she looks around.

"You spent a lot of time in here?" I ask.

She nods and approaches the punching bag. Her hand pushes it, and it sways slightly back and forth. She grabs the two boxing gloves and tosses them to me.

"Put these on."

"Ten."

I fit them over my hands.

She puts her hands together above her sternum and rubs them together, like someone trying to start a fire would.

"You're not as strong as Aji yet, so we'll start easy," she says.

I step closer.

"Thirty-nine. You want me to punch the bag?"

"Repeatedly for three minutes straight," she says, and looks up at the clock that is mounted onto the wall.

"Thirty-three. Sounds easy enough," I say.

She laughs, but I don't see what's funny.

"Now?" I ask.

She shoots her eyes back to the clock and waits until the secondhand hits twelve.

"Now."

I count three letters in my head and swing, hitting the bag with my left, then my right. It moves, but not much. I continue this for another thirty seconds. I see now why she was laughing. My arms are beginning to burn and feel as heavy as elephants. My heart pounds. My breathing changes. I begin to sweat. My punches feel like they're moving in slow motion, through quicksand.

"Two more minutes to go," she says.

Her letters fill my head. I focus on each word, keeping my mind away from the exhaustion setting in. *Two* equals three letters. *More* is four letters. *Minutes* is seven. *To* is two, and *go* is two. I add them up as they squeeze my skull.

"Eighteen," I release them into the air.

My voice is pleading with my breath. She claps her hands frantically. I'm slowing down. My hands are dropping. I'm about to stop.

"Don't give up!" she shouts, sending a small burst of energy back into my body.

"I won't!" I reply as I pound away at the bag.

I look up and see there's only one minute left. This should give me some relief, but this last minute feels like an hour already. I can barely lift my arms. I dig down to search for any reserves my body has and send them straight into my hands. I fight through the fact that they feel like they are on fire. I want to stop, drop, and roll . . . but I don't. For her, I keep punching.

"Time!" she announces, and I drop to my knees and catch my breath.

"Four," I say in between my panting.

Orenda bends down to me and pushes my sweaty hair back, away from my face.

"You feel stronger yet?" she asks.

"Eighteen. I feel dead," I say, and she belly laughs.

"Good. You gotta feel dead to appreciate life sometimes."

"Forty-five."

She walks over toward a small fridge against the wall. I didn't even know it was there. Orenda knows my home better than I do. She pulls out a bottle of water and tosses it to me. I tell my arms to lift, but they don't move. It hits me in the chest. Orenda laughs again.

"We'll work on your catching skills tomorrow," she says.

I reach down and open the bottle of water. I put it up to my lips and drink the entire bottle in a matter of seconds. H_2Oh my God, water has never tasted so good!

"Thirty-six," I say as I pull the empty water bottle from my face.

"Interesting," she says, and nudges me in the butt with her cane, signaling me to stand.

"Eleven. What's interesting?"

"You already got a bit stronger."

"Twenty-five. What makes you say that?" I ask as I struggle back up to my feet.

"When I said, 'Don't give up,' you didn't count my letters."

I try to play it all back in my head, but I'm honestly too exhausted to remember that far back. Is it true? Did her words slip past my mind undetected? *Don't give up*, huh? I know it's ten, but if I didn't total it up for her, then simply knowing the total doesn't matter. But as I think of this small breakthrough, her current sentence floods my brain.

"Forty-one. Did I really not say ten?" I ask.

She nods.

"How did it work?" I ask her, becoming a bit more excited now that my energy has started to replenish itself.

"Not sure, but we aren't done yet," she says, and pushes the punching bag with her cane, swaying it.

"Twenty-four. What do you mean?" I ask.

"That was only round one. Time for round two," she says, and looks at the clock, getting prepared to set the time.

"Thirty-four. Are you serious?"

She smiles and crosses her arms.

"Begin," she orders.

"Five," I say, and take a deep breath.

I start whaling away at the punching bag. The words *don't give up* play over and over in my head, on a constant loop. Partly because I forgot to count them, but maybe also because, for the first time in my life, I am starting to somehow believe in myself.

CHAPTER SIXTEEN

- ⟪◆⟫ - ⟪◆⟫ -

THE STORYTELLER

Somehow, I survived all three rounds of boxing. I can now barely lift my arms. They feel like two fire hydrants attached to my shoulders. I wonder how easy this was for my brother. I lie down and watch Orenda, with her cane, slowly walk toward my next assignment: reading.

She selects a book from the long and crowded bookshelf. She balances it under her arm as she approaches me—still on the ground, still exhausted.

I should tell her that I don't read very often except for the occasional comic book. But I don't want to come off as weak *and* stupid.

She places the book on my chest.

"This is an excellent book," she says, and carefully lowers herself to the floor near my head. It's not so easy for her. But once she's in position, I forget about all the wrongs in the world. I just stare into her eyes. Right now, with her beside me, the whole world is perfectly perfect.

"You want me to read this entire book? Are you serious?"

"Yes and yes," she replies.

"Nine."

"*Nein* means 'no' in German. Wrong answer. If you want to ever be strong, you'll read this book."

"Seventy," I say, and pick up the book and read the cover.

It is titled *How to Hang a Witch*.

"Is it scary?"

"It's a thriller. Why? Do you scare easily?"

"Thirty-one. No, but."

"Woman up. Time to look fear in the face and slap it silly," she says.

"Forty-four. Okay . . . is this a chick book?" I ask.

She tilts her head, and her eyebrows rise. "Says the boy who just asked if it was scary?"

"Thirty-four. Good point. I'll read it."

"The main character in it is a total badass. Like me," she says, and pushes it toward my face. "It was one of Aji's favorites."

I tally up her letters then ask her a question I've been wondering all day, "How well did you know him?" I ask.

Her eyes lower, like she doesn't want me to notice her vulnerable side. But I do.

"Very well."

"Eight. I wish I had the chance to know him."

"You're getting to know him right now. You're punching his bag, reading his books, and hearing his story."

Wait, what? His story? Then it dawns on me.

"Eighty-one. That was Aji?" I ask. "The recording?"

She nods.

"That was my brother?" I repeat, even though she already answered me.

She nods again.

I don't know how to feel. I can't believe I heard my brother's voice. I picture the urn in the living room. No, I scrub that image away from my mind and instead imagine the young man in the military uniform framed in the hallway. He sounded like he was so full of life. And he was, until he wasn't. He sounded happy. I hope my brother was happy right up until the very last moment.

I won't dare ask her or my mom how he died exactly, because it doesn't really matter. After all, war is war, and in war horrible things happen to people. I'll leave it at that.

"Can I hear more of the story now?" I ask her.

She looks up at the clock. "I have to go."

"Nine. Please?"

"Read the book. Then, if your arms have any strength left, come to the tree house to hear a bit more of your brother's story," she says, and slowly walks out of the garage.

The door closes before I can give her the number of letters in her last sentence, but that's okay; no one wants to hear it anyway. But after I release it under my breath, I take another look at the book I'll be reading.

I'll read this if it gets me closer to my brother . . . The moment I think that thought, I smile. Even though my brother is gone physically, Orenda just showed me that there are still ways to get to know him. He'll be beside me as I punch the bag and read the book. I can still have a brother. Orenda is a genius.

I want to jump up and tell her that I get it. I see why reading is a part of my warrior training. Reading is just as important as punching the bag. In fact, maybe even more important. I will get as strong as Aji. My brain will be like a huge crocodile, and my arms will be like . . . two more crocodiles. (I admit, I need to work on my creativity. But books should help that too.)

This is weird. I mean, I am legitimately excited to read a book! And if I don't give up, I'll soon be a brave. And braves <u>fight</u>. I'll be able to defeat my counting condition.

All this wonderful news engulfs me. I can't keep it in, so I spring up to my feet and run after Orenda. I barrel through the house and head out to the backyard, where I see her slipping through the fence. I run up and squeeze through, scraping my elbow on the wood.

"Orenda!" I yell.

She turns around. "You read the book already?" she asks jokingly.

"No, I just wanted to say I get it."

She smiles and plops down into her wheelchair like it is a loyal horse waiting for her.

"Right now, you're so afraid of words. They terrify you because you trained your brain to count the letters. I figure, if you fill your head with an entire book, your brain might forget about counting, and maybe, just maybe, you'll listen to the story the words tell instead."

Her letters swirl above and behind my eyes like kids on a merry-go-round. There are so many of them. I wait for them to stop, and when they do, I tally them up as quickly as I can. Orenda knows patience. She watches me and waits for my response.

"Two hundred and fifteen," I say.

"Wow. That's a lot."

"I know."

"But did you hear what I said?" she asks.

"Twenty-two. I did. And I promise you, I will read the book. It may take me a while, but I won't give up."

She smiles again and folds her arms, waiting for me to do

something. But what? Her eyes shift to the handle of the wheel-chair. It finally clicks.

"You want me to push you to your tree?"

"We're still training you, aren't we?" she says with a smirk.

"Twenty-seven. Yes, we are," I say, and begin pushing her through the yard.

"Watch out for the peaches," she warns.

The wheelchair glides easily over the grass, which is good because my arms aren't offering much help right now. I blurt out "Twenty-one" as we stop in front of the tree. She climbs out and grabs hold of the rope. It still amazes me how strong she is.

"Can I ask you a question?" I say, even though I just did ask her a question, technically.

"Shoot."

"Five. Were you always like this?" I ask.

She begins her climb. "Like what?" she asks.

"Eight. Not able to walk, like other people," I say.

Before she reaches the top, she stops and looks down at me. "No."

"Two. Then what happened?"

"I've already told you . . . I'm changing," she says, and disappears into her tree house.

I wonder if I stepped over the line by asking her again. If she wanted to tell me what's going on with her, she would. Is she sick? I hope not. And what does "I'm changing" even mean?

Seven greets me as I walk back into my yard. She's hungry. I don't read many books, but my dog's eyes are an easy read. Together, we enter my house, and she leads me into the kitchen. I open a can of dog food my mother got from the market and dump it into her bowl. Within seconds, the food is scarfed down and Seven takes off.

"How was school today?"

I turn around and see my mother walk in with an armful of groceries. She sets them on the counter and hugs me. Do I look like I need a hug? Maybe I'm an easy read too.

"Seventeen . . . It was fine."

"Fine?" she presses. "I guess that's a step up from 'worst day of my life.'"

"Forty-two. How many steps are there? I'm exhausted," I say, and mimic taking large steps up an invisible staircase.

"Maybe forty-two steps?" she says and laughs at her own wordplay.

She begins to put the groceries away. I stop my exaggerated steps and linger in the kitchen with her. "Eighteen," I say while I watch her place the peanut butter onto the shelf.

She turns to me, smile paused. "Just ask," she says.

"Seven. Do you know what's wrong with Orenda?" I ask.

She places the almond milk into the fridge and shuts the door. But before grabbing the bread, she touches my nose, trying to gauge my level of worry.

"What do you mean, wrong?"

"Eighteen. Come on. Obviously, something's wrong with her."

Am I the only one that thinks that an otherwise healthy-looking girl being bound to a wheelchair for the rest of her life is strange?

"Something's wrong with everyone, Collin," she replies.

"I know that. But why can't she walk?" I ask.

"What did she tell you?"

"She said she's changing. But I don't know what that means."

My mother pauses, carefully choosing her words. Then smiles, like she just dug up a fond memory from the storage room in her brain.

"Her mother is a great woman. Did she tell you about her?" she asks.

"No. What about her mom?"

"She changed too."

"I don't understand. Where is her mother now?"

My mom has the same look in her eyes that she had when I asked where Aji was. It's a mixture of happy and sad. Which makes me think that Orenda's mom is also dead. And if that's true, does that mean Orenda is dying?

"Ask her to take you to see her mother tomorrow," my mom says, and continues to put the groceries away.

Take me to see her mother? So maybe she's not dead? Or maybe she's in an urn too? As Mama turns away from me, I notice her touching her face. I have my answer. My mom is wiping away tears, which means Orenda's mom is dead. And she thinks Orenda is dying. To change must mean to die. Change is not good.

But I refuse to believe it. My mom must be wrong. How can Orenda be dying? She is by far the most alive person I have ever met.

I should run back to Orenda and find out what is exactly going on with her. No more riddles, I'll say. I want the truth. Just tell me what's what. I should tell her all of this now . . . But . . . I also swore to her that I'd read that book. I need to keep training. And I need to remember that Orenda will tell me what she wants me to know. I can't force her to tell me about her legs or her mom, and I certainly can't go over there and ask her if she's dying. She's currently the only friend I have, so I better not scare her away by asking her too many personal questions. I need to be smart about this. I need to be strong, which brings me back to training.

I decide that I'll do what my mom suggested, I'll ask her to introduce me to her mom tomorrow. And whatever happens happens. Right now, I have a book to read.

I grab the book that she left me in the garage and carry it to my room. Reading is fun, I keep telling myself as I pace back and forth near my bed, but my mind is too occupied with Orenda.

The thought of her being sick makes me want to punch the walls, but my arms are too weak and I've already damaged this house enough. So I grab my pillow and scream as loudly as I can into it.

It doesn't help. Orenda is still sick. And the worst part is, there is nothing I can do about it. Or is there? I can keep boxing and start reading. Maybe if I read this book, I'll be working to defeat my counting condition, but also, perhaps, my body and mind will be strong enough to help her in some way?

I've been here less than a week, and I already didn't count two sentences. That's huge. Is it my Native American blood waking up after being dormant for all these years?

Is that even possible?

The strange thought makes me realize that Minnesota is getting to me. In a good way.

I collapse onto my bed and open the book. The first couple pages are about the Salem Witch trials in 1692. I don't see how this story will help me, yet, but I remember learning about this back in California. And if anyone was bullied, it was these women and men who were accused of witchcraft. I turn to the first chapter and begin reading.

CHAPTER SEVENTEEN

- ‹‹◆›› - ‹‹◆›› -

GUN THREAT

The alarm on my watch goes off at seven fifteen. I immediately regret putting it across the room, but I guess that's the point. I have to get up to make it shut up. I wipe the sleep from my eyes, yawn, and sit up. The book falls off my chest. I stayed up most of the night reading it. I usually don't remember my dreams, but last night, mine were filled with ghosts, witches, Salem, and magic.

I see why Orenda chose this book. It puts into perspective how gossip travels as fast as fire and spreads from home to home, causing friends to not trust each other, neighbors to turn on each other, and an entire town to be overly suspicious of strangers. Gossip sucks. A few years back, a rumor started that my counting condition was contagious. No one would come near me for the rest of the year.

This book also showed me that I don't have it all that bad. I mean, don't get me wrong, I absolutely hate my counting problem, but at least I'm not being accused of witchcraft and getting executed. If this was a few hundred years ago, that would be my fate.

I'm sure the lesson Orenda wants me to take away from this book is that we all have a past, but the past doesn't determine our future. I've been called a freak for so long that I actually started to believe it. But I don't have to anymore.

Maybe counting isn't the curse that I think it is. I mean, it's no gift either, but maybe I don't need to fear words and letters as much as I do. There will always be bullies. But that doesn't mean I will always be bullied. I need to ignore what people say about me and just work on being the best me I can be. Plus, bullies exist because people give them power. They feed off the attention.

From now on, I'm not going to give them any power. I'm just going to . . . be late for school! Crap! It's now seven thirty. I finally leap out of bed, turn off my alarm, and get dressed as quickly as possible. As I hop through the hallway, trying to fit both my shoes on, I take a quick glance at my brother's photograph.

"Good morning, Aji," I say.

I enter the kitchen and feed Seven before I feed myself. I'm so hungry that I scarf down my bowl of cereal almost as quickly as Seven finishes her breakfast. My mom walks in and eyes my outfit: black pants, black shirt, black hooded sweatshirt, black hat, and black shoes. Even though I'm always in black, she examines me more than usual this morning.

"What?" I ask.

"You ever notice you look remarkably like a witch?" she says, while chomping on a banana.

I tally up her sentence and grab the broom that rests beside the fridge. I put it in between my legs and strike the witchiest pose I can.

"Hop on. I'll drive," I say.

She laughs and grabs her car keys. And like every day, we race to the truck, and like most days, she wins.

As I get into the truck, I realize that my dad hasn't checked on me since I began my new life without him. To be fair, I haven't called him either. I guess this is how it's always been between us. We never talked. Now that we're two thousand and eighty-six miles from each other, why would that change? But there is a nagging feeling tugging at the back of my head. It's a feeling that's kind of new to me. I want to tell my dad everything that's happened to me so far. The good and the bad. And I want to talk about Orenda. I want him to know that there's a girl who actually talks to me. I wonder if he'll believe me.

The moment we drive off of the reservation, the radio kicks in. I quickly switch the station from a country song to the local hip-hop station before my mom can stop me. I gave country a shot; now she'll give rap a gander.

Even though my mom definitely has never heard this song before, it doesn't matter. Just like every other song on this planet, she sings along—loudly. She makes me forget about school, which is maybe her plan, because I cannot stop laughing at her attempts at rapping.

We pull into the parking lot and sit. I really wish I was brave enough to go to class without needing a pep talk, but here I am, looking at my mom, who pulls out a stick from the back seat and hands it to me.

"I already played this game with Grandma," I say.

"Then you should be good at it," she says.

I tally up her letters and examine the stick.

"A very long pencil," I say.

She smiles. "A microphone," she says, and uses it as the song on the radio comes to an end.

"A guitar," I say, and take it back, strumming it in my hands.

She laughs, claps in excitement, and snatches it from me.

"Let's see . . . A telescope!" she says, and holds it to her eye, aiming it up to the sky.

"Good one. A sword!" I say as I take it from her and slice through the air, cutting it in half.

"A fishing pole!" she says, and mimics someone fishing. She even pretends to catch a fish and struggles with bringing it up. "But we catch and release. Fish have families too, ya know," she says, and tosses the invisible fish out of the window.

She hands me the stick. I think hard. "A magic wand," I say, and point it toward her. "You will turn this truck around and take us both to the movies," I say, and zap her with the wand.

She laughs. "Are you a Jedi using the Force or a wizard using a wand?"

"Whichever gets us out of here," I say after tallying up her letters.

She snatches the wand out of my hand and pretends to run in place. She moves her arms like she's sprinting, breathing in and out, tiring. She hands me the stick. "I'm having a wonderful morning . . . I pass you the baton, so you can have a wonderful morning . . . at school!" She finishes her run-in-place.

I take the stick and nod. There's no way out of running this race. I open the door, and my mom takes the stick from my hand.

"This stick was a dozen different things. So can be this school. Is it prison? Is it camp? Is it a theme park? Hogwarts? Or maybe just an average school where kids go to learn stuff. It's what you want it to be, Collin. Have whatever kind of day you want to have . . . Which is?" she asks.

"A good day," I say.

She smiles, and I step out of the truck. I turn to face my school and the bustling sea of students. "Walk," I tell myself and take a step, but I hear a loud honk behind me.

I turn around and see my mom stop the truck and get out with the stick. And it's not just me who's watching her. Heads turn. What is she doing?

"Last one! It's a horse!" she shouts, and places the stick in between her legs and rides it like it's a wild horse in a full circle around her truck. My jaw drops. I can't believe my mom just did that. I turn and see everyone staring at her. This is so embarrassing. But as soon as she gets into her truck and drives off, people go about their business, like nothing happened.

Huh. Maybe I do care what people think too much. I should be more like my mom. That doesn't mean I'm going to pick up a stick and ride it like a horse to class, but no one really cared when she did it. And that's the point. Maybe I make everything a bigger deal than it actually is. Imagine that.

Halfway to my first class, a group of four kids approach me, blocking my way to the main building. I recognize one of them. It's Josh. The buzz cut who messed with me the other day.

"Hey, freak," Josh says.

"Eight," I say, and I immediately put my earmuffs on. I hit PLAY on my phone and crank the music up to its loudest volume.

I watch them laughing, but all I hear is the song blaring into my skull. One of the guys tries to grab my earphones, but I step aside, and he nearly trips down the steps. I know I just punched a bag for three full rounds yesterday, but punching a person is very different; they punch back. And I really don't want to get in another fight this soon. My nose has just barely recovered from the beating I received in California.

I see my opening and run up the remaining steps. I can't help but feel like the lucky gazelle that just evaded a pack of laughing hyenas.

When the coast is clear, I remove my earmuffs and make a bee-line to my first class. I start to take a seat, but no one is sitting. The teacher looks a bit shaken up. What's going on?

Mrs. Hagadorn grabs her purse and snaps her fingers to get everyone's attention.

"Class . . . there's been another gun threat today. We all need to go outside," she says.

Another gun threat? We had a few drills in California, but I don't remember ever being evacuated because of a real threat.

Our class merges with the rest of the classes as we all shuffle down the halls. The students are a mixed bag of walking emotions. Some are anxious; some appear to go about their day like this is nothing out of the ordinary. Some students seem bored, and some are smiling as if they enjoy this time out of actual class.

Me, well, I'm hoping whoever they think has a gun is actually just carrying around a stick.

There's an eerie feeling in the air. We are all escorted off campus and into the parking lot. The teachers look nervous.

As we wait for the police to search the campus, the principal and an officer approach us. The cop looks on edge, like this is a part of his job that he wishes wasn't. But the principal looks relieved. He forms a small circle of teachers, and they huddle for about a minute before they break back into their class sections.

"The threat has been resolved," he says aloud, and gives two thumbs-up.

Resolved? What does that even mean? Does it mean it was a prank? Was someone arrested? Resolved only makes me more nervous. Are they sure?

As everyone starts filing back to class, I find myself walking through the parking lot, away from school. I know I should go back to class, but too many scary images have filled my head. I need to leave school and be as far away from guns as possible. Plus, if I manage to find my way home, I get to see Orenda much sooner. My mom will understand. Safety always comes first.

I walk off campus and down the main road. The parking lot is jammed with cars driving in. I guess parents were notified and have come to pick up their kids and take them away from danger. I wonder if my mom was notified? If she was, and is on her way to get me, she'll see me walking home. At least I hope so.

Thirteen songs later, I enter the reservation. It's pretty windy, so I muster up all the energy I have in me and speed walk to the house. I'm skipping the forest adventure again. Not only because it's cold, but also because I don't see Grandma waiting for me on the road.

But as the house comes into view, a warmth replaces all the coldness clinging to me. Who would have ever thought I'd feel so much joy from seeing my grandma? But there she is, fixing the screen door on the porch. This time her color-changing dress is blue.

"Hey, Grandma," I say, and head over to see if she needs a hand.

She dusts her hands off and extends them for a hug. I wrap my arms around her and squeeze. She must have been outside for a while, because she's as cold as ice cubes. "Do you need some help?" I ask.

"Oh, because you're so good at fixing things," she says, laughing.

She has a point. I have broken more than I've fixed since I've been here.

"I can try?" I say.

"No. I enjoy fixing things. You're still a kid. Go break stuff. You'll be old as me before you know it," she says, and gets back to work.

"All right. Let me know if you change your mind." I head to the backyard.

After I give Seven a kiss and wrestle her for a few minutes, I squeeze through the opening to Orenda's yard. It's a feeding frenzy. There are more peaches and even more butterflies fluttering above the grass, dipping and diving like a dance.

Her wheelchair is under the tree. I grab hold of the rope and begin my ascent. My arms are sore and weak, but the thought of seeing her propels me to the top quicker than I have thus far. How about that? I am getting stronger by the day.

I crawl into her tree house through the opening, but before I can get to my feet, something presses against the back of my head.

"Did you read the book?" she says, and nudges me with whatever she's holding. Her voice sounds a little different, almost as if she was out of breath, but I don't bring it up. Instead I count her letters.

"Seventeen. I'm halfway done. It's great so far. I mean, I had to check under my bed for ghosts before I went to sleep, but—"

"Prove it. Are you Team Jaxon or Team Elijah?" she asks.

I count her letters and give the best British accent I can. "Elijah, obviously," I say.

She releases me. I turn around and see it was her cane being held to my head. Strange. This morning at school there was a gun threat, and then miles away, she does this.

"Aren't you supposed to be in school?" she asks.

"There was a gun threat, so I left."

Her eyebrows rise, but not in surprise.

"And now you're here," she says.

"And now I'm here."

I stand up and notice her legs are shaking a bit more than usual.

"Are you okay?" I ask.

"I just need to sit," she says, and leans on her cane as she slowly walks over to her bed.

I follow her.

I sit beside her and wait. She knows what I want. She holds strong for a few moments, then breaks into a smile.

"Fine. You can hear a little more. But you're not ready for all of it just yet." She reaches under her pillow, pulling out her earbuds.

"I'm ready."

I close my eyes as she hits PLAY. My brother's voice makes me immediately smile. It's smooth and rough at the same time. I sink into Orenda's bed as he pulls me back into his story.

Life as a wolf was very difficult for the human baby. He was far more dependent than the other cubs and relied on the mother wolf for even the most basic things. But time crawled on, and soon he was no longer a baby, but a little boy. He was getting better at wolf life, but was still far from that of the other wolves. When they played, he was often the last one chosen. When they ate, he was often the last one fed, and when they learned to hunt, none of the wolves wanted to be teamed up with the boy—he was far too slow and far too loud.

But there was one advantage to having him around. When the mouse or squirrel evaded the young wolves and scurried up a tree, the boy climbed the tree and shook the little snack out. No other wolf could do this, so in time, they allowed him to join their hunting parties. That is, if he could keep up with them.

And even though he was technically a part of the pack, the boy didn't really have any friends. The other wolves were too busy being wolves. He often felt left out and unwanted. The only love he got was from the mother wolf that took him in. But even she knew that there'd come a day when the boy would become a man. And wolves feared men. In fact, all the animals feared men. But for now, he was a boy, and all boys need love.

One day, years later, when the boy was a teenager, he—

It stops playing. I open my eyes and see Orenda's face so close to mine that I nervously swallow. I can smell her breath. She must have just eaten a peach. A peach that was raised by strawberries. She smells so good.

"That's it for today," she says, and stuffs the earbuds back under her pillow.

"He was a really good storyteller," I say.

"*Is.* Not was. He's telling you a story now, not then," she shoots back to me like I somehow offended her.

"Sorry. *Is.*"

And even though I was the one listening to Aji, it is Orenda who looks on the verge of tears.

"Are you ready for your rematch with the punching bag?" she asks, changing the subject.

"I am, but I don't think my arms are ready yet."

"Well, let's see if they follow you to the garage. If they do, they're ready," she says.

"Sounds like a plan. And after boxing, I was hoping you could do something else for me."

"What?"

"I was hoping you'd introduce me to your mom."

Her eyes go wide, and it looks like she is forgetting to breathe. Should I tell her to inhale? Exhale?

"Are you okay?" I ask.

"You want to see my mom?"

"I do."

And just like that, her eyes are smiling. She walks over to the opening and grabs hold of the rope.

"We'll punch the bag tomorrow. Let's go see my mama," she says, and climbs down.

I'm not really sure what I just got myself into, but as long as I get to go through it with her at my side, I'll go anywhere and do anything. I follow her out of the tree house where she is waiting for me, sitting patiently in her wheelchair.

CHAPTER EIGHTEEN

-《◆》--《◆》-

KALEIDOSCOPE

Orenda wheels herself through her backyard and stops at the gate. She pulls out her cane and opens the latch. The door swings open, and she wheels herself out. I close it behind me and try to catch up to her.

She's heading toward her dad's truck.

"We just got to find the keys to this horse," she says as she taps her cane against the passenger door, signaling me to begin searching.

"Wait, what? Huh? You can drive?" I ask.

"No, I can't drive. I was hoping you knew how," she says.

"Nope," I say, and wonder if this is where I should be more of a warrior and less of a wimp. "But how hard could it be?" I say, which sends a huge smile across Orenda's face.

I climb in and search the truck. After a few failed attempts at finding them, I flip the visor down. The keys fall right into my lap.

On the set of keys is a key chain. It has two words on it. Seven letters total. BE BRAVE. I can't believe how much this little key chain applies to me right now. I must be brave. For her.

"Got 'em," I shout.

Orenda hops out of her wheelchair and climbs like a monkey into the passenger seat. I stick the key into the ignition, and the engine roars to life.

"Now what?" I ask.

"Seriously? You really don't know how to drive at all?" she asks.

I tally up her letters and answer her. "I'm almost thirteen. All my driving experiences have just been as a passenger."

She laughs. "Throw the gear in D and step on the gas. Oh, and steer."

I yank the gear lever down to D. It locks in, and I slam on the gas. The truck flies forward, and we barrel into three empty trash cans near the curb.

Orenda reaches over and shifts the gear to PARK. In between snort-filled laughs, she pulls the key out of the ignition.

"I'm driving! You drive as good as you fly," she says, and climbs across to the driver's side.

"Okay, but at least I kept my clothes on this time," I say, and try not to realize I just reminded the both of us about my epic naked fall out of the window. We both laugh as we switch seats.

I can hear Seven barking from the backyard. Of course she's worried about me. I yell out that I'm okay as loud as I can, and just as if she understood me completely, her barking stops. But still, we've got to move quick before all this noise brings adult human attention to us.

"You know what you're doing, right?" I ask.

She grips the wheel and turns to me. "We shall see," she says, and gives a sinister laugh.

She flips the truck into reverse and we speed backward. She slams on the brakes. Our bodies jolt forward. She shifts to D and steps on the gas again, trying to turn in time before we hit the trash cans again . . . But . . . We crash into the already toppled-over trash cans once more.

We laugh so hard we can't breathe. Seven starts barking again. Orenda parks the truck, pulls the keys out, and places them back behind the sun visor like none of this ever happened.

"New plan . . . So, my grandpa was the size of four regular men," she says.

"Super random, but good to know," I say.

"When he got too old to walk, he refused a wheelchair. Mainly because he couldn't fit into one . . . So my dad had a great idea. And his idea is now my idea." She hops out of the truck.

I walk as slow as she does, but try to make it look perfectly natural, which I think she appreciates because she doesn't say anything about our snail's pace. I hope we get where we're going before her dad sees our destroyed trash cans. And as if she read my mind, she turns to me and says, "Go clean up our mess, then meet me in my garage."

Already a few of the other neighbors have gathered outside to see what all the commotion is about. I need to move quickly.

I reach the trash cans and set them back up onto the curb. There. Good as new. I ignore the neighbors' eyes and run to Orenda's garage. Halfway to it, I see my grandma standing at our house, watching me. She doesn't look upset; in fact, she looks quite amused.

"Am I in trouble?" I ask her.

"You will be if you two don't hurry up and hit the road," she says with a smile, and walks back into the house, not waiting to hear how many letters she just tossed me.

I quietly sneak into Orenda's garage. It's dark. Where is she? I flip on the light. It flickers to life and hums. The space is neatly organized and way too clean to be a garage. At the back wall, Orenda stands in front of a large object that is completely hidden by a blue tarp.

"What is it?" I approach her.

"I call her the Beast," Orenda says, and pulls off the tarp with one single yank.

It falls to the floor, revealing a white golf cart. I laugh.

"She's terrifying," I say jokingly.

"Fear not. This Beast and I have history," she says as she steps inside of it, gliding her hands across the frame.

"We're in the belly of the Beast now," I say, and climb into the passenger side.

"Yes we are. Hold on tight." She presses the button on the clicker attached to the golf cart.

The garage door slowly lifts, letting in the sunlight. Orenda grips the steering wheel and turns the ignition button on. It rumbles to life like a vending machine on wheels.

I grip the bar in front of me and read the bumper sticker plastered onto the dashboard. It says WHEN TIMES GET BAD, DON'T GET SAD—GET MAD.

Orenda kisses her index finger and shoots it like a gun toward the sky. "That's my grandpa. He was a madman," she says.

I tally up her letters. "Was he a wise man too?" I ask.

"Yes," she says, and points to an enlarged framed photograph mounted on the garage wall. It shows a heavy man with the same eyes as her, smiling at the camera. His long black and silver hair drapes down toward his belly. He wears a shirt that has a red alien on it. The alien has two feathers sticking out of its huge head and is holding up two long skinny fingers: a peace sign. On the shirt it reads I DRUM IN PEACE.

"Very wise," she says.

"He looks full of . . . wisdom," I say, which causes Orenda to laugh.

Her grandpa looks like a very happy man. I wish I could have met him.

We're interrupted as the door that connects to the house opens.

"Orenda, that you in there?" a man asks. Her dad?

"Crapola! Let's go!" she says, and steps on the gas.

We don't fly out of the garage—it's more of a cruise at a comfortable, safe speed, which makes the situation even funnier.

We exit the garage and joyride down the street at about the same pace as a speed-walker. In fact, her dad could easily catch us, but when I look back, he's standing with his hands on his hips, smiling. I have yet to get a good look at him. And this time is no different, him being cast in the shadow of the doorway.

Orenda, on the other hand, is treating this whole excursion like she's the getaway driver and we just robbed a bank. We pitch from side to side as we approach the main road.

"Is your dad going to be super pissed at you for this?"

"No. The good thing about being a rebel is acts of rebellion are expected from you. He'll huff and he'll puff, but he won't blow the house down. Don't worry about Foxy. He may be big and strong as five men combined, but when it comes to me and my shenanigans, he's a total softy."

"Your dad's name is Foxy?" I ask.

"Yep. Don't tease him, though, he hates being called the foxy fox named Foxy," she warns.

"Good to know," I say, but I didn't need her warning. Teasing a man that size is the last thing I'd ever do.

Every car passes us as we ride on the shoulder. Even a few horses trot by, but Orenda doesn't seem to care. She looks so happy. It's freezing, but her eyes look like she sees an open road on a sunny day. She's tasting freedom. She is drinking air and eating light. I watch her in awe. This is the most free I've ever seen her, ever seen anyone, and it's contagious. I howl up at the sky that's watching us. Orenda howls too.

"Is that all you got?" she shouts to the strong breeze fighting against us in our little motorized golf cart.

"Bring it on!" I chime in and challenge the wind with her.

And almost as if it heard us and admired our courage, the air relents. Orenda smiles in victory as we drive smoothly down the road on a now calm and sunny—but still cold—afternoon.

I am fully aware that no one is perfect, but Orenda is the closest any of us humans will ever get. She reaches over and flips on the radio. Her eyes ignite when a song comes on. She turns the volume way up, and just like my mom does, Orenda sings along, loud enough for all the birds flying above the clouds to hear.

I don't sing along. Instead, I watch her as she serenades the sky and everything under it. I want to know what it would feel like for my lips to be pressed up against hers. I've never really wanted to kiss anyone before, so this feeling is new to me, but it feels like the most obvious thing in the world. Like my lips were made to feel hers. Like we were both born for our lips to one day meet and grow old together. Humans only have lips because one day a boy named Collin and a girl named Orenda would meet, and when they did, they'd need a way to show how they felt about each other. So lips were fastened to our mouths to act as cushions for when our faces inevitably collide. Just for us . . . She just doesn't know it yet.

Orenda snaps me out of my daze by elbowing me in the shoulder and raising one eyebrow. "What are you looking at?" she asks.

"Just . . . nothing."

"Oh, I'm nothing?"

"No, you're not nothing. You're everything. I was just looking at you. Not in a creepy way. I swear."

She smiles, and with her free hand, she grabs mine and holds it. My heart nearly beats out of my chest as her palm rests into my palm. I am sweating. We are holding hands. Orenda and I are holding hands. This is why hands were made too. For this moment right here, right now. There's no use trying to hide the happiness on my face, but I'm glad each end of my smile is not sticking out both sides of this golf cart.

Our hand holding is short-lived, though. Safety first. She places both hands on the steering wheel and focuses on the road ahead of us.

I try to calm my heart, but it's at a theme park right now. It's running past the long lines and jumping into the fastest roller coaster on earth.

"We're here," she says, and veers the golf cart right as we take an exit marked ANISHINAABE.

"Anishinaabe. That's our people. In our mother tongue," she says as we drive out of the forest area and into a green clearing. I focus on the word. It's eleven letters. Sounds like ten, but the last *a* has a twin.

She pulls the cart over on a small bluff that overlooks a vast field of green grassy hills below us. All reckless sense of adventure in her eyes is gone and is now replaced with a calm collection of every emotion lying perfectly still on her face, like a frozen lake. In her eyes, I see happy. I see sad. I see excitement. I see fear. I see courage. I see heartbreak. I see bliss. I see longing. I see joy. I see a strong young woman, and I also see a nervous little girl.

She picks up her cane. I jump out of the golf cart and run around it to meet her while she stands.

"Thanks," she says as I help her out.

Together, we slowly walk toward the cliff, which makes me

really nervous, given that I'm super clumsy and her legs don't work very well.

"We're here," she says as she stops inches from the edge.

"Eight," I say, and my jaw immediately drops at what I see next.

In the center of this green field of grass that is spread out in all directions, bookended by forest, there lies a beautiful garden with a small, thin, crystal-clear river running through it.

Our eyes take in the hundreds of colorful flowers.

"Wow," I say, and she slips her hand into my hand again.

"Isn't it beautiful?" she says, not bothering to wipe the escaping tear from her eyes.

"It's the second most beautiful thing I have ever seen," I say.

Her eyes leave the paradise in front of us and meet mine. "The second most?" she asks.

"You're the first," I say, and squeeze her hand, hoping that if I apply enough pressure, our hands will merge into one, so I will always be holding her.

Her smile grows, but the rest of her face is still crowded with other emotions, and I think I know why. We are here, but I don't see her mother. As the thought leaves my head, she turns back to the garden in the middle of the clearing.

"They're coming to meet you," she says.

I look toward the clearing. "Who?"

"My family," she says, and a few more rogue tears run down her sun-kissed cheeks.

I squint. "Eight. Where?" I ask.

And before she can answer, I see something. Movement. I squint and focus . . . And then I see it. An entire troop of butterflies flutter up from the garden and head toward us. They're flapping, zigzagging, and floating in the air like a multicolored cloud, moving closer and closer. I stand perfectly still as they reach us. They dance around Orenda and me, spinning around us—watching us. Like an exploded rainbow caught in a slow and gentle tornado.

"Is this real?" I ask.

She takes in a deep breath. "Very real," she says, and as she exhales, her warm breath forms a cloud.

The butterflies range in sizes from small as a nickel to as big as my hand. And even though they don't make sounds, there is a constant hum from their beating wings. The kind of comfortable hum that would put a baby to sleep.

Orenda extends her hand and waits. And a few moments later, one butterfly with brown and yellow wings breaks from the group and lands on her fingertip. It moves its wings up and down, twitches its antennae left and right, and nods its head. In return, Orenda smiles and lets the tears flow freely down her cheeks. The butterfly launches off her finger and joins the group.

"This is my family," she says.

"You have a very . . . colorful family."

"Everyone's family is colorful . . . but not everyone's family can fly like mine." There is such pride in her voice.

Orenda is inches away from the edge of the bluff. I want to reach out and grab her, but she seems steadier than ever.

"Meet the Count," she says to the butterflies.

Then all the butterflies change direction and begin to circle me.

This is by far the most amazing thing I've ever experienced. This is magic. Magic is real.

The same butterfly that was on her fingertip breaks again from the rest and flutters over toward my face. I keep perfectly still as it lands on my nose. My human eyes are inches away from the butterfly's eyes. It's so close, it's hard to focus on it, but then it spreads its beautiful yellow-framed brown wings, which immediately eases my vision, almost hypnotizing me. Wait a minute! I recognize this butterfly. It looks exactly like the one that was in my bedroom the night before I arrived in Minnesota. How is that even possible?

"Hi," I say, and my cold breath moves across its little body. It bats its wings at me, gives almost a full-body wiggle, then lifts off of my nose and floats back to Orenda, this time landing on her nose. They share a moment of silence together. Orenda is smiling, and I don't know how I know this, but the butterfly is smiling too.

"Yes, Mama," Orenda says.

The butterfly extends its wings and slowly bats them twice. They are communicating. Orenda speaks Butterfly.

Then it lifts off of her nose and rejoins the group.

And after another full circle around Orenda, the butterflies ride the wind back down to their lush floral paradise. Orenda and I stand speechless for a few moments.

"You know what a group of butterflies is called?" she asks.

"No, what?"

She takes my hand and pulls me close to her. Our bodies are almost touching. Her lips are near mine. Her eyes are near mine. I can feel her breath on my cheeks.

"A kaleidoscope," she says, and the exact moment the word leaves her mouth, she leans in and kisses me.

I've been alive for almost 400 million seconds, but this second happening right now is the only one that matters. She pulls away and looks me in the eyes. I don't know what to say. I should say something. I don't even know if I remember how to speak. I'm just smiling . . . but so is she.

"Thanks," I finally blurt out.

She laughs. "You're welcome?" she says, and with her cane in hand, she slowly walks back to the golf cart.

I try to join her, but I'm frozen. My legs are still thinking about our kiss. They won't move. I tell my brain to get back to work, but it's too busy reliving that moment. The most interesting girl on this planet just kissed me. I finally force my arms up and touch my lips, just to make sure they are still on my face. I'm numb. Not from the cold, but from Orenda.

My brain finally kicks in, and I turn around. Orenda is in the golf cart, waiting for me. But this time she's in the passenger seat. I guess she doesn't want to drive away from her family.

She kissed me. I should have kissed her back. That's all I can think as I slowly meander back to her—that and hope my wobbly legs don't give out on me. I sit down in the golf cart and turn to her.

"You said 'Yes, Mama,' to that butterfly. Yes, what?"

"She asked me a question about you."

"What question?"

"You'll find out soon enough," she says.

I tally up her letters and reach for the radio. She stops my hand. "No. Let's hear the wind this time."

CHAPTER NINETEEN

- ‹‹◆›› - ‹‹◆›› -

SECOND KISS, FIRST FIGHT

Orenda doesn't say much to me when we finally arrive home. She has been in her head since the breathtaking butterfly spectacle. I haven't said much either, although I have a thousand and one questions for her now. I met her family—well, I met a kaleidoscope of butterflies that she believes to be her family, and if that's the case, then I not only met her mom, but her mom actually stood on my nose. Maybe I'm dreaming?

What I do know is that her mother was a human once. And if she is now a butterfly, that means she's no longer a human, but has changed. And my mother says Orenda is changing too. So does that mean Orenda believes she will die and become a butterfly? Nope. I still refuse to believe it. I'd rather believe her doctors will find out what's wrong with her and will help her.

After dinner, after my three three-minute rounds of boxing, after my shower, I'm in my room, ready for more reading.

I open the book to where I left off, but I can't stop thinking of Orenda. Our kiss plays on a constant loop in my brain, like a movie. And it's the best movie I've ever seen. I've titled it *My Kaleidoscope Kiss*. Starring Orenda and the Count. Playing now in my head. Over and over.

I even told Seven all about it, but she doesn't find romance flicks all that interesting. She prefers action movies with tons of food, slobbery tennis balls, and dodgy squirrel villains.

But this is no movie. This is reality. And in reality, not every story has a happy ending. I need to find out what's going on with her. I need hope.

Oh, great. Now I'm crying. I need to calm down. I need to focus. I bury my head in the book and continue reading.

It's three thirty in the morning. I'm in tears. Chick book? I'm such an idiot. This book was amazing. If anyone is afraid of ghosts, all they have to do is read this book and they'll no longer be scared of them, but instead want to be best friends with one. Maybe even develop a crush on one. Imagine that.

I close the book and realize that it is in no way only for girls. Because this story was of a true fearless warrior. And the coolest part is, our hero didn't start off fearless. She was scared and alone, in a new place with no friends, just like me. But she found her courage by believing in magic and, more important, by following her heart, instead of giving in to her fears. That's what I need to do. I need to follow my heart if I'm ever going to defeat this numeric beast in my brain. I hope I can figure out how. All I know for sure is that if I did follow my heart, it would lead me directly up into a certain tree house. But first I need to sleep. I have to wake up in four hours for school. I pull Seven up to my chest, listen to her heart song, and drift off to sleep.

"Good night, Orenda."

I'm in the middle of math class, where the teacher has suggested I sit in the back, so I don't bother anyone with my counting. I stare at my worksheet and can't help but see the irony. All these numbers we are working on, and solving, are perfectly normal. No one bats an eye at them. No one protests them. No one crumples their paper up in frustration because there are numbers written on them . . . but if I happen to respond in numbers, people label me a freak.

Literally every single person the teacher calls on blurts out the answer, which is a number. Seriously! I keep my head down and ride it out until the bell rings. The good thing about being stuck in the back is that when we're dismissed, I am the closest to the door. I dart out of class so fast, you'd think it was filling up with lava. Not only because I am excited to get out of class, but I have a more pressing reason . . . I need to pee, really badly.

Buzz-cut Josh is in the bathroom with two of his buddies. They are writing on the mirrors with black Sharpies, and as I run in, they stop and look at me. This is going to suck . . . but I have to go, so I make a beeline to the urinals.

I unzip and piss an entire gallon before I hear their footsteps approach me.

"Hey, freak," Josh says.

"Eight," I say back, hoping this is all they have.

But I know it isn't. "Just leave me alone, guys," I say. "I've heard it all a hundred times."

"A hundred times? Interesting. Now, are you sure it's a hundred and not a thousand?"

"Maybe it was a million?" one of his friends chimes in.

"Or maybe it was a hundred million?" his other friend adds.

Their numbers fill up in my skull. I try to think about clouds, hoping they'll save me. But before I can tally up the letters, they begin laughing.

Warm. Then immediately followed by cold. Now I know why they're laughing. I turn around and see Josh with his pants pulled down. He's peeing on me. First the back of my thigh, but now that I've turned to face him, his stream is hitting my front.

Anger boils within me. I know what I should do. I should treat them all like my punching bag, but I don't. Last time I threw a punch, I was the one who was expelled. And I don't want to be sent away again. I think of the book I read last night, but that won't help me right now because I don't know any spells to place on these jerks; plus, I'm not a witch. So I try my very best to let the anger dry up inside of me, even with wet pants. Josh stares at me, waiting for me to do something. I think he wants me to hit him. I think he's looking for a reason to beat me up, but instead, I zip up my pants and stare back at him.

"You done?" I ask.

He smiles and zips up.

"What are you going to do about it?" he asks.

"Twenty-six. I'm gonna . . ."

He laughs. "You're gonna what?" he says, and steps forward, getting right into my face.

"Fourteen. I'm gonna wash my hands," I say, and sidestep away from him.

I head to the sink. I glance at the mirror and see them staring at me. I try to ignore the wet-cold-sticky feeling on my leg as I scrub.

Josh walks up to me, pushes me out of the way, and writes *FREAK* on the mirror with his Sharpie. He wants a reaction, but I don't give him one. Sure, I want to pound his face in. Instead, I grab a few paper towels and dry my hands.

"You pissed?" he says, emphasizing the word, which causes his friends to laugh.

"Nine. That's *no* in German," I say, and walk out of the bathroom.

I try to collect myself as I walk down the hall. I didn't even realize how fast my heart was beating and how shaky my hands were. I just want to get home and change my pants.

I walk out of school and get on the bus as fast as I can. I don't know what's worse, people thinking I pissed myself or people thinking I just let someone take a piss on me.

I take a seat and try ignore the smell coming from my jeans. The bus fills up, and we pull off of campus. I slip my headphones on and hit PLAY. As the song starts, I search for the one positive thing to come out of this pee-stained situation . . . Well, I've had a lot of things happen to me from bullies in school, but being peed on is definitely a first. At least I wasn't pooped on. There. I guess that's a good thing.

Do I tell my mom what happened to me today? I know I should, but she'll most likely want me to report it to the principal. Her intentions will be good, but that would only make things worse for me. Back in California, the principals said things like "boys will be boys" or "these kids will someday grow out of this phase and become better people—let's not make life harder for them over this one incident."

Which totally sucks, because it completely dismisses what the bullies did. And somehow, it always becomes my fault. I had to transfer. I was the distraction. It's never them who suffer. Even my dad said I shouldn't take this stuff so personally, because this is how kids are. But it's not. I'm a kid, and I'd never pee on someone. I think kids only act this way because sometimes adults let them.

As I step off the bus and begin walking to my house, I find myself stewing in anger again. I don't want to hate people. I need to think of people that are good. I know they are out there. Like my mom, who has not yet once showed any sign of fatigue or frustration when speaking with me. She's a good person. And like my grandma, who barely notices my counting problem. And when she does notice, she makes me feel like it's some hidden gift that I just don't know how to use yet. Even those two little kids are good people. They see life the way it should be seen.

And like Orenda.

None of these people seem to be annoyed or frustrated with me. In fact, they are nicer to me than I am to myself. I should follow their lead and give myself a break sometimes. But it's difficult not being normal, especially in your own head. Half of me agrees with what Josh wrote on the mirror, but if being normal means picking on people that are different from you, well then, maybe I don't want to be normal after all.

My jeans are still wet because it's so cold out. I think the pee froze into the denim, which is pressing tightly against my leg, giving me the shivers as I walk up my driveway.

Orenda's dad is sitting cross-legged in the center of his front yard staring up at the sun with his eyes closed. What is he doing, meditating? This is the first time I actually get a good look at him. Yesterday when we drove off in the cart, we were in such a hurry, but now I can focus on him and notice his features, which are quite impressive. He has long straight black hair, like his daughter, and his body is lean and strong-looking. If I thought it was possible, I'd work out every day and devote my life to being able to look like him one day. But it's not possible. I'm too pale and scrawny. His skin is a shade darker than Orenda's, probably from doing what he is doing now, meditating out in the sun. I'd be sunburned in twenty minutes. But this guy just sits and soaks it all in . . . In fact, is he even awake?

I tiptoe toward my backyard so I don't disturb him, but more because I don't want him to see that my pants have a huge pee stain on them.

I quietly open the gate and shut it softly behind me. I take two steps in and wait for Seven to slobber me with kisses, but she doesn't. Where is she?

"Seven?" I shout.

Nothing. I look around the entire yard, but Seven isn't here. I pull the sliding glass door aside and search the house. Where is Seven?

Finally, when I reach my room, I see a note on my bed. It says *Took her on an adventure. Love, Grandma.*

I sigh in relief and grab another pair of black jeans out from my closet and run into the bathroom. I want to brush my teeth, just in case I get to kiss Orenda again.

After dousing my leg with a wet soapy washcloth, I slip my clean jeans on and rush out of the bathroom. The thought of kissing her again makes me nervous. And this sudden nervousness makes me try to run faster than my feet will allow, and at the same time, it feels like my feet are each a hundred pounds of wet cement. I leave the house and make it to the fence while trying to look as cool and calm as possible. I don't want her to see me so clumsily smitten.

The rope is down, waiting for me. I smile and grab hold.

This time, it takes less than ten seconds to reach the top, which is easily my best climb yet.

Orenda is in her wheelchair, painting. She doesn't turn around.

I move closer to her to see what she is working on. Wow. She's painting yesterday. It is the two of us holding hands, standing at the edge of the bluff. There are butterflies all around us, in every imaginable color. That memory has been locked into my brain from the very moment it occurred, and she captures it perfectly.

"That's beautiful," I say to her.

She turns and sees me. So she wasn't listening to music; she was just really in the zone. She is wearing a purple baseball cap. By the look of how worn it is, I'm guessing it was her dad's once—or even her grandpa's. I recognize the logo on it. It's a football team my dad always rooted against. I can't remember their name to save my life, but if I had to guess, I'd say they're called the Minnesota Angry Blond Guys? Her black strands flow freely out of it, framing her beautiful fire-skinned face.

I realize that as cool as I try to act around her, the moment she looks at me, I melt off any coolness and become . . . well, me. Which, strangely, feels . . . good.

I can actually be myself around her. For the first time in my life, I don't need to hide who I am in front of someone. And it feels really good. And feeling good is better than trying to feel cool. Both are four letters. Both are double *o*'ed, but they are so different from one another. I'd rather be seen as a good person than a cool person.

"Did you finish the book?" she asks.

Her voice sounds much thinner today, like she's really tired.

"Nineteen. I did. I cried."

She smiles and positions her wheelchair to face me. I notice her movements are a bit more forced, like her limbs aren't moving as fast as her brain is telling them to.

"I love happy endings," she says.

"Seventeen. Me too."

She extends her hand. I take it and hold it. Her skin is cold.

Much colder than the air outside. "But like all good stories, the end is just the beginning."

"Forty-five. What do you mean?" I ask.

"It means there is a sequel. And yeah, it's scary," she says, and lets out a tired giggle.

"Thirty-six. Can you stand?" I ask.

She purses her lips together. "Not very well today," she says.

"Sixteen. Why? What happened?"

"I told you, I'm changing—"

"I know you're changing. But I need to know what that means."

"Hey! Look at that," she says.

"Look at what?" I ask.

"You're not counting my letters."

What? I play it back in my head. And sure enough, she's right. I didn't. Two whole sentences! This is huge. I want to celebrate this victory, but I can't yet. I first need to know what is happening to her.

"Twenty-five. What do you mean by changing?" I'm back to counting, but for once I don't care. Numbers are the last thing on my mind, even if they are the first things on my mind right now.

She releases my hand and rolls to her bed. I watch her carefully lift herself onto the mattress. It's as if she's moving in slow motion.

"I don't really want to talk about that right now," she says.

"Thirty-eight. Orenda, please."

"You know what you need to know. Can't that be enough?"

"Forty. No."

"Why not?"

"Six. Because I don't think you're telling me everything," I say. "And I'm worried."

"I never asked you to worry about me," she says.

"Twenty-eight. That's not how worrying works. Just tell me what's really happening to you."

Her eyes shoot daggers at me. I've never seen this side of her. Her eyebrows dart down, and her focus zeros in on me.

"Are you calling me a liar?"

"Twenty. No, I'm sorry—"

"Get out!"

She tries to stand, but her legs fail. She hits the floor, landing on her knees, and winces. I rush to help her, but she pushes me away.

"Get out! Six! I did it for you, now leave!" she yells.

Her words bubble and grow inside of me like storm clouds eating a clear sunny day. They darken, chew, and pour onto my brain. I want so badly for them to disappear, so I can try to make this better with Orenda, but they swell and flood my thoughts, causing me to seal my eyes shut so numbers don't leak out of them.

I drop to my knees, too. *Please, numbers, get the hell out of my head!* But right before I'm about to drown in the inundation of letters, I open my mouth and let them all surge out of me. "Thirty-five," I shout.

Orenda's smile cracks open. First a light chuckle exits her mouth, but before I can ask what's so funny, she bursts out laughing.

Her laugh is contagious, and soon we are both laughing hysterically. A whole new current of tears streams freely down my face. Not upset ones, but uncontrollable laugh-tears ... One minute, shouting at each other, and the next, we're laughing so hard that we can barely breathe.

"That was our first fight," she says.

"Twenty. Yeah, I think you won."

"I don't know, your 'thirty-five' was pretty good," she says, which makes us laugh again.

She wipes the funny from her cheeks and climbs back into her bed.

"Thirty-six," I say, and sit beside her.

We just had an argument and an epic laughing session within

two minutes. Both have left me exhausted. Maybe I'll just lie here for a bit and—

"My mom really likes you," she says.

And just like that, I am right back to needing answers.

"Nineteen. You really think you're turning into a butterfly, don't you?"

"I know I am," she says.

"Eight."

"You don't believe me, do you?" she asks.

"Twenty-one. I don't know what to believe."

"That's all right. You will," she says, and offers me her hand again.

I take it. We stare into each other's eyes, and I'm suddenly okay with us being the two biggest weirdos in Minnesota.

"Twenty."

She smiles at the number I whisper and leans into me. Her eyes close, and her mouth opens slightly. Here it is. I close my eyes and lean in toward her. Our lips touch. At first, it's soft like two pillows pressing against each other, but her other hand grabs the back of my head and pulls me even closer.

My entire body immediately goes warm. I touch the back of her head. I gently pull the baseball cap and run my fingers through her hair and then, something shifts. She pulls back and sits up. As she does, her black hair nearly slides off of her head. It's a wig.

"I have to go," she says, and climbs back into her wheelchair.

I can't believe I just ruined the moment.

"I'm sorry," she says as she fastens the wheelchair to the rope, but her arms aren't cooperating with her. She tries to shake it out, flapping her arms into obedience, but the frustration in her face mounts.

"Sixteen. Orenda, let me help you."

"I don't need help. I never need help, got it?" she fires back at me.

Her words stop me in my tracks. "Thirty-two. Okay," I say, and watch her struggle to get her wheelchair ready for its descent.

She does need my help. She's basically hyperventilating, and I'm just standing here. I rush forward and reach for the rope, but as I do, she loses her grip on it and the wheelchair plummets to the ground. It makes a crash so loud that it brings her father into the yard almost instantly.

"Orenda! Are you all right?" Foxy shouts.

"I'm fine. Please just go back inside!"

I look through the hole in the floor and see him staring up at us. He doesn't move. I wouldn't either. I put my hand on her shoulder as she begins to cry.

"It's okay," I say to her.

But she shrugs my hand away and grabs hold of the rope. She takes two deep breaths and begins to lower herself. My entire body tenses. If she falls, hopefully Foxy will catch her. Before she leaves, we lock eyes again.

"Don't forget to train tonight," she says, and lowers her head out of the tree house opening.

I watch Foxy reach up and guide her into an embrace. She wraps her arms around his neck and buries her head into his shoulder. I can't hear her crying, but I know that she is.

She's sicker than I thought. I drop to my knees and look directly below me. I see the overturned wheelchair lying on its side in the grass. It's a pretty accurate representation of how I feel right now . . . Broken.

CHAPTER TWENTY

-《◆》--《◆》-

BEAUTIFUL WINGS

I stay up all night, not hitting the punching bag, and not even playing back everything that happened with Orenda in the tree house. I can't sleep because Seven and my grandma haven't come home yet. After pacing back and forth in my room until about three in the morning, I finally pass out.

I wake up still fully dressed, and with Seven sleeping right beside me. I didn't know that grandmas stayed out so late. Aren't old people supposed to be in bed early? I didn't even hear them come in. I need to have a talk with her about this. I have enough things to worry about right now. At least it's Saturday so I don't have to go to school looking like some sleep-deprived zombie.

I get up and walk toward the kitchen to find some food. My mom is on the phone, and from her tone of voice and animated body language, I glean that she's in a really good mood. I wonder why.

I fix Seven her breakfast and eat three large slices of blueberry buckle. I don't know if my mom made it or if my grandma did, but whoever it was, they should win an award for this deliciousness. Seven scarfs down her second bowl of food before I am finished washing my plate. She's always hungry, but this is some next-level appetite. She must have had quite the adventure. My mom gets off the phone and enters the kitchen.

"You like weekends too, huh?" I ask.

"Why?"

"Because you look so happy," I say.

She does a spin and strikes a pose, which makes me laugh.

"What is it?" I ask.

She takes my hand, and I can feel her blood moving though her veins. She's incredibly warm, and her skin is so soft it makes me sleepy.

"Well?" I press her.

"Ronnie is coming home in two weeks," she says, and practically bounces off the walls in excitement.

I want to bounce with her, but I have no idea who Ronnie is.

"That's so great. Who's Ronnie?"

"My . . . your . . . I'm not sure how to say?"

"Just say it, Mama. I've never seen you this delighted."

"I'm happy!" she says, and does an impressive pirouette, then picks up a piece of the blueberry buckle and stuffs the entire thing into her mouth.

"Who's Ronnie?" I ask again.

"Mmmm sonomnomnom," she answers while chewing her food.

"Mom? Chew. Swallow. Speak. Who's Ronnie?" I ask for a third time.

"My soul mate," she squeals out. And just hearing it out loud makes her do a little happy dance.

Out of all the ways to say it, that's her choice? Her soul mate.

My mom is so cheesy. I mean, she could have just said her . . . Wait! What? My mom has a boyfriend?

"You have a . . . boyfriend?"

"Yes. He's been deployed overseas for the last year. That was him on the phone. He's coming home!" she says, and her feet just can't stop floating off of the floor.

"Seventy-three."

"Seventy-three, wow," she says.

"Fifteen. Wait. He lives here?"

"Of course."

"Eight. There's no 'of course' about it. A minute ago I didn't know he even existed!" I say.

"Well, sweetie, a lot can happen in one minute," she says.

"Does he even know about me?"

"Of course."

"Eight. No more *of course*s! I mean, does he know about *me*?" I say, and point to my head.

"Oh, not yet, but he won't care."

"Twenty-one. Everyone cares, Mama."

"Do I?"

"Three. No, but you're different."

"Around here, we're all different, Collin. Have you not picked up on that yet?"

She does have a point. Normal does not live anywhere near us. Whatever normal is. Was my dad normal? Not really. Are the kids at school normal? Is Josh McPee-on-people normal? No. Bullying is not normal. I guess my mom is right. Around here, we're all different.

"Fifty-nine. I see your point."

"So you'll give him a chance just like Seven here gave me a chance?" she asks as Seven licks her leg like a kid with a lollipop.

"Fifty-one. Yes. I'll give him a chance if he gives me one."

My mom wraps her arms around me and squeezes. I feel a couple bones crack from the pressure. I sigh in relief. I really needed that.

My mom dances her way into the living room. Her words linger in my head, not for me to count, but to reflect on.

No one is normal, and we all have issues. We all deal with our problems differently. I usually hide in my room with mine. My dad drowns his problems in beer. Josh pees on people. I want to be there for Orenda and help her in any way that I can. Sometimes, the best we can do is be present.

I need to be there for her.

"I'll be right back," I shout to my dancing mom and rush out of the house.

Seven runs with me until I reach the fence opening. "Stay here, girl," I say, and squeeze my body through.

The wheelchair is gone. I reach the rope and climb up into the tree house, but Orenda is not there. I need to tell her that I don't care about her hair, that she is beautiful no matter what.

I go down the rope so fast that my hands nearly burn. I run up to her back door and knock three times. After a few passing moments, her father answers the door. Wow. Foxy is so much bigger up close. He stands over six feet tall and his shoulders are almost the width of the doorway. She wasn't exaggerating when she said he was as strong as five men. But he has her kind eyes, or maybe she has his.

"Hi. Is Orenda home?"

He looks me up and down.

"Are you the boy who kissed my daughter?" he asks in the deepest voice I have ever heard.

I swallow. "Thirty-one. Ummm. Yeah. Sorry. I mean, I'm not sorry. Unless you want me to be sorry, then I am. Is she home?"

He cracks a smile. "We're about to leave, so make it quick," he says, and steps aside, allowing me to barely squeeze through the door frame we are sharing.

The house is full of Orenda's artwork. There are beautifully knitted butterflies hanging on the walls, paintings of butterflies, and photographs of her family (in human form). I stop and stare at one in particular. It is a framed picture of a younger Orenda, her father, and her mother, who looks so much like her daughter. Long black hair, golden skin, and a smile that makes me instantly sad that I will never see it in person.

"That's her mother," Foxy says from behind me.

"Fourteen. They look identical," I say.

"They were one and the same, those two," he says, and leads me toward Orenda.

"Twenty-nine," I respond, but his strides are long, and he's already too far ahead to hear me.

Foxy opens the door to one of the back bedrooms and steps aside for me to enter. Orenda is lying in bed, wearing a red knitted beanie on her head.

She sits up when she sees me. I just now notice that her dad and she are wearing matching denim button-up shirts. They are one and the same too.

"Ren, I'll be out in the truck. We're running late," Foxy says.

"I'll be right there, Dad," she says, and gives him a look that demands privacy.

Foxy gets the hint and walks out of her room, which is mostly decorated with plants and exotic flowers.

"So this is your other room, huh?" I say, and take a step closer to her.

"Yeah. I call it my garden."

"Nineteen. It smells really good in here."

"Look, about last night . . ."

"No wait . . . Hold on . . . Eighteen . . . Let me go first."

"Okay," she says. "What ya got?"

"Thirteen. I don't care about your hair. I don't care about that stuff at all. I just want to be around you. I feel really good when you're near me. And if I upset you or made you feel embarrassed, I'm sorry."

She lifts herself out of the bed and climbs into her wheelchair. It looks fully repaired. Foxy must have stayed up all night fixing it. But I also take notice of the way she is moving. It's much slower and much more forced, like someone cautiously walking on thin ice. She takes careful, steady steps.

"I loved my hair," she says. "And when you love something, you got to be able to set it free."

"What do you mean? You set your hair free?" I ask.

"Where I'm going, I won't need hair."

"I'm confused. Your hair didn't fall out?" I ask.

"I gave it away to people who need it. My mom did the same thing before she changed."

"Wow. Well, I don't care whether you have hair or not. As long as you're here, I'm happy."

My words make her pause. Maybe because what I said was from my heart, or maybe because she doesn't plan on being *here* much longer. I can't tell.

I reach out my hand to her.

She takes it. "I guess I totally ruined our kiss, huh?" she says with a smirk.

"I'm the one who probably ruined it," I say.

"I guess we'll just have to try again," she says.

I lean toward her, but her dad honks the horn from outside. I perk up.

"I swear he's psychic," she says.

"I think my mom is too," I say, smiling.

I shove my hands into my pockets, just in case he's not only psychic, but can also see through walls.

"I gotta go," she says.

"Where are you going?"

"I'm going to pick out my wings," she says, and rolls past me and out of the room.

"Twenty-three."

Near the front door, she grabs a bag of peaches from the shelf and hands them to me. "Will you feed the butterflies while I'm gone?"

"Thirty-six. Of course."

I follow her out of the front door and down her driveway. Her father waits with his arms crossed, leaning against the idling truck, eyeing me suspiciously.

"I noticed a new ding on my bumper. You wouldn't know anything about that, would you?" Foxy asks me.

"Sixty-five. I—"

"I already told you, Dad," Orenda says. "Those trash cans attacked the truck. We fought them off. You should thank us."

Foxy laughs. "Oh yeah, I forgot. Thank you guys for that."

"Thirty-two. It was nothing, sir," I say, and look down at my shoes to avoid seeing his reaction to my obvious fibbery.

He steps forward, and in one motion, scoops his daughter out of her wheelchair and places her in the passenger seat. Foxy puts the wheelchair on the truck and climbs in.

She leans her head out of the open window, and I meet her at the passenger side door. I close my eyes and lean in for a kiss, which is weird because her dad is right there, but why else would she be leaning her face out the window? Orenda laughs. I open my eyes. I see her dad just staring at me, while Orenda laughs.

"I'm sorry, I thought—"

"You thought what?" Foxy asks.

"I was just going to tell you, while I'm away, I'll be as brave as a brave if you will be too. Deal?" Orenda asks.

I unpucker my lips. "Deal."

The truck drives off. Orenda shouts, "And keep training while I'm gone."

"Twenty-six. I will," I shout back.

Orenda and I stare at each other for as long as we can, seeing who will break eye contact first. It's a draw. Neither of us looked away.

She's going to pick out her wings. I bet that translates to a doctor's appointment or something. I hope she isn't scared. It's hard to imagine Orenda being scared. I'd be kicking and screaming if I was in her shoes. But I'm in mine, and she's in hers. And we all gotta walk with the feet we were born with . . . unless you can grow wings and fly.

As I stroll back to my house, I look down at the bag of peaches in my hand. Well, if I can't hang out with her today, at least I can hang out with her friends.

CHAPTER TWENTY-ONE

- ‹‹◆›› - ‹‹◆›› -

WISE TORTOISE

After eating two peaches and tossing the rest of them out her tree house window, I collapse onto her bed and lay my head against the pillow, and as I do, I hear a crinkle underneath me. I reach under the pillow and pull out a folded sheet of paper. It reads *Hey, Count, listen to the rest of your brother's story. Love, Ren.*

I flip the pillow over and see her earbuds wrapped around her recorder. I unravel the cord, stick them into my ears, sit up, and hit PLAY.

One morning, the wolves were awakened by a horrible sound. The forest was screaming in pain. The humans had entered and were ripping the trees out from their roots with heavy machines and chopping them down with axes. The wolves were losing their home. In a panic, they all gathered together and fled the forest in search of somewhere new. But the human boy was much too slow to keep up with the pack. The mother wolf saw the boy lagging behind and turned back to help him, but the humans with axes and chainsaws scared her off, and they took the teenage boy.

The boy was sent to the city of humans and was placed in a school and forced to go to church, so he could be a good human boy. But soon the humans knew he was far too different to live amongst them. He acted like a wolf, not a boy. He ate differently, he walked differently, and he even howled at the moon. So the other teenage boys and girls stayed away from him, making him feel alone and unwanted.

The boy fell into a deep depression. He wasn't wolf enough to escape the humans, but was too wolf to live with the humans. He didn't fit in. So he decided to run away. That night, he snuck out of the human city and ran as fast as he could for as long as he could. He ran over the hills, he ran through the fields. He ran across the farms, and ran past lakes and rivers and even mountains. And when he finally stopped running, he found himself in a desert.

He thought since there was no one around, there would be no one to not want him. So he decided to stay in the desert. Weeks went by, and he grew so lonely that he no longer wanted to be alive. Life isn't worth living if you have no one to share it with, so he lay down and waited for the sun to melt him. Just then, an old desert tortoise slowly approached him.

"What are you doing?" the tortoise asked the boy.

"I don't belong anywhere, so I will leave this world," he said.

The tortoise laughed.

"Why are you laughing at me?" asked the boy.

"Because, silly boy, everyone belongs somewhere," said the tortoise.

"Oh yeah? Where do you belong?" the boy asked.

"Wherever I go is where I belong," the tortoise said and then showed the boy his shell. "You see, no matter where I go, I am home. And to belong, all you need is a place to call home."

"But I don't have a shell!" the boy shouted, jumping up.

"A home isn't always a shell, silly human. A home sometimes is a family. Have you no family?"

"I had a family, but I wasn't a wolf like them," the boy responds.

"Well, who are you like?"

"The humans, but I'm not like them either. I was too wolf."

"Well, it's simple. Stop trying to fit in. Be different. Different is good. It makes you unique. Look at me, I was raised by ducks."

The boy sat down and thought about what the tortoise said. He began to look back at his life and realized the wolves were his true family, even though he looked different from them. He began to see that he was so afraid of not fitting in that he made himself feel unwanted and alone. His fears parted like clouds, and his memories began to clear. Even though he was picked last in the wolf games, he was still picked. Even though he was the slowest, he was still included to run with them. And even when they hunted, they wanted him along to climb the trees for them.

If the boy had just accepted that he was different, then he would have been able to look past that and live his life with his family. They still loved him. He still howled at the moon with them. They shared their food, and they even let him grow up around them knowing he'd be a man one day. Even when wolves were taught to fear humans, these wolves trusted him.

"I've been so scared of not fitting in that I didn't ever realize I was already a part of the pack," the boy tells the tortoise.

"See! Family doesn't always mean blood. A family is the ones around you, protecting you, living with you. And that makes a home."

"So what should I do?" asked the boy.

"I don't know, but if you want to help some wolves out, there's a whole pack of them a mile back that are stuck in the desert, searching for a den to hide in to escape the hot sun."

The boy thanked the tortoise and ran as fast as he could toward the wolves. And once he reached them, he saw that it was his family. His *mother wolf rushed up to him. "I thought we lost you," she said as she embraced him.*

"No, Mama, you found me a long time ago, and now I found you."

"But we lost our home, and now I fear the hot sun will kill us all."

"No, Mama, I have a plan."

The boy ran all the way back to the city and since he was a human, he was able to speak to the people and have them agree to give him some of the wood they cut down from the forest. He carried it back to the desert and built the wolves small wooden dens. He then ran back to the river, and with human tools, he dug a path through the desert, giving the wolves flowing water.

The wolves were so thankful that they called the boy Ma'iingan, which means "our brother wolf" in Wolf tongue. And soon, the pack regained enough energy and strength to make the long journey north, to find a new forest to live in, far away from the machines that kill trees.

The boy who had always felt like he didn't belong now felt special. Even though he was a human, he was also a wolf. And even though he was a wolf, he was also a human. He was able to live in both worlds. He taught humans that wolves aren't the scary monsters they're made out to be, and he taught the wolves that not all humans are evil and want to kill them.

And over time, the two worlds became so close, they started to blend together. Some humans became wolves, and some wolves became human.

And today, many, many, many years later, there are people who still have wolf blood pumping through their human hearts and there are wolves that still have human eyes. This is why man and wolf must get along . . . Because even though we look different, we are family.

The end.

There is silence. I open my eyes and hit STOP on the recorder. My face is dripping onto my shirt. I didn't even know I was crying. And although it's just a tale my brother made up and recorded for Orenda, I realize that I am the boy in his story. I am from two different worlds. I am different in both of them. I've always believed my counting was a curse.

But how could Aji make up such a beautiful story about me? Or was it about him? Did he feel unwanted? Unloved? Was he from two different worlds too? But didn't everyone love him?

Including Orenda? Was she in love with him too? Did he love her? If he is a squirrel now, does his heart break every time he sees me with her?

I notice a photo album on the shelf by her bed. On the cover of it is a hand-drawn image of a black-and-orange squirrel riding a large red-and-blue butterfly. That must be Aji and Orenda. I open it.

My heart sinks as I flip through the pages. Each photograph is of them growing up together. Snapshots of their lives show me what happiness really looks like. It's a past that I don't have. I see him as a teenager, building the tree house with her father as she watches them. There are photos of them boxing, reading, hopping off the roof, climbing trees. On every page, they look happy. The last photo is the most recent. It is of Aji at prom. He's standing there, with a confident grin above his velvet blue tuxedo, but Orenda isn't with him. Some dude is. He also wears a blue tuxedo. They look like cloudless skies, embracing. Orenda is too young for prom, which explains why she wasn't his date, but who is this guy with him? Is it his best friend?

Then I wonder if Orenda is training me to be strong and smart, so I can be more like him?

I close the photo album and put it back. I'm not sure how to feel. I can't blame her for loving Aji. He seems perfect. I'd kill a king to be half as good-looking as him, half as smart as him, half as strong as him.

Seven barks for me. I walk over to the opening and look down. She's right below me, looking up.

"I'm coming, girl," I say, and climb down the rope. Together, we walk through her yard, squeeze through the fence, and return home.

My mom is in the living room. She's sitting at the coffee table with a stack of paper in front of her.

"What are you doing?" I ask.

"Paying bills," she says, keeping her eyes on the work laid out in front of her.

"Why didn't you tell me Orenda was in love with Aji?" I ask.

She looks up at me and smiles.

"They loved each other very much, but they weren't in love," she says. "And honey, if they were, that's news to me."

"How did you not know?" I ask.

She laughs again. "Did Orenda tell you this?"

"She didn't have to. But you should have. And stop laughing."

"For someone who wants so many answers, you sure don't ask many questions," she says.

"I'm asking you now. Tell me about Orenda and Aji," I say.

"Go get Orenda. Let's all talk together. I'll start a fire," she says.

"I can't. She left to go pick out her wings," I say.

My mom's expression changes. She gets up and walks over to me. And just when I think she's gonna finally level with me and tell me what's really going on with Orenda, she forces a slight smile onto her face and hugs me.

"Well, I'm sure her wings will be beautiful."

I know she means well, but sometimes it's better to face reality head-on and let it crush you.

"Why can't anyone just tell me what's going on? No more riddles! No more lessons! Just tell me what's happening!" I say.

"My sweet boy. This is a part of her story that only she can tell. It isn't mine to give to you. When she's ready, she'll reveal it to you. Be patient. And as far as her and Aji, he was like a big brother to her," she says, and sits back down to continue paying her bills.

"I'm not asking for a story. I'm asking for the truth," I say, and walk out of the room.

As I enter the garage, I realize another reason why Orenda wanted me to read that book. In that story, gossip spread across the town and people were killed because of it. Families were ruined. Friendships were destroyed. If they all handled a rumor the way my mom would, nothing bad would have happened. Salem would just be another town in America and not be shrouded with such a dark history. They would be like, "Is she a witch?" and the neighbors would be like, "I don't know. That's her story. Go ask her." Done. Problem solved. Everyone would have survived. So the answer to the title of *How to Hang a Witch* is clear now, and it's simple . . . You don't. You simply just talk to the witch. And who knows? Maybe, just maybe, you'll see how we're all not so different from one another.

I spend the rest of the day in the garage with Seven. She gnaws on a rubber bone while I hit the punching bag for hours. Visualizing the bag as Orenda's un-talk-aboutable illness keeps me swinging, even though my arms feel like mashed potatoes. But I'm not giving up on her; I will beat this bag to nonexistence.

But no matter how many times I swing, it's still there, and so is Orenda's sickness.

CHAPTER TWENTY-TWO

‑«◆»›‑«◆»›‑

BILLY BEAR

Orenda still isn't home yet.

Last night I hit the punching bag for a total of three hours. Today I've gone jogging with Seven for two miles, and I even found another book to read. When I put the one I read back, right next to it was the sequel, *Haunting the Deep*. So naturally, I plucked it out and started reading it. I can't wait for Orenda to come home and discover that I began a new book. She'll be so impressed.

This time, our hero, Samantha Mather, deals with the sinking of the *Titanic*. And if the first book was about stepping up and accepting who you truly are, this book deals with privilege and how we view people different from us. That and a ship full of ghosts, curses, spells, and magic. In both books, our main hero is in love with a dead boy named Elijah. I hope Orenda didn't recommend this book because she knows I'm falling for her and she is preparing me mentally for the day that she dies. I hope she wants me to read them just because they are super-cool books. Although, if she did die, I'd search through every page to find the spell to summon her back to life. But it's just a book. And this is real life.

And in real life, a whole lot of people went down with the *Titanic*. They died. And Orenda is right: There are people that have it way worse than I do. I count letters, but at least I'm not drowning in the freezing Atlantic <u>O</u>cean. Problems come, and sometimes we can't control the outcome. Some problems get the best of you, even if you're a strong warrior. Sometimes, the problem wins the fight. And that terrifies me. I know Orenda is just trying to prepare me for what's ahead, but I'm not going to listen to her this time. I refuse to let whatever it is that's hurting her win this war. I refuse to lose because I refuse to lose her.

It's now midday. I haven't gotten out of bed yet. So much for my weekend. But my mind and body need a rest. I've been reading and punching every day since Orenda started training me. And tonight I'll probably just draw something. I haven't drawn in a while and my fingers are going through with*draw*als. Plus, my mom took a picture of a deer yesterday that was nibbling on a wineberry bush in the front yard. Maybe I'll surprise her with a drawing of it. I keep thinking of things to do to occupy my mind, but no matter what I engage in, every twenty minutes I keep checking to see if Orenda is home yet. It feels like she's been gone forever.

There's a knock on my door.

"Come in," I shout.

My mom opens the door. Her hair is down, and she's wearing a red flowing dress with black flying birds on it, maybe crows.

"Get up. We're going out," she says.

"Where?"

"To meet your ancestors," she says.

"I'm tired. I think I'll just stay home."

"Okay," she says. "I'll tell Orenda you said hi." She begins to walk away.

"Wait! What? She'll be there?" I say, and launch myself out of my bed.

She smiles and walks out of the room. Meet my ancestors? What does that even mean? I have more family I didn't know about?

I put my black denim jacket on and slap on a hat. Through all the excitement about seeing Orenda, I completely forgot about how I felt about her having feelings for Aji. I know it's absolutely stupid for me to be jealous. I mean, he is no longer here, and besides, he did meet her first. And by the look of all those photographs, he made her happy. That's all that should matter. But then the fear grabs my neck. Can I make her as happy as he did? He was older, stronger, and better-looking. And did she become sick because he is gone? Can love cripple the body like that? If it can, then maybe love can heal the body, too?

My mom honks the horn. I kiss Seven goodbye and rush out of the house. Since the radio doesn't have reception this deep in the reservation, my mom is compensating for it by belting out one of her favorite rock songs a cappella. I climb into the truck and use her nose as a volume knob and turn the dial down . . . way down.

As we drive, my nervousness kicks in. All I can think about is Orenda. And the weird part is, I like it. I like her being the strong fist squeezing my brain and making everything I say, see, hear, smell, and think be all about her.

"Wanna sing with me?" my mom asks.

"Is Orenda really gonna be where we are going?" I ask, ignoring her question.

She smiles and starts singing again. Ignoring my question. I guess if she doesn't get an answer, I don't either.

As we cross the invisible line out of the reservation, the radio kicks in. And it happens to be the exact song she's been singing since we started our drive. I don't know how my mom does stuff like this. It's either Native American magic, or she's a descendant of one of those Salem witches. Either way, she's pretty freakin' cool.

We drive through the forest, on a thin one-lane gravel road. As we head deeper and deeper into the thick of the trees, it becomes so dark that all we can see are the truck's headlights and ten feet of gray road in front of us. It looks like we are headed straight into a black hole. I clutch the sides of my seat as the drive becomes more bumpy the farther we venture in.

A good ten minutes later, my mom pulls off the road and into a hidden dirt lot. There is a faint source of light ahead of us, way off in the distance.

As we drive closer, the light becomes more visible, and I can now make it out to be a large campfire. There are a dozen parked cars, even a few horses tied to wooden poles.

"What is this place?" I ask her.

"Like I said, it's time for you to meet your ancestors."

She parks the truck, turns off the radio, and turns to me. "Give me your face."

"I don't know what that means. It's mine," I say.

She laughs, pulls out something small, encased in cloth, and carefully unwraps it. It's a thin black piece of charcoal, I think. Maybe it's chalk?

"Closer," she says, and I lean my face toward her.

"What is that?"

"What's in it? Let's see here. There's clay, berries, plants, minerals, all wrapped in burnt tree bark. You'll wear this for Aji," she says, and with her index finger she rubs against the thing, coating her fingertip with a deep black paste. She then presses on my forehead and streaks her finger down toward my eye. I close them instinctively as she drags her finger farther down my face, stopping just below my cheekbones.

"I feel like I'm going to battle."

"You've been in battle your entire life. This, my son, will help you win."

The air in here just got thick, like there's a presence sitting in between us. She feels it too because she takes a deep breath and closes her eyes. It's almost dizzying.

"What is this?" I ask.

"You feel it?" she asks.

"Yeah."

"That's our blood waking up," she says, and gets out of the truck.

I whisper, "Twenty-one," to myself.

Together, we walk through the dark dirt lot, passing the parked cars and stationed horses, lit only by the moon hanging above us. I'm hearing sounds I've never heard before. It's like a concoction of voices: talking, screaming, laughing, and singing all at once. There's a vibrating drumming that reminds me of the night I saw Orenda up in her tree house while I was freezing my naked butt off. It shakes my feet with every step, getting louder and stronger as we get nearer. Maybe this is the way all family gatherings sounded, before we made electronics and machines that covered up everything.

When we finally arrive, there are a dozen people dancing around a large fire. They look like giant birds, feathers bouncing off their bodies as they dance. They never leave their feet on the ground for more than a second, as if the earth is too hot to stand on.

Surrounding the dancers is an even larger outer circle of people sitting and clapping along. I hear their voices, but I can't tell who is singing which parts. It all blends together like a symphony.

In the outside circle, I see Orenda, sitting in her wheelchair. She hasn't seen me yet. She has her eyes fixed to the fire-dancers.

"I'll be right back," my mom says, and walks off into the darkness toward a few tents on the outskirts of the event. My eyes scan the crowd. Everyone here is Native American. I've never seen so many before—outside of a Western movie. I'm the palest person here, by far.

I don't know these people, and I don't know what I'm supposed to do. I don't know how Native Americans handled people like me, but if this was a couple hundred years ago in Europe, my numbers condition would be labeled as witchcraft and I'd be tossed into that enormous fire.

"Who invited the white boy?" a voice says behind me.

I turn around and see three teenagers walking toward me. The one that spoke is tall and thin, he wears a bandana around his head, and his hair is separated into two long braids that hang down to his chest. The second one is short and heavy. He actually looks pretty friendly, but I'm not going to count on it, literally. The third one, I can't really tell if they're a girl or a boy. Either way, their face is striking, and their hair is in tight black cornrows. I take a mental photograph of his or her face, because it's definitely one I'd like to draw later.

All three of them are dressed in vests covered in beads and what looks like bones. Most likely, I'm about to catch a beating, but I must admit, they do look really freaking cool.

I don't count his letters because technically they weren't meant for me, although I know he said it loud enough for me to hear him. His chubby friend laughs as they get close enough to see my face.

"Who are you?" the first one asks me.

"Nine."

"Nine? Your name is Nine?" the third one says, and even hearing their voice, I still can't be certain if they are a he or she.

"Eighteen," I reply.

"Nine Eighteen? That's a dumb-ass name," the first guy says.

"Twenty-nine. And what's yours? Boy Who Steps in Horse Poop?" I say in return.

He immediately looks down at his feet.

"Made you look," I say.

Both his friends laugh, but not so much at my dumb joke. They laugh at the fact that I just talked crap (literally) to a guy who is clearly much bigger and stronger than I am.

He steps forward and gets right in my face. I know what comes next. I've been here before. This is where I get punched. Usually, I'd close my eyes and hope it all happens quickly, but I'll keep my eyes open this time. Maybe if he swings, I'll swing too. I know how to throw a punch now. I've thrown thousands at a bag since my last beating. I don't want to fight, but I'm not going to curl up in a ball and welcome a butt whupping either, especially with Orenda here. I guess what happens next all depends on this guy. I wait . . .

But instead of shoving me, or punching me, or slamming me down onto the ground, his eyes focus on the black design my mom painted onto my face.

"Wait . . . You knew Aji?" he says.

"Fourteen. Knew him? He's in my blood. I know him," I say.

They all look confused.

"Hey, Joey! I wouldn't mess with him," says a voice behind the group.

Joey turns around, as do his buddies. A guy is splitting the group in half as he approaches. Whoever this guy is, he commands respect. I immediately recognize him from the prom photo under Orenda's bed. He was the guy standing with Aji.

"Hey, Billy," says Joey, whose body language dramatically changes now that Billy has arrived.

"Don't 'Hey, Billy,' me. This is Collin," he says to the group.

"And?" Joey says. "Are we supposed to know who he is?"

"You should. He's Aji's brother," Billy says as he puts his hand on my shoulder.

After a long silence, Joey approaches me and offers his hand.

"I meant no disrespect, Collin. Aji was good people."

"Forty. It's okay," I say, and shake his hand.

"Why didn't you say you were Aji's brother, homie?" the chubby friend says, and gives me a bear hug, lifting my feet off the ground.

"Thirty-seven."

"Is that, like, code or something?" he asks.

I tally them up again. "Twenty-five. Something like that."

He catches on and pretends to zip his mouth shut with the invisible zipper in his hand, which is fine, but after he locks his mouth closed, he opens it and eats the invisible key. Then laughs at his own joke. I laugh too.

"Nice to meet you, Collin," the third friend says. "I'm Deo."

And by the look, the voice, and even the name—I still have no idea of his or her gender. I guess it doesn't matter. I guess it's just Deo.

They walk off and leave me with Billy. He is maybe even more attractive than my brother was, if that's possible. He has short black hair, a scruffy face, and green piercing eyes. He doesn't share the same facial features and skin color as any of the people here, so I'm not sure if he's Native American or not. If I had to guess, I'd say Egyptian or from somewhere far away like that.

"Thanks," I say.

"Don't mention it," he says. "You probably heard a lot about this town's high school football legend, Billy the Bear, well, that's me."

"Ninety-four. I don't know about football stuff, sorry . . . So, you and Aji were friends?" I ask.

He laughs. "You can say that. So you really do count everyone's letters, huh?" he asks.

"Fifty. Yeah, it's my superpower. What's yours?"

"Me? I just kick butt and look good doing it," he says, and laughs.

"Thirty-three. Wanna trade?" I ask.

"No thanks. I suck at math," he says.

As I count his letters, my mother sneaks up from behind and wraps her arms around me.

"Making friends, I see," she says.

I look at Billy: "Nineteen to you." And turn my face to my mom: "Seventeen to you."

"Hey, Billy," she says, and hugs him. "How are you?"

He squeezes her tightly. By their expressions, I can see they are both happy to see each other, but also, it's not easy. Too many memories flooding back.

"I'm good. Just trying to stay positive, you know?" he replies.

"We all are. You can still come around, you know? We miss you."

He exhales a heavy breath. "I will. I'm just not ready to be back there yet."

While they talk, I look back at Orenda, smiling at me, from a distance.

In the glow of the campfire, Orenda looks as if she set the world ablaze with her beauty. She wears a black Western hat, and her eyes shine through black paint covering her face like a bandit. Her sweatshirt is red with black sleeves; in the center, over her chest is a black painted handprint. She wears tight jeans and heavy brown boots.

As she approaches me, I notice that even her wheelchair looks cooler; the two wheels have been upgraded to have tires much thicker than the originals, like a dirt bike's tires, made for rough terrain.

"I leave for a bit, and you're already almost getting into fights?" she says.

I tally up her letters. "He started it," I say.

She wheels herself even closer. "My rebel. Come on, let me feel those arms," she says, and reaches out for me.

"Thirty-one."

I bend down, and she grips my biceps. As she squeezes, her eyebrows rise very slightly. "You've been training hard!" she says excitedly.

"I told you I would. Did you pick out your wings?" I ask.

"I did. They're beautiful. Speaking of beautiful, I see you met Billy."

"Yeah. He actually saved me from me getting my butt kicked," I say, which causes her to laugh.

"No. With those arms, my money's on the Count."

"Were Aji and him close?" I ask.

"As close as two can be," she says with a smile.

"Closer than you and Aji?" I ask.

She looks at me strangely. Very strangely, like she's examining my face, searching for the reason why I asked such an odd question.

"Why are you looking at me like that?" I ask.

"Interesting."

"What is?"

She traces my face with her finger. And her eyes focus on all my features, like an explorer studying a map before a great voyage. "Serious face. Sad eyes. Confused brows. Stubborn nose. Nervous lips. Ask me what you want to ask me before your face explodes," she says, and drops her finger into her lap.

"Were you in love with my brother?" I ask.

She laughs the same way my mother did, although I still find no humor in my question.

"He was like my older brother, you bozo," she says.

"But did you want to one day grow up and marry him?" I ask.

Her eyes widen. "That would be impossible," she says.

"Why?" I ask.

"You didn't know?" she says. "Aji was gay."

Wait a minute. No way. My mom said all the girls loved him. She said everyone wanted to be him. She said he was the most popular kid at school . . . But she also said he had to work for it. She said he was bullied early on. That he had to fight and gain everyone's respect.

Now it all makes sense. Wow.

"I had no idea."

"Clearly. And you met his boyfriend," she says.

"Who?" I ask.

Orenda puts her hands on her wheels and thrusts forward. I follow her all the way until her wheel bumps into the back of Billy's leg. The guy that just saved me from getting beat up was my brother's boyfriend. Duh, they went to prom together. How did I not figure that out?

"He didn't know you and Aji were a thing," Orenda says to him, and points to me.

Billy smiles. "Was he shocked?"

Orenda turns to me. "Are you shocked?"

"Surprised, I guess."

She turns back to Billy. "He's surprised, he guesses."

Billy walks up to me and puts his hand on my shoulder. "Aji was the best person I've ever met. Orenda here, maybe the second best. Keep an eye on her. She's quick."

As I count his letters, Orenda sees her chance and takes off in her wheelchair, rolling through the crowd, maybe to prove how quick she really is.

"Eighty!" I shout to Billy, and take off running.

She weaves in and out of the crowd, maneuvering her wheelchair like a rocket ship avoiding asteroids in space. After a full sprint, three almost falls, and two near collisions, I finally catch up to her. I grab her wheelchair. We stop.

We are alone at the very end of the dirt lot. We can still hear the drums and singing, but they are now joined by the crickets making their own music. How are crickets out when it's this cold? I try to focus on the ground to see them, just to check if they are wearing tiny cricket coats and scarves, but it's much too dark to see anything out here. I hear an owl too, but it's impossible to tell where it is exactly because its *hoo*s are echoing off of every one of the million trees.

"Billy's right. You are quick," I say.

"Like lightning," she replies.

"Thirteen. I miss you," I tell her.

I drop to my knees. Our eyes are level. I take both of her hands into mine.

"You shouldn't miss what's right in front of you," she says, and leans forward.

"Thirty-seven."

"Thirty-seven nothing," she says, and kisses me.

I close my eyes. The crickets give us a standing ovation, cheering us on.

CHAPTER TWENTY-THREE

-《◆》--《◆》-

SPIRIT QUESTING

"Orenda!" her dad shouts.

Our faces pull away from each other. I stand up and take a step back, hoping he'll forget that he just saw me kissing his daughter.

"It's time," Foxy says to her.

Orenda's eyes light up. "Yes!" she says excitedly.

"Time for what?" I ask her.

"You'll see," she says, and wheels herself toward her father.

I take a few minutes to myself before I walk back toward the crowd. There are so many crickets around me, churning their legs to keep the moon aglow, which is so big and yellow, it looks close enough to touch. I hear the owl still hooting from a tree. I hear branches swaying with the breeze. I'm not alone. I realize right then and there, that when you finally open your eyes and ears to nature, even when there's no one around, you'll never be alone.

I bid adieu to all of earth's hooters, crawlers, and swayers and walk back to the crowd of humans. Everyone is having such a good time that it feels nice just to watch them. I guess we are a part of nature too. We just forget that sometimes. But everyone here hasn't forgotten it; in fact, they're celebrating it. I watch them laugh, dance, and flirt with one another and have yet another realization: My people are really cool. They get it. Life is about finding your family, and once you find them, you stick together and dance along to this song that we call life.

"There you are!" my mom says, and rushes up to me.

"Hey, Mama."

"I was looking all over for you," she says, and grabs my arm, pulling me toward the tented area.

"I kissed Orenda. It was so—"

"Magical?" She finishes my sentence.

"Yeah. How'd you know?" I ask.

"All the good ones are."

"Where are you taking me?"

She walks me to the very last tent, which isn't a tent at all, it's an actual teepee. I've seen black-and-white photographs of them in history books, but I've never seen one in real life. And it's much bigger than I imagined. A whole family can live in one, well, if you forgo the whole "needing privacy" thing.

My mom pulls back the opening flap and leads me in. Inside is black as pitch, until a torch is suddenly lit and carried over to the center. A man that looks at least two hundred years old sits cross-legged and still. The fire is placed between him and me. My mom pushes my shoulders down, signaling me to sit, so I do.

"I'll be right outside," she says.

"Seventeen. Okay."

She leaves, and it's just this old man and me. And silence. I wait for him to speak but he is too busy staring into the flame to be bothered, so I go first.

"Um, should I just meditate or something?" I ask.

Instead of speaking, he claps his hands together, just once, loudly.

And within seconds, four people wearing long robes enter the teepee. Each robe is a different color: one red, one black, one yellow, and one green. Each person holds a pair of tongs. Gripped in each tong is a different color stone, matching the color of the robe they're wearing.

All four people kneel down and place their stones into the fire. The stones sizzle to life, sending gray clouds of smoke into the teepee. The heat immediately engulfs my body. I've never been to a sauna before, but I imagine this is what it feels like.

The four people leave without saying a word. The heat intensifies once we are alone. The air quickly becomes so hot and thick that I want to run out of here and check my clothes for flames, but I don't. Because the old silent man finally speaks.

"There is battle within you," he says. His voice is deep and cracked like a long-forgotten sidewalk.

In my head, his words resemble the smoke clouds forming above us in the teepee. My sweat begins to sizzle on my skin, so I move slightly, causing the sweat to run down my body. I start to breathe in deep, but my lungs feel like they're boiling, so I keep my breathing as shallow as I can. Is it supposed to be this hot?

The old man sees my suffering and smiles. "Become the heat," he says.

"Thirty-five. That doesn't make sense."

He waves his arms in front of me, mixing his hands with the flames. How is he not burning? I see the flames touching his skin, rolling over his wrinkled hands, through his spread-out bony fingers. The sweat in my eyes stings and doubles my vision. I wipe it away, but the blurriness doesn't leave.

"Close your eyes," he says to me.

I close my eyes. Now all I see is black, and it still feels like I am trapped inside of an oven. "Thirteen," I say through my hot breath, hoping my teeth don't melt in my mouth as I speak.

"Do you see the battle inside you?" he asks.

"Twenty-six. I don't see anything. Just black."

"Look deeper. Not outward, but inward," he says.

"Twenty-nine. I just see . . . Wait . . ."

As I look through the blackness, I see something. It's me. And I'm floating toward myself. What is going on? And I don't stop. I literally collide into my own body and merge into one. Now it's just me again.

What the heck was that?

But I feel different. Like this black all around me isn't nothingness any longer. It's my mind. I'm standing inside my mind. At least, I think I am. I lift my hands up, and I see them in front of my face. I count all ten fingers. I'm all here.

I must be inside my mind, because I know on the outside I'm sitting in a steaming hot teepee with an old man and my eyes are closed.

I take a step forward. Wow. I can even walk inside my mind. I turn in all directions, but there is still only blackness everywhere I look. Outer space at least has stars and planets, but my mind has nothing. Maybe there's a light switch in my head somewhere?

"Hello?" I shout, and hear my voice echo four or five times until it falls silent again.

I walk forward, and even though I see no ground, I feel like I'm getting closer to something. The more I walk, the stronger the feeling is. So I run. And the feeling becomes a sound. It's a faint whimper. I slow down to a walk and follow the noise . . . And as I get nearer, it gets louder and louder.

Then I see it. It's a wolf. Immediately I think of the story Aji recorded for Orenda. But this wolf is large, gray, and angry. It sets its black eyes on me. It growls and drools, revealing its sharp fangs to me. They look like they would easily sink into my skin like knives through butter. I stop and feel my heart beating through my chest. This is fear. My hands are shaking. A thick, heavy rope is tied to the wolf's back leg. It looks exactly like the rope I climb to reach Orenda's tree house. I instantly wonder if I'm out of reach or not.

I look down and see that there's now a large knife in my hand. The same knife Orenda uses when she cuts peaches. How the heck did I get her knife?

The wolf growls and steps toward me. As it moves, black numbers and letters shimmer in its fur, the way a dragonfly's iridescent skin shimmers when it flies.

I know two things. I'm inside my head, and this wolf is made of numbers and letters. So maybe this is the battle within me that the old man was talking about? Am I supposed to fight this wolf? I can barely fight off bullies in school—how am I supposed to fight a wolf?

Will slaying this numeric beast finally cure me? I mean, a part of me knows this isn't real, but also, a part of me thinks it may be. After all, magic is real. I've seen it many times since I've moved here. What if that old man somehow transported me to face my fears by literally putting a hungry, large wolf in front of me? Oh, crap. What if this wolf can really kill me?

Fear grips my entire body as the wolf slowly walks toward me. Should I run? Would Aji run? No, he'd fight. Would Orenda run? No, she'd fight too. Would I run? Yes. I've run my entire life. But running never got me anywhere but farther away from where I want to be, from who I want to be.

I'm done running. I reach my hand deep into my gut and find whatever small amount of courage I have inside and pull it out. I hold the blood-dripping bravery in my hand and watch it sizzle and smoke in my fist.

"Be the heat," I say to myself, remembering the old man's words.

I stuff my courage into my mouth and eat it. My senses heighten. I feel taller, stronger. No longer afraid.

I grip the knife as tightly as I can and charge toward the wolf. It snaps its jaws as I get closer. I lift the knife above my head, and right when I'm about to drive it down toward the wolf, it launches up, opens its mouth, and bites down on me. I drop the knife, and I fall to the invisible ground. The wolf is on top of me, tearing my flesh from my bones. It hurts. I hear my bones crack and my skin rip. I scream.

My eyes burst open. I'm still screaming. But the pain is gone. And all the courage I was feeling is quickly replaced with the sudden returning burst of heat. I am back in the teepee. The old man sits across from me, watching me.

"What the heck was that?" I say.

"You failed," he says, and points to the entrance, which is also the exit.

"Nine. But I tried. I tried to face my fear. I tried to kill the wolf!" I say.

"Courage takes many forms. Now go," he says, and turns his eyes from me back to the fire.

"Twenty-six," I say, and rise to my feet.

Cold air immediately pats me down as I exit the teepee, brushing off the sweltering heat still holding on to my body. It feels better, but I don't. I feel awful. I feel like a failure.

My grandma approaches me, seeing the disappointment on my face. "Next time," she says, and kisses my forehead. This time her dress is yellow.

"What kind of test was that?" I ask her.

"It's called a spirit test. Or is it called a spirit quest? I can't remember . . . Oh, that's right, the test is a quest. Did you try your best?" she asks.

Even after I failed her, she's still having fun. Rhyming and giggling.

"I did, but my best wasn't good enough . . . Where have you been?" I ask her.

"Traveling," she says.

"How many adventures does someone your age need?" I ask her.

"Just one that never ends," she says.

"Collin!" shouts my mom, and I turn to her. Even she looks a bit disappointed in me. My grandma pushes me toward my mother and walks off to join a group of people.

"Six. I failed."

"But you didn't run. Learn from your failures. They are your best teachers."

"Fifty-eight."

Leave it to my mom to dish out some deep wisdom right now. She puts her arm around my shoulder and walks me back toward her truck. As we pass the remaining parked cars, I can't help but be moved by this whole experience, whatever it was. Losing fights isn't new to me, but I've never fought an imaginary wolf before in some spirit test-quest battle that all took place inside my head while my body was cooking in a teepee. I mean, maybe I'm not a brave yet, but I do feel like I'm getting closer to something big. Maybe there is a method to Orenda's madness. Maybe her training will someday cure me. I just need to figure out how to defeat the wolf.

"Where's Orenda?" I ask my mom as we climb in her truck.

"She had her test."

Orenda had a test, too? Did she beat the wolf? Did she have to fight it while sitting in a wheelchair?

"Did she pass hers?"

"Yes. Foxy took her home to celebrate," she says. She drives through the rough terrain of the dirt lot until we once again enter the forest.

If Orenda passed her test, does that mean she is no longer sick? Can she walk now? The thought of her being cured gives me hope. I imagine her running, dancing, and . . . us kissing again. That was pure magic. Crickets sang. Lightning struck. Owls hooted. And . . . I almost forgot . . .

"Why didn't you tell me Aji was gay?" I ask my mom.

"You never asked."

"Fair enough."

My brother was gay. That's it. And Billy seemed like a great guy. Those two were lucky to have each other. And to top it off, Orenda had him as someone to look up to. She saw him as her older brother. I couldn't think of a better life.

My mom must miss him so much, but she's so strong about it. It must be hard to be strong all the time. I reach out and grab her hand.

"Can I ask you a question?"

"Of course," she says.

"Why didn't you and my dad work out?" I ask.

She takes a moment, assessing how to respond. "When your father and I . . . met, I was in a dark place. A few years earlier, Aji's father was killed in a car accident. I fell into a depression. Aji and I had to move back in with my mother, on the reservation. It was a tough adjustment. A friend of mine took me out to a concert, and I met your father. One thing led to another, and there you were. Having another child was going to be very tough for me, but I was ready to do it . . . But your father's parents were very adamant about raising you, giving you the life I couldn't. I wanted you to have all the opportunities I never had, so I agreed. I'm sorry."

I tally up her letters and wipe a tear off of her cheek as she drives. We don't say another word, and she doesn't even turn on the radio. We just drive in silence together, both of us thinking of the coolest guy to ever live: my brother, Aji.

CHAPTER TWENTY-FOUR

-《◆》-《◆》-

REBOUND/REVENGE

Me and gym class. It's a love-hate relationship. I love it for the same reasons I hate it; there is very little talking involved, I'm always the last picked for whatever sport we're playing, I never get passed to, and I never get asked to participate in the team-building huddles. I never really have to do anything besides stand around.

In California, I could wander around the field and go unnoticed, but here in freezing Minnesota, we're all crammed together in the gymnasium. It's much harder to not be seen.

Today we are playing basketball, and if I can find any source of light to this situation, it is this: I'm glad my dad isn't here to see this disaster.

We all line up at the baseline. The teacher picks one person randomly to step forward and shoot a free throw. If he makes it, he steps aside and lets someone else take a shot at it. If he misses, we all have to run the entire length of the court as fast as we can. And so on and so on.

I must say, Minnesota breeds some really good basketball players. Over half the class has already shot the free throw and made it. These are natural-born athletes. Must be nice. Their fathers must be really proud. But I am at the end of the line, and I am pretty sure I am going to be public enemy number one by the time class is over.

Finally there are three people left to shoot the ball. One girl, one guy, and me. The girl walks up to the free-throw line. The gym teacher, Coach Alomits, passes her the ball. She dribbles three times and sets her aim. I watch her take a deep breath, bend her knees, and shoot. The ball bounces around the rim before it falls through the hoop. The class cheers. She bows to the class and joins us at the baseline. The guy next to me is tall and muscular. He looks like he plays basketball for breakfast. He struts to the free-throw line and waits for the ball.

Coach Alomits passes him the ball, and with no focus needed, he catches the ball and immediately shoots. Swish. Nothing but net. He dusts off his shoulders and strides back to the baseline. Everyone turns their focus to me. I feel like a floodlight just shone on me, onstage, and everyone paid good money for me to entertain them.

"Step up," Coach Alomits says to me.

"Six," I say, and begin to move my feet toward him.

A few students laugh, but reality sets in. If I get too flustered and miss the shot, they will have to run. So quickly the gymnasium becomes silent . . . dead silent.

"Since he's the last to shoot, we run until he makes it," Coach Alomits says to a crowd of sighs—already assuming my first attempt is going to be a miss.

He passes me the ball as I reach the free-throw line. I bounce it once to get the feel of this round orange leather glob, and it hits my foot and rolls away. The class knows they're doomed. I run after it and return to the free-throw line.

"It's simple, Collin. Just put the ball in the hoop," says Coach.

"Thirty-eight," I say, and bounce the ball again, this time more carefully.

The class watches me like they're about to see a car crash. I try to block them out and think of one thing only. Ball, meet hoop. Be friends. Please. I hold the ball and line it up to the hoop. And right before I shoot, I stare at the class, who are standing as if the baseline is the edge of a cliff and it's up to me whether they plummet to their deaths or not.

I scan each of their dread-filled faces and realize that this is what power must feel like. Before I shoot, a familiar face catches my eye. It's Josh. The jerk who peed on me.

Wait a minute . . . This can be fun. Sure, I'll probably get stuffed in a locker for it, but at least I can make them so exhausted that they'll only hit me once, maybe twice. I stare at Josh and smile. They say revenge tastes sweet. Well, let's see if that's true.

"This one's for you," I say to Josh, and shoot the ball.

Brick. It hits the rim and ricochets back to me.

"One," Coach Alomits shouts, and on cue, the class runs full speed up and down the court.

He passes me the ball again. And again, I bounce the ball a few times to at least appear like I know what I'm doing. I remember how the pee felt running down my thigh, making my pants stick to my skin.

"Take your time," Coach says to me.

But I don't need time when I'm out for vengeance.

"Twelve," I say, and interestingly enough, this time, no one giggles.

I shoot the ball up again; this time it veers left and bounces off the rim.

"Two," he shouts.

Again, the disgruntled class race up and down the court. I have to say, this is by far the most fun I've ever had in gym class. No one is laughing now.

"Third time's a charm," Coach Alomits says, and passes me the ball again.

"Sixteen."

I look at Josh. He's huffing and puffing on the baseline, with his hands on his knees. He shoots daggers at me with his eyes and clenches his fist, threatening me in between his gasps for air. While keeping my eyes on him, I toss the ball up and hear it clank off the steel rim. I smile as he stomps his feet like a spoiled brat.

"Four," Coach shouts.

The class takes off, this time much slower. I watch them travel the entire court and stop back at the baseline. Hands clutching knees. Deep gasps. Cursing under their huffed breaths. Even moans.

"Clearly, this may take a while, and I have a sneaking suspicion there is more here than meets the eye," Coach says to the line of tired students.

He turns to me. "Collin, choose one lucky person to stay and continue this. The rest of you are dismissed."

"Seventy-one," I say, and point to Josh.

His nostrils flare. His chest puffs out. But the rest of the class sighs in relief as they leave the court.

"You . . . *pissed*?" I ask Josh.

"You're dead," he fires back to me.

"Nine. Not if you're dead . . . tired," I fire right back.

Josh tries to milk the time by taking in as much air as he can before the ball is given back to me. Coach Alomits hand delivers it to me this time.

He leans into my ear. "I got all day, kid," he says, and gives me a wink.

Good to know. This coach hates bullies, too. I'm going to enjoy this.

"Thirteen," I say, and accept the ball.

Josh stands alone on the baseline. Waiting for more punishment. He's probably thinking of the many ways he's going to hurt me. But I don't care because right now, the ball is in my court and I'm in control. I pretend that I'm really going to try this time, but as I release the ball, I veer it right. It bounces off the backboard and returns to me.

"Five," Coach Alomits shouts, and Josh runs up and down the court.

Payback does taste sweet. And it's surprisingly easy. I haven't even broken a sweat. And the greatest thing about it all is, even if I felt sorry for this bully, I'd maybe attempt to make the shot, but I suck. So, I'd still be exactly where I am now. It's a win-win for me.

By my lack of talent and athleticism, I am forced to punish this jerk. All the years of sucking at sports has led me here. Maybe my dad wouldn't be proud, but if every kid that was ever picked on, or peed on, by bullies like Josh saw me now, I know they'd be cheering me on to miss as many shots as I possibly could. And it makes me so freaking happy to do them all a favor like this. Hopefully Josh will think twice before picking on someone again, especially someone who sucks at sports. He'll be forced to pick on some star athlete, but then he'll get his butt whupped because star athletes are exactly what I am not, physically gifted.

And after half a dozen more misses, I take a moment to allow Josh a few seconds to catch his breath. He is now barely standing. Sweat pours from his wobbly body. It's great. I bounce the ball, snapping him out of his much-needed rest and prepare to shoot.

"Wait!" Josh shouts in a pathetic sigh.

"Four," I shout back.

All Coach Alomits needs is a bag of popcorn and a Coke. He's loving this just as much as I am.

"I know why I've been missing this whole time. Duh. I've been shooting with my right . . . I'm left-handed. Oops," I say, and I hear Coach Alomits laugh from the sideline.

Josh grunts in pure agony and drops to his knees.

"Line up!" Coach Alomits shouts, and slowly Josh stands.

"What are we at?" I ask Josh.

"No more," he whimpers back.

"Six. Why? Do you need a break? Do you gotta pee or something?" I say, and I look at the rim.

"I'm sorry," he says, and looks down.

Did he just apologize? Did I break him? Or better yet, did I finally win at something?

I immediately feel bad for him as he hides his eyes by looking at his feet. I know that feeling. I've done it hundreds of times. It's pure humiliation. And I don't wish that feeling on anyone. If I keep missing and making him run, wouldn't that make me a bully now? I fought my battle and won. I taught the bully a lesson; now my lesson should be to know when to stop. The last thing I want to do is pick on someone who already admitted defeat. I need to be the bigger person now. I had my fun.

I spin the ball in my left hand and imagine Orenda standing beside me. I envision her saying that if I make it this time, her illness will vanish. Motivation. Is. All. I. Need.

I bounce the ball, bend my knees, set my aim, and release it off my fingertips. It spirals through the air and hits the rim once, twice, and on the third bounce, it falls into the hoop.

Josh collapses in relief. I jump for joy, thinking I just cured Orenda, but then realize Orenda isn't really here. It's just me, Josh, and a very amused gym teacher.

I walk up to Josh and bend down, so we're eye level.

"You retaliate in any way, then the next chance I get, it won't stop until you start growing a beard," I say, and walk away in my first ever victory.

Surprisingly enough, the whole time in the locker room I was anticipating getting punched and having my head shoved into a toilet, but it never came. In fact, Josh quietly changed and left me alone. I suspect Coach Alomits gave him an additional talking-to.

I change back into my all-black outfit and shut my locker. I feel good. I may have lost to a wolf, but I just stood up to and defeated a bully, and that feels like a step in the right direction.

While I walk to the bus pickup area, I see Billy out in the field. He's too old to be at this school. What is he doing here? He's surrounded by a bunch of kids, like he's a coach leading a huddle. He sees me and runs through the field toward me. I watch him run and can't help but think of the extremely hot model guy running in slow motion in one of those shampoo commercials. And I'm not the only one to notice; a few girls walking in front of me stop and drop their jaws—and books.

He approaches me. The chain-link fence is between us.

"Well, if it isn't Mr. Basketball Star himself!" he says as he grips the fence with his hands.

"Thirty-five. Wow. Word travels fast. What are you doing here?" I ask.

"I run an after-school program. Keep kids off the streets and on the field. Today I'm teaching football. You interested?" he asks.

I tally up his letters and look for the best way to pass on his invitation. "I'll stick with basketball," I say, which makes him laugh—by now, he knows how bad I suck.

"Well, if you change your mind, you know where to find me," he says.

"Forty-three. Thanks. Can I ask you a question?"

"Sure."

"Four. Did Aji know about me? I'd ask my mom, but I don't want to make her sad by bringing up the past so much."

Billy nods and briefly looks away. I guess I just made him a little sad.

"Your mom told him about you, but she made it this elaborate story about how these two little wolf pups were separated by humans but will one day find each other and live happily ever after. He was looking forward to that day. But life had other plans for him. Plans none of us were ready for," Billy says.

I tally up his letters and see the pain in his eyes. "I wish I got to meet him," I say.

"You will, one day. Maybe not in this world, but I know him. He'll find you in the next one," he says. "I gotta get back, but tell your mom I'll be stopping by soon."

"I will. Thanks."

I get on the bus and think about my brother the entire ride to the reservation. I feel so close to him but, at the same time, so far away from him. Our lives are intertwined, even now, but we are still separated betwixt life and death. I wish he was still here. I wish I could see him. But all the wishes in all the worlds won't bring him back. I need to accept that.

The bus drops me off, and I immediately hope to see my grandma waiting for me, but she's not. I was hoping to ask her for any clues or hints on how to defeat the wolf—if I ever get another chance.

As I reach the driveway and head into the house, I see Orenda's dad outside, covered in white paint, hosing himself down. If my grandma was here, she'd see it differently. I'd say it's a man hosing the white paint off his body, but she'd say, *No, it's a warrior that was eaten by an angry cloud. And just before he was about to die, he ripped through the cloud's belly and made an escape* . . . Wow. I'm beginning to see things differently. Those books are doing their job. Orenda's training is working. My grandma is rubbing off on me. My Native American side is waking up.

"You slayed the cloud!" I shout to Foxy.

He stops what he's doing and looks over at me. I give him a thumbs-up.

"It was a cumulus cloud. Caught me when I wasn't looking, that sneaky devil," Foxy shouts back to me. "Let this be a lesson to you, kid. Always keep your head up."

CHAPTER TWENTY-FIVE

- ·《◆》·-·《◆》·-

STAGE THREE: PUPA

My grandma stands at the open fridge and drinks orange juice straight from the carton. I reach into the cupboard and grab her a glass. Today her dress is orange, matching her drink.

"Hey, Grandma," I say, and hand her the glass.

"No, thanks. I'm done."

She twists the cap back onto the orange juice, shakes the carton, and places it back in the fridge.

"Where's Mama?"

"She went to go pick something up."

"What, dinner? I'm starving."

"So is she. She went to get her man."

"Wait, that's today?"

She nods and pulls out a carrot from her pocket; it too matches her dress. She crunches it so loudly that it reminds me of how Seven eats carrots. I wonder if she sees the fear in my eyes. I can't believe my mom's boyfriend arrives today. Today came too soon. I'm not ready. Now I have to worry about how another person is going to handle my counting.

"I was gonna take Seven on an adventure today. Is that all right?" she asks.

"Sure. I'll just go check on Orenda," I say.

"Okay, dear. *Pupa* is four letters."

"What's pupa?" I ask.

"Go see for yourself."

She walks out of the kitchen. "Come on, girl. Let's go world hopping!" She calls to Seven, who couldn't be happier about the idea.

I head toward the backyard and squeeze through the opening in the fence. As I approach Orenda's tree house, I see it is no longer brown, but now freshly painted white.

Either Foxy painted it or the cloud is trying to eat Orenda too. I hurry to the rope, but it has been replaced by a large wooden ramp that descends from the side of the tree house to the ground. It doesn't take a genius to realize why. Easier access. This must mean she is weaker. Too weak to hold up her own body weight. But she passed her test! Isn't she supposed to get better now?

As I run up the ramp, there are children making their way down. Each neighborhood kid carries a butterfly painting. What's going on? Why is she giving away all her paintings?

I reach her tree house, which now has a freshly painted white life-sized door on the side of it. When does her dad have time to build all this stuff? He must not sleep at all. I open it and step inside. It looks like an art exhibit. The walls are painted white, with brown and green strands of yarn streaking across the room like veins. White cloth is draped over the canopy of her bed, in layers, encasing it to resemble a white tent. The opening in the floor is gone, and the floor that was once brown wooden planks is now replaced with one large white rug, completely covering the room.

"Orenda?" I say.

"In here," she says from within the white-fabric-encased bed.

"Six," I say, and brush the white fabric aside to see her.

Her bed is now completely white—the pillows, blankets, and sheets. A once colorful, vibrant room now looks like the insides of a super-clean futuristic space ship.

She lies in her bed, wearing a white hoodie and white beanie. She looks frail and a bit pale . . . but still just as beautiful as ever.

"What's going on?" I ask.

"Phase three," she responds with a smile that reveals her teeth, which perfectly match the room.

"What does that mean?" I ask.

"Stage one, I was a hatched egg. A baby. I was born into this world," she says.

"Okay. Go on," I say, and sit down beside her.

She looks at my hand but doesn't reach out for it. So I take her hand into mine. Even her hands feel weaker now. Her thin fingers rest in my palm like fragile baby birds in a nest.

"Stage two. I was a caterpillar. A girl. That's how you know me," she says.

I'm not sure how to feel or even what to think of all this, so the least I can do is bring humor into this insane conversation.

"I was kissing a caterpillar?" I ask, making her laugh. Mission accomplished. But even her laugh is shallow and strained.

"It's time for me to become what I've been preparing to be. My dad painted all this to be my cocoon. This is where it will happen," she says.

"Where what will happen?" I ask, fearing/knowing what she'll say.

"Where I become a butterfly," she says.

Her letters pinball around my head, then morph into little white numbers. So, I count them and let them fly out of my mouth like little butterflies: "Twenty-two."

We sit in silence for the next few moments. I, not knowing how to respond to that, and she, not needing to say anything more.

"Don't be sad. This is how life works, for all of us," she says.

"No, this is not how life works. Kids don't turn into butterflies. They turn into adults."

She laughs and tries to sit up, but can't quite position herself upright.

"We are born. We live a magical life. We change. Then we're reborn. And so on and so on," she says.

"If I can't save you, what was the point in all of my training?" I ask, wiping a tear from my eye.

"You want to know why you're stronger now?" she asks.

"Yes."

"Take me outside," she says.

"Thirteen."

I get up and scoop her into my arms. And as I lift her, everything falls into place. I am strong enough to carry her now. My arms couldn't hold her weight when I first arrived. What a clever girl.

I lift her up to my chest and feel her heart beating against mine. I scan the room for her wheelchair.

"It's outside," she says.

"Ten," I say, and carry her out of her cocoon and down the ramp. She sighs in bliss as the sunlight hits her face. "Hello, sun," she says, so loud that I'm pretty sure the sun actually hears her.

Foxy stands in the yard and watches us, and even though he

looks kind of sad, he also looks happy. I bet he's just so relieved to see his daughter in such great spirits right now.

We reach her yard, and Foxy opens the gate for us. He avoids eye contact with both of us. I'm not really sure why, but if I had to guess, I'd say it was because if Orenda and he did lock eyes, he'd start crying uncontrollably.

It's colder than usual today, and we both feel the chill once we are out in the open. Her wheelchair is in the front yard, near the sidewalk, waiting for us. Foxy left her thick red blanket in it. I walk her to it, wrap the blanket around her, and gently place her in the wheelchair.

"Where to?" I ask.

She points out toward the forest. I grab hold of the handles behind her and push, rolling her toward the giant trees. We don't speak for quite a while. I imagine she is just taking in the beautiful earth that surrounds us.

What I once saw just as rows and rows of identical trees now looks like a whole new world, teeming with all kinds of life. Nature has always been just a background for me, a thing outside, a place people go camping in, but since I moved here, it's been much more than that. Nature is now a part of my life. A friend.

People pretend to live with nature, and sometimes people try to avoid it by building roads, buildings, and walls, but the truth is, nature is in everything and in everyone. My family is nature. Orenda is nature. I am nature. It lives in all of us. Maybe that's why it feels so good to walk in it, to swim in it, to live in it, because when we're in it, our bodies feel at peace, like we just returned home. Without nature, we are nowhere and no one.

Orenda has a better eye for all of nature's gifts than I do, though, because as we enter the forest, she spots and points out every hidden creature she sees.

She shows me lizards darting past us, birds high up in the branches, bugs scurrying up the tree trunks, spiders designing their webs, squirrels running, leaves falling, wind blowing, and she even points directly up, high above the trees, to a passing plane, which she mentions is technically nature too, because inside that plane is full of life. Lastly, she points to the many rocks by our feet.

"The rocks are lying perfectly still for us," she says as we pass a congregation of gray, beige, and black stones.

"Really? So, if we weren't here, they'd be doing what?" I ask, trying to keep her speaking now that she started.

"Dancing," she says.

"And how do rocks dance?" I ask.

"They rock. And roll," she says, looking back at me to see if I find her wordplay cute. And I do.

"Why did you want to come out here?"

She raises her hand, signaling me to stop. "We're almost there. Pick me up," she says.

"Almost where?" I ask, and lift her out of her wheelchair.

She points forward, so I carry her. We weave in and out of the trees, the same way we wove in and out of the dancing people at the ceremony the other night. But I was running then, and she was wheeling.

"Run," she says, almost as if she was reading my mind.

I run. And with my new strong arms and powerful legs, I pick up speed. She is smiling as we dodge the incoming trees and bushes. Her eyes close, and she spreads her arms out as far as they can be stretched.

"Run faster," she shouts in pure joy.

So I do. And about fifty trees later, she opens her eyes.

"Stop!"

"Four," I say, and slam my feet into the ground, causing us to slide a few more feet before coming to a stop. She laughs because of how careful I am with her in my arms, like she's a glass of fruit punch I'm carrying over a white carpet.

In front of us, propped up against a large earthy gray rock, is a white canvas, and beside it is a palette full of colorful globs of paint and a paintbrush.

"I want you to paint me," she says.

"As you wish."

I set her down beside a fallen log, and instead of explaining to her I am more of a sketch artist than a painter, I keep my mouth shut and sit down beside the canvas.

"I belong in this forest," she says, more for her to hear herself than for me to hear it.

"Nineteen," I say, and a few butterflies shake from the trees and sky-dance around us.

Orenda smiles as she watches them flutter back to the trees, giving us time alone.

I pick up the paintbrush and study everything about her: her eyes and how they reflect the brown-covered ground when she looks down and turn slightly green when she gazes up at the trees; her perfect fire-colored skin that matches a few of the rocks around her; and her body, resting against the fallen log, covered in moss, making her look like she's part of the forest herself. She's right. She does belong here.

"You're the most beautiful person I have ever met," I say, not caring how cheesy I sound.

She smiles and takes a deep breath, inhaling the cool air. "Show me; don't tell me."

I plunge the brush into the brown glob of paint and make my first stroke onto the white canvas. I can see she's a bit uncomfortable, sitting on the cold ground and propped against the dead tree, but she's a warrior and doesn't complain, just as she wouldn't want me to keep asking if she feels all right. So we both silently do what we came here to do. I begin painting, and she begins blending into the world around her.

I wonder if she's thinking about death. It would constantly be on my mind if I were in her shoes. I'd hate it. I'd be so afraid. But she doesn't look afraid at all. She looks happy.

How can she be fearless? Doesn't she realize that if she's gone, all the things she loves so much, she will never get to do again. She'll never paint again. She'll never read another book. She'll never cut up peaches and toss them out her window . . . She'll never kiss me again.

As I outline her face and add the shades to it with a deep orange color, her carefree smile fades, and she begins to cry. I stop momentarily.

"No. Keep painting," she says, and lets the tears stream down her face like two sad waterfalls.

Every instinct inside of me wants to drop the brush and comfort her, but instead I do exactly what she asks.

Although Orenda crying is the saddest thing I have ever seen, I can't help but see the beauty in the situation. She brought me all the way out here to paint her at her most vulnerable. That is a strength I have never experienced. I mean, when I cry, I make sure the bedroom door is locked, and I cry into my pillow to make sure no one hears me, not even Seven. But this brave girl, this warrior, is showing me and the entire forest her true self. She is afraid. Maybe not afraid of where she believes she's going, but afraid of leaving behind what she has here now.

And as hard as I fight it, her weeping crawls off of her face and jumps onto mine. Tears leak from my eyes as I paint. My vision blurs. And as impossible as it sounds, my ears even begin to blur. It's like I hear the forest weeping alongside us. Perhaps all the rocks, lizards, bugs, trees, and birds are as sad as we are.

As we cry, the sky begins to pull the dark blanket over the forest. The beams of sunlight splicing through the trees disappear as the sun descends behind us. The coldness slithers over the forest floor, wrapping its frigid fingers around the both of us. Night is here. I wipe my paint-covered hands over my face, erasing all evidence of my tears, but covering my face with smears of colors, and she suddenly gasps.

"What is it?" I ask.

Her eyes are fixed on the painting of her. I look at it for the first time as a whole and know why she reacted with a gasp. I think this is the best thing I have ever created. It looks exactly like her, but at the same time, I realize how someone might see a butterfly instead of a girl. I have no idea how my portrait of her turned into this. This shouldn't be possible, but here it is, staring at me.

"It's beautiful," she says.

"Twelve," I say. "Did I really make this?"

"You really did."

She crawls over to me, but it looks forced and painful, like she is narrowly escaping invisible quicksand. So I crawl to her, meeting her halfway.

"Collin."

And before I can tell her, "Six," she wraps her arms around my neck. I pull her into my chest and hold on to her, tightly, just in case the night tries to take her away. "Not yet," I whisper to all the nature surrounding us.

CHAPTER TWENTY-SIX

-《◆》-《◆》-

MY BRAND-NEW DAD

Orenda gave me the painting, which is weird because it was right after I handed it to her. But she said where she's going, there's no need for paintings, and this way I can look at her all day and all night and remember what she looked like as a human. I know that sounds crazy, but she's really convinced she's turning into a butterfly ... So I accepted it and hung it above my bed, right next to Seven's portrait. I'm not sure if it's my imagination or not, but when I look at it, I still smell the forest.

Which reminds me, where is Seven? Where is Grandma? They've both been gone since this afternoon. What kind of adventure are they having?

Orenda told me to come visit her tonight around eleven. So naturally, I've been checking the clock every ten minutes. It's only eight thirty. Maybe I'll finish reading *Haunting the Deep*. I need to see if Samantha and her charming ghost boyfriend end up together, but I'm kind of avoiding reading it too, because if they don't end up together, I'll be sad, and I'm trying really hard to stay away from sadness. Perhaps I'll work out instead? I've grown quite fond of getting stronger. And it shows. I actually have muscles now. I think my dad would be proud if he saw me.

As soon as I open my bedroom door, the smell of the forest is quickly eclipsed by a very familiar smell. A smell I haven't experienced since leaving California . . . Pizza.

I follow my nose down the hall and reach the living room. As I turn the corner, I see two pizza boxes on the table, and my mouth instantly salivates. But that's not all I see.

My mom stands before me, beaming with happiness. She looks like she just found the pot of gold at the end of a rainbow. And standing next to her is her pot of gold in the form of a tall, dark, and handsome black man.

"Collin, this is Ronnie," she says.

I have to look up to meet his eyes. Not just up, but way up, like I'm looking at the ceiling. He definitely had to duck down, under the doorway, when he entered the house. My eyes are instantly distracted by his muscles. I mean, just moments ago I was thinking I had muscles, but this guy . . . He is muscles. Like, a hundred of them just piled onto each other. They bulge out of his sleeves, barely fitting inside his shirt. His chest presses against the fabric, like trapped inflated balloons; even his neck looks like it could overpower a bear.

I immediately wish that I had his complexion. Not only because black is obviously my favorite color and it's all I ever wear, but also because his skin looks so smooth and flawless. My pale skin always has blemishes and freckles and red spots forming from who knows where, but his skin looks perfectly wrapped around his muscles, with not a scratch on it.

By the way Ronnie and my mom are just staring at me, I realize I have been staring at his body for far too long. Her letters are bouncing around behind my eyes, waiting for their withdrawal. "Eighteen. Sorry. Hi, Ronnie."

He smiles. His teeth are even whiter than Orenda's. Wow. He must brush them three times a day, at least.

"I heard a lot about you, Collin. Nice to finally meet you," he says, and extends his hand to me.

I shake his hand. I bet our handshake resembles a large bald eagle swooping down and grabbing a field mouse.

"Forty-four. You're not at all how I pictured," I say.

He laughs and pulls me in for a hug. As my body hits his, I realize he could easily crush me if he wanted to. His body is hard like steel, not an inch of fat anywhere. He must work out three times a day as well. Right before brushing his teeth, I assume. He pats me on the back, nearly knocking the wind out of me, before he releases me.

"Who'd you picture? Some marine with a buzz cut smoking a cigar?" he asks.

The truth is, I didn't picture anyone. I didn't think about this guy at all. In fact, I actively tried to avoid thinking about him as soon as my mom brought up his existence to me. I count, and even his letters seem cooler than other people's letters.

"Forty-nine. I don't know. You just look famous, I guess."

He laughs again and wraps his huge arms around my mom, like a python clutching a fox, and kisses her forehead, which he has to bend down to do.

"I love this kid already," Ronnie says to my mom.

"He's mine. What's not to love?" She reaches up, on tippy toes, to kiss him back.

Now I'm just standing here watching my mom and her boyfriend trade kisses. Which is super awkward since my mouth is still drooling from the pizza three feet away from me.

"I should probably go," I say to them and reach for the pizza, but Ronnie reaches out and grabs my arm.

"Not so fast, little man."

"Eighteen. Huh?" I ask.

"I got you something," he says, and reaches down into his duffel bag and pulls out a silver chained necklace.

I've seen this type of necklace before, in war movies. They're called dog tags. The soldiers would take them off their dead friends to identify who was killed in action. Ronnie places the chain over my head and lets it drop, where it settles near my heart. There are two dog tags attached to it. I hold it close to my face and read the first one. It's his. Staff Sergeant Ronald B. Spicer III. Even his name is cool.

"Sixteen. Spicer?" I read aloud.

"I call him Spicy," my mom blurts out.

"I'm sure you do," I say, and look at the other dog tag.

My mind goes numb, momentarily. It's my brother's dog tag. I immediately picture Aji smiling. And this guy attached Aji's dog tag to his own. I don't know much about the military, but I'd assume that means a lot. My heart drops a few inches as I realize Aji must have meant a lot to Ronnie.

"He'd want you to have it," Ronnie says to me.

"Eighteen."

I look at my mom and she nods. I can see that this moment means everything to her. Like everything she went through in life has finally come full circle. She has a man again. A son again. Her family has changed, but we are a family nonetheless.

"Thank you," I say, and let the dog tag slip through my fingers, where it lands above my heart and rests with the necklace my mom gave me on my first day here.

And at this very moment, I feel something I haven't really felt before from a man . . . I feel wanted. And at this exact moment, I find myself feeling sorry for my dad. Being wanted feels really good, so I'm pretty sure wanting someone feels just as good. My dad and I lacked both feelings. I never felt wanted, and he never necessarily wanted me. How easily we could have been happy if we just accepted each other for who we are, flaws and all.

"I'm not trying to replace your dad, but I want you to know that you got one here, at home, if you have room for another," Ronnie says.

"Ninety. I'd like that," I say.

We both stand and stare at each other awkwardly, like two men not used to being vulnerable. Should we hug? Do men kiss on the cheek like sons and mothers do? Should I shake his hand again? He gives me a thumbs-up, so I mimic him. My mom laughs.

"Okay. As your new dad, my first rule is to never let hot pizza go cold," he says, and hands me the pizza box.

I smile and accept it. And it's still warm. "Fifty-three. That's a good rule."

"Now, Collin, if you don't mind, Spicy and I have some making out to do," says my mom.

Wow. She went there. And by the way they are both grinning at each other like little rabbits, I take the hint.

"Fifty-two. You two have fun," I say, and carry the pizza toward the sliding glass door.

I know I was going to work out as I chewed time waiting for Orenda, but why chew time when I can chew pizza? I'll just wait for her in her newly remodeled cocoon. Maybe I'll even save her a slice. Maybe.

I'm not even completely out of the house before my mom and

Ronnie go at it. I hear the lip smacking as he picks her up and rushes her down the hallway like she's a football and he's destined for the end zone. And yes, there is definitely a touchdown happening. Their door slams shut.

I pick up my pace and squeeze through the opening. As I near the ramp, I open the box and pull out a slice. It smells heavenly, if heaven is coated in melted cheese. I bite into it. OMG. It's so good! There is no rooftop to the joy I'm tasting.

A whip cracks the sky. It's so loud I nearly drop the pizza. I look up, and the entire sky flashes from lightning bolts behind the clouds. Thunder rolls through the sky like bowling balls crashing against the pins. Dark clouds are squeezed, releasing a sudden heavy rain.

I carefully walk up the ramp, balancing the pizza box in one hand and my half-eaten slice in the other. I kind of miss climbing the rope to get in here, but like Orenda says, things change. I stuff the rest of the slice in my mouth and chew.

The moment I enter, Foxy looks up at me. He is applying wet rags to Orenda's skin as she lies in bed. The room is lit only by candles, but I notice Orenda immediately reaching for a hat and placing it on her hairless head as she sits up.

"Oh, I'm sorry. I know I'm early. I'll come back later," I say.

"No, stay. We're done," Foxy says, and rises to his feet.

"Fourteen."

As he passes me, he says, "It'll cost you a slice, though."

I open the box, and he reaches in and takes the largest slice and smiles.

"Thanks," he says as he leaves the tree house.

Even though pizza makes everyone happy, I saw the pain in his eyes. He's losing his daughter, and there's nothing he can do about it, because if there were something to be done, he would have done it, because Foxy's that kind of dad. The kind that swallows the pain and lets his daughter think wild thoughts like she's not dying but instead turning into a butterfly. It must eat him alive to witness this, not once, but now twice. From both of the loves of his life. Ronnie is tough and built like a tank, but Foxy is easily the strongest man I have ever met.

I approach Orenda and set the pizza box on her bed.

"Hungry?" I ask.

"Don't have much of an appetite these days," she says, and pulls her knees up so she can rest her elbows on them.

Neither of us pays attention to the way her limbs are vibrating.

"Thirty-three."

She smiles. "Thirty-three drawn out looks like two butterflies cuddling," she says, and with her index finger, she traces the number into the air.

"Fifty. Yeah, I see it," I say.

Her voice is so thin and shallow now, and it looks like it hurts every time she moves. I wish I could take her pain away. I'd happily feel it all if it meant she would feel better, but I also know she would never let me. It's hers. It's part of her story.

"Is it painful?"

"I invite pain in sometimes to remind me how beautiful being alive is. But sometimes it overstays its welcome," she says.

What an amazing way to say it hurts. And I guess there's some truth to it, I mean, if it weren't for pain, we wouldn't really value it as much when we feel good. Everything has its counterpart. We wouldn't love bright sunny days if we didn't know a day could also be dark and gloomy. We wouldn't love kindness if the world was never cruel. And I wouldn't know what being wanted feels like, if I hadn't experienced feeling so unwanted most of my life. Orenda has shown me how great life is, because I know how awful it can be sometimes.

"I don't know how you're so strong. I'm such a wimp. Seriously.

Pain scares me. Just the thought of getting hurt kinda hurts," I say, which causes her to laugh.

"You're a dork," she says, which now causes me to laugh.

"Only dorks still say the word *dork*," I say, and put my hand on her knee.

She stares at my hand, each finger, before she lifts her eyes to meet mine.

"I'm gonna miss you, you dork," she says.

"You shouldn't miss what is right in front of you."

She smiles, remembering she once told me that exact thing. She leans forward and holds up her index finger. "Describe me in one word."

One word. How do you describe the girl that a million words could never come close to describing? There are not enough words, not even if you combine every word from every language. So, I'll keep it simple and speak one word from my heart. "Pretty," I say.

She gasps, and her tired eyes widen. "Pretty? Is that it? I'm pretty?"

"Yes. You are pretty. You are pretty kind. You are pretty funny. You are pretty smart. You are pretty amazing. Orenda, you are pretty much perfect," I say.

My words hold her still. I don't know what she's thinking, but I see tears forming under her eyes. But the dam holds back the flood; she doesn't cry. She just smiles and lets the moment pass by us, float out of the window, and disappear into the storm.

"Wanna do something totally crazy?" she asks, with newfound twinkles in her eyes that resemble the billion stars outside.

I wonder what this girl considers crazy, because by all accounts, she is already *pretty* crazy.

"Should I be terrified?" I ask.

"Yes," she says, and shakes from excitement, letting out a sinister laugh as she points to her wheelchair.

"You want me to put you in the wheelchair?" I ask.

"I do," she replies.

"Three. All aboard," I say, giving my best attempt at sounding like a train conductor.

This is already a bad idea, but the truth is, I'd do anything for this girl. I get up, scoop her into my arms, and place her softly into the wheelchair.

"Now what?" I dare ask.

"Hop on the back. We're riding down the ramp," she says.

Okay. She's finally lost her mind, I mean completely. "Thirty-three. No way."

"Fear ceases to exist once you confront it," she says.

"Thirty-four. Forget fear, how about it being incredibly danger-ous?" I ask.

"As long as we don't fall off the side, we'll be fine," she says in a voice that resembles a little girl asking to go on a roller coaster.

"Thirty-eight. We can get hurt! No. We're not doing this," I say.

Her eyes narrow in on me, and her lips pull to one side. "I am. You with me or not?" she asks.

She's serious. She's really going to do it. And now the ball is in my court. Will I just stand by and watch her do this incredibly stupid act, which also does sound kinda fun, or will I throw caution to the wind and hop on board and let whatever happens happen?

"Seventeen. I'm in."

If she could jump for joy, she'd be doing it now. But we'll have to settle for her smile.

"You do know it's raining outside, right?" I ask.

"It won't be," she says.

"What do you mean? I can hear it. It's a storm. Look!" I say, and wheel her toward the door. I swing it open to show her the downpour—except . . . the rain is gone. The thunder and lightning and the black foaming clouds are gone. It's just cold. "Where's the storm?" I ask.

She laughs. "I am the storm. Let's do this," she says.

"Twenty-one," I say, and wheel her out.

We stop at the top of the ramp. I look at the steep path ahead of us. This is a bad idea.

"You sure about this?" I ask.

"Hold on . . . I'm ready," she says.

I pause, which makes her laugh. "No, I mean, hold on *tight*. I'm ready," she clarifies.

"Thirty-eight. If something goes wrong, you got to share this wheelchair with me," I say jokingly, but also I kind of mean it.

"We'll never forget this. Whatever happens, you and I will forever have right now," she says, and places her hands on both sides, gripping them tightly.

I can't believe I am about to do this. This is insane. But . . . this is love, and maybe love is crazy. Maybe everyone needs to try to be a little less normal and a bit more crazy.

She takes a deep breath. "As brave as a brave." She exhales.

I don't count her letters because they weren't for me. They were for her.

I put one foot up on the bar behind the wheelchair, I grip both handles behind her as tightly as I can, and I push off. We begin to roll, so I lift my other foot up and set it on the bar. I feel the cold air push against my face and hair. I close my eyes and hold the image of Orenda in my mind. If I die, I want hers to be the last face I ever see.

We pick up speed, and my stomach drops. Orenda lets out a loud battle cry, which makes me forget about the danger ahead and brings a smile to my terrified face. We race down the ramp and careen through the grass at a way faster speed than I anticipated.

I open my eyes, I see the fence coming straight for us, but we are going much too fast to stop. I decide to embrace it. Like she says, "Fear ceases to exist once you confront it," so I let out the loudest battle cry I can before we collide into the fence.

As the front of the wheelchair hits, we are launched off of it and flung forward. We both slam into the fence and hit the ground.

I turn my head to check on Orenda, but she is far from needing help. In fact, she is lying on her back, laughing hysterically. I sit up and watch her laugh. She looks so happy.

"You have grass in your hair," she says, and erupts in laughter again.

I reach up and pull a patch of dirt and grass from my head.

Foxy rushes up to us. "What just happened?" he asks as he helps his daughter up and places her back into the wheelchair.

"I tried to fly, Papa. But I can't yet," she says to him.

Foxy turns to me and offers me his hand. I take it, and he hoists me up with one hard yank, bringing me face-to-face with him. "You let her do this?"

"Fifteen. She won't know if she can fly until she tries," I say.

Foxy sighs at my response, but Orenda doesn't. Instead, she smiles at me as if that was the greatest thing ever said. She thinks I finally believe her about the whole butterfly thing. Which, obviously I don't, because that's impossible, but it feels really good to make her feel really good right now.

"Are you hurt?" Foxy asks her.

"No, Papa. I feel great," she replies.

"You're fixing this," he says to me, and points to the fence.

Wow. We broke the fence. That's two fences I've broken now since I've been here. "Fifteen. Yes, sir."

Foxy begins to wheel Orenda back toward the house, but she stops the wheelchair abruptly by grabbing both wheels. She spins it around and looks at me. "My rebel," she says, and releases the wheels.

"Takes one to know one," I say.

Foxy continues pushing as I watch them enter the house. I feel a knot forming on my forehead and rub it. Ouch. I hit that fence harder than I thought. Maybe it was my head that broke it.

CHAPTER TWENTY-SEVEN

- ‹‹◆›› - ‹‹◆›› -

ANIM ALS

My new dad. That's still weird to me. I know he'd love it if I called him Dad. Maybe Aji did, but I still need to get to know him a bit more. For now, I'll just call him Ronnie. For damn sure I'm not calling him Spicy.

Ronnie said I can skip school today so he and I can do some male bonding. As cheesy as it sounds, I'm still a kid, I'd do anything to skip school. Plus, it kinda sounds cool, since my dad and I never really bonded. Bring it on.

I imagined we'd do what men do with their sons on TV—you know, like shoot at targets with a gun, toss a ball around the yard, or maybe go camping somewhere deep in the forest, but nope. We went to the hardware store.

We're now in Orenda's yard, and he's sitting on the cooler, just watching me try to figure out the correct way to repair the fence.

"You broke it, you fix it," Ronnie says.

I've been out here for an hour, and I've accomplished absolutely nothing. It's not funny, but he sure thinks it is. He watches me try to line up the wood evenly while trying to balance the nails before I swing the hammer. I'm hopeless. I have managed to drop the same nail eight times now. I guess he thinks I've suffered enough, because he finally joins me and takes the hammer from my hand.

"Don't they have fences in California?" he asks.

"Yeah, millions of them. But once they break, we just leave them like that. Everyone's too busy to fix things," I say.

He twirls the hammer in his hand like a gunslinger with his revolver and tosses a nail into the air and catches it between his lips. I'm impressed. And he knows it.

"Watch and learn, buddy," he says, and grabs <u>one</u> of the new planks of wood.

I take a step back.

He gets to work. By the looks of it, he's broken many fences in his day. He's good at everything, it seems. I don't know who the better catch is, him or my mom. This town m<u>u</u>st seethe with envy whenever they are seen together.

He tries to show me how to properly repair the fence, but my eyes repeatedly drift from Orenda's back door and up to her tree house. I haven't seen her at all today. And I don't think she's grounded or anything like that, because by the looks of it, she has Foxy wrapped around her finger. He'd do anything to keep her happy, even immediately forget the danger she put herself in last night.

"They left early this morning," Ronnie says to me, snapping me out of my thoughts.

"Twenty-four. Do you know where they went?"

"You want the truth, or you want their version of it?" he asks.

Finally! Someone is going to tell me what's really going on and not replace every single detail with some magical explanation.

"Forty. I'd love the truth for a change," I say.

Ronnie looks around, making sure we're alone.

"All right, but you can't tell your mama I told you what's what, you hear?"

"Fifty-four. I won't say a word," I say, and drop to my knees beside him, so he can whisper.

"They went to the hospital," he says.

"Twenty-one. I figured that, but why?" I ask.

"Good luck counting this one . . . amyotrophic lateral sclerosis," he says slowly.

The words scrape against my brain. I count each letter as it moves forward, like huge trucks at a toll road, waiting for their turn. "Fifty."

"Damn. That's impressive, buddy. Also known as ALS."

I remember learning about ALS back in California. It was when the world came together and did all those ice bucket challenge videos. Our teacher did one and had us film it and post it online. It went viral, too.

"Thirty-eight. Orenda has ALS?" I ask, more to hear the question out loud for myself.

"Her mother did too. But goddamn, can those women fight! I mean, her mama fought tooth and nail to the very end. That was a sad day. I was deployed soon after. Then Aji was deployed. He hated leaving Orenda here, all alone. But she has you now."

His words hit me like a ton of bricks. One thing I remember from learning about ALS is that there is no cure for it. My brain drops into my throat, and my throat sinks into my heart, and my heart drops into my gut. Orenda is dying. For real dying.

As Ronnie's letters pile into one another in my head, they turn into horrible little numbers and crawl across my tongue. I just need to vomit them out and breathe.

"One hundred and eighty-five," I say, and gasp for air.

Ronnie looks at me like I just resurfaced from the bottom of the ocean. He pats my back and nods. I know that nod. It's a "sorry for talking so much" nod, but I don't want him to stop. I want to hear more. Everything. Anything.

"Two people in one family getting it . . . The chances were one in a billion," he adds.

"Fifty-six. One thing I know about Orenda . . . She's a one in a billion kind of girl. I guess her mama was too," I say.

"They both are. Some people get lucky. Some people get unlucky. That's how it goes," he says.

"Sixty-three. She knows what is really happening to her, right? I mean, she saw her mom go through it, so why does she say she's turning into a butterfly? Why doesn't she get treatment like other people? Maybe doctors can help?" I ask.

"In the end, does it matter?" he asks.

"What do you mean?" I ask.

"Orenda believes she's changing. Maybe she is. We don't know what's real and what isn't. None of us do. We guess. Sometimes we're right, sometimes we're wrong."

Sometimes we're lucky, sometimes we're not. Sometimes were right, sometimes we're not. Ronnie looks at life so simple. I don't know if that's good or bad. But he does have a point. Orenda is pretty darn convinced she is gonna be a butterfly. But wait . . . Why would she be at a hospital if she didn't believe the doctors can help her? Maybe there's hope. "So why is she at a hospital, then?" I ask.

"She's probably doing what her mom did," he says.

"Thirty. And what's that?" I ask.

"Donating her hair to cancer patients. Donating her blood to science. Letting them run more tests to better understand the disease. Even now, when she's in pain, she hides it. But not only that,

she's out there trying to help the world. Just like her mother did."
Ronnie rises to his feet.

He sees how broken I feel, so he extends his hand to me. I need it. I accept it. He hoists me up to my feet, but I don't think I can stand. I feel empty, hollow, and weak. I look down and prepare to collapse at any moment.

But this feeling is nothing compared to what Orenda feels every day. Suddenly, my letter counting condition doesn't seem so bad. I steady my wobbly legs and focus on the numbers in my head.

"Two hundred and four. I know this is a weird question, but I just need to hear the answer for my own sanity. So is she or is she not turning into a butterfly?" I ask.

Ronnie dusts his hands off and gives me a look that I can't crack.

"Life is strange, kid. I don't have that answer. No one does but the Father," he says.

"You mean God?" I ask.

"Father Time. Only time will tell what happens. The important part is to just keep your eyes open, so you don't miss it," he says, and walks back toward the opening in the fence to our house.

I scramble his letters into numbers as quickly as I can, so I can ask him another question before he makes it to the end of the yard. A question I can't ask anyone else.

"Ninety-two, Ronnie," I yell to him.

He stops. I approach him, trying to figure out how to ask.

"Aji . . . How did . . . he die?"

"Aji lost his dad when he was just a kid. But that didn't stop him from idolizing him his entire life. And rightfully so—his dad was an amazing guy. He was military, like me. Naturally, Aji wanted to be like the guy. He enlisted the day he turned eighteen. His plan was to serve two years and have the corps pay for his college. That dude loved to learn. He was a hell of a soldier too. I was actually here, with your mama, when it happened ... And she knew. To this day, I still don't know how she knew, but at ten twenty-seven A.M. she collapsed on the floor, clutching her chest, screaming your brother's name. That day we got the official word: His unit went down in a helicopter during training. Eight boys died that day," Ronnie says, and fights back the pain in his eyes.

I tally up his total and divert my eyes to the fence. I know Ronnie doesn't want me to see him like this. It hurts too much. I walk back to the broken fence and let Ronnie walk away from whatever emotion he wants to escape.

Aji loved his dad so much. I hope he's finally with him now. I hope my mom thinks they're together, so she doesn't always have to walk around with a broken heart. Hearts break so easily. Like fences. But not everything that breaks is sad. Sometimes breaking something leads to something better. That fence that I broke and was somehow magically repaired and then magically broken again led me to Orenda. I love that fence. It's my passage to her, and I need it now more than ever.

I turn to see the other fence, the one Orenda and I broke last night. Ronnie has completely repaired the damage I caused, with not much help on my part. It looks as if nothing happened at all.

Life is weird like that. One minute there's a gaping hole in the fence caused by two crazy kids crashing a wheelchair through it, and the next minute it's just a normal fence again. There's no trace of our crash. No trace of our adventure together. But I know it meant a lot to her. She was testing fate. She was living on the edge. She faced down her illness and screamed like a banshee as we raced toward danger. And we met it head-on. And we lived to tell about it. Her fear no longer exists because she confronted it, and I helped her do it.

I squeeze through the fence and step into my backyard. I realize that Seven is still out with Grandma. They've been gone since yesterday. I know I should be worried, but for some reason I'm not. Maybe it's because if there is one person that I don't ever need to worry about, it's my grandma. She's smart and tough, and has been around long enough to know how to stay alive. But still, what can an old lady and a dog be doing for so long?

I close my bedroom door behind me and hop onto my bed. Ronnie let me borrow his laptop, so I open it and type *ALS* into the search engine. About three dozen sites pop up. I guess it isn't as rare as I thought. The next two hours are spent reading all about it. It's terrifying knowing that Orenda is going through all of this. One of the sites says that no two people with ALS are alike—the signs and symptoms vary from person to person. I wonder if she feels it spreading throughout her body? She must be exhausted. It's a constant war being waged under your skin. And they list the pain as excruciating. A ten out of ten. How is she so strong? How has she not given up?

I continue reading . . . ALS begins in the brain and attacks the motor neurons. The most common symptoms are impaired speech, excess saliva, difficulty sleeping, and weakness in the hands and feet. That is why Orenda can no longer walk and why her speech has slowed down and thinned so much. That's why her hands are giving her so many problems. That's why she made me paint in the forest, because she physically couldn't.

I'm so mad that some stupid disease has chosen such a good person to torment. It's not fair. I used to think it wasn't fair that I got stuck with this counting thing of mine, but I couldn't care less about that now. Orenda deserves nothing but happiness. She should be able to grow up and become a teenager, a woman, a mother some-day, then a grandmother, then a great-grand . . . argghh. I'm so mad. The world is so lucky to have her in it, and what does it do with this luck? It hands her ALS.

I get up and grab one of my markers. It's blue. I walk over to my wall and write in huge letters *ALS*, so I have a constant reminder of who my enemy is. I want to stare at it, and I want it to stare back at me. I want it to know I am going to fight it. This is war.

My eyes trace each letter. Hate boils within me. A hate I didn't know I had in me . . . But then I turn my head and look at the portrait of Orenda, and the hate instantly dies. I know that Orenda wouldn't want me filled with hate. She wouldn't want me to be obsessing about what it does and what I should expect to see. To her, she doesn't have some life-threatening disease diagnosed by some doctor who is telling her she's going to die. No. Orenda doesn't live that way. She believes, with all her heart, that she is changing into a butterfly, just like her mother did. And when she is a butterfly, she will be free.

So, in front of the large blue *ALS* letters, I write four more letters—*ANIM*—and step back and smile. There. That's much bet-ter. Orenda would like this.

Now all I gotta do is draw them. I will stay up all night filling my room with sketches of as many of them as I can fit onto these walls. I put marker to white wall and begin drawing. My first sketch will be of a rooster . . . And I won't stop drawing until the rooster crows. Before morning, my wall will be covered in *A-N-I-M-A-L-S*.

CHAPTER TWENTY-EIGHT

-《◆》-《◆》-

THE INVISIBLE MAN

A week has gone by since I last saw Orenda. My mom has been in contact with Foxy and assures me that she's okay. They are doing tests at some fancy hospital up in Canada. I want to call her all the time, but my mom said she is having trouble talking on the phone right now. I can't imagine Orenda's voice disappearing. Everything inside me wants to hop on a train and go see her myself, but I promised Ronnie and my mom that I wouldn't miss any more school.

The last seven days have been pretty much the same. I go to school, avoid as many interactions with people as possible, although, since everyone now knows Aji was my brother, no one messes with me anymore. In fact, most people are pretty nice to me now, and Josh, well, he even passed the ball to me when we were playing basketball in PE. But I am too busy right now for friends. I am way too preoccupied with worrying about Orenda.

After school I come home, work out, and read. Every morning and every night, I peek outside to see if Orenda is home yet. But she's not. I've been slicing up peaches and tossing them out into her yard for her, though. She'll be pleased to know her butterflies are well fed.

And it's not only Orenda's absence that is driving me crazy . . . My grandma still hasn't come home with Seven. But again, my mom assures me that everything is all right. Apparently, my grandma took Seven on an adventure that led them on a weeklong journey to Canada.

The way Ronnie tells it is that a few elders from the reservation went to comfort Orenda and her dad, and my grandma hitched a ride with them. And since Seven was with her at the time, they took her along, too. Yep. My dog went to visit Orenda, and I didn't.

If there's anything positive I can take from this week of isolation, it is that I have successfully transformed my white-walled room into a room completely full of animals. From floor to ceiling. It's like I sleep in a National Geographic special. Also, I am basically now an expert in ALS . . . I've read all there is to read about it. It's a terrifying disease, and knowing Orenda has it makes me incredibly stressed. And when I'm stressed out, I release it by hitting the bags. I am pretty much a fantastic boxer now. Ronnie took over in training me while Orenda's away. He boxed in college. I feel sorry for whoever stepped into the ring with him. He hits harder than a truck. The bag goes flying.

As a result, I now have muscles in places that I didn't even know muscles could be. And in a certain kind of light, I resemble Aji more than the kid I was when I first arrived here.

Strictly out of habit, I find myself looking for a reason to dislike

Ronnie—but the truth is, he's a really great guy. The more I get to know him, the more I hope to be like him when I grow up. I guess that's what a dad should be to a son. I even accidentally called him Dad this morning when he dropped me off at school. We both looked at each other in shock, mostly me. But I can tell he liked hearing it, and a bit of me kind of liked saying it.

I didn't really learn anything new today. Well, at least not at school. But I did learn something when I got home. I learned to make a lot of noise when I enter the house. I learned it the hard way. I walked in and saw Ronnie and my mom making out on the couch. They sprang up like startled rabbits when they saw me. Then they burst out laughing. I'm glad they found it funny because I most certainly did not.

Now it's nine o'clock, and I'm in Orenda's tree house. I come up here sometimes just to sit. It feels better than sitting alone in my room. I feel closer to her in here.

As I lie in her bed and think about her, a noise from outside makes me sit up. I rush over to the window and hope to see their truck pull into the driveway with Orenda sitting in the passenger seat, but it's not them. It's actually the second-best scenario. It's my grandma and Seven walking up the road. Finally! They're home!

I run down the ramp and race through the yard to meet them in the driveway. Before I can run to her, Seven runs into my arms. The force knocks me back, and I fall on my butt. Seven kisses me for every minute we were apart. Which is in the thousands. I wrap my arms around her and give her half as many kisses in return. My grandma, her dress in purple now, watches us, smiling.

"We had quite the journey," she says.

"You sure did. I was worried sick," I say back to her.

"Is Mama home?" she asks.

"Yes, but knock before you go in."

My grandma clasps her hands together in joy. She loves affection. The thought of her daughter finding happiness again makes her equally happy, maybe even more. She walks off and leaves me alone with Seven.

"Wait. How is Orenda?" I ask before she enters our yard.

"Ask her yourself," she says, and continues walking.

"What? How?" I shout as I rise to my feet.

Just then, two headlights hit me full blast. I turn around and see their pickup truck turning into the driveway. It's too dark to see inside, so Seven and I rush up to them. As I reach the truck, I see Orenda.

She sits in the passenger seat, smiling like she always does. Our eyes meet and do a quick little flutter dance before I open the door for her. Foxy flashes me a smile. He looks so tired. I can't imagine what he's feeling right now.

"I'll give you two some time to catch up," he says and exits his truck.

"I missed you, too," Orenda says before I have a chance to tell her how much I missed her.

I try not to give her any indication that I notice the shift in her voice. She talks even slower now, and there's saliva sneaking out the corners of her lips, like the words are heavy bags of water that she has to drag out of her mouth and her teeth are tearing holes in the bags, causing them to leak.

"Thirteen," I say, and move in for a hug, but her arms and hands don't move to receive it. At all. They just lie completely still on her lap. I hug her anyway.

"My human limbs aren't working too well these days," she says, and instead returns the hug with her wild eyes.

"Forty. You can use mine," I say, and unfasten her seat belt for her.

"And I can't fly yet," she says.

"Fourteen. Then I shall carry you," I say, and lift her into my arms.

Either I am getting much stronger or she weighs much less than she did the last time I carried her. Maybe both.

Her head rests against my neck as I walk through her yard and up her ramp. She takes in a deep sniff as the breeze hits us and smiles. "You've been feeding the butterflies," she says, somehow picking up the scent of sliced peaches.

"Every day," I reply as we enter her tree house.

I set her softly into her cocoon bed. I read that sometimes massaging the limbs can feel good for people with ALS. So I begin rubbing her arms, up and down, and it works. As soon as I begin, she relaxes a bit and breathes easier.

There are so many questions I want to ask, but she looks so peaceful lying in her bed, with her eyes slowly closing.

"Do you want me to leave so you can sleep?" I ask.

"Stay."

She scoots over as best as she can, which is hardly any movement at all. But it's more than I need to understand what she wants. I lie down beside her and wrap my arm around her, pulling her frail body against mine.

"Four," I say, and kiss her forehead.

I kick my shoes off and get comfortable. I take notice of all the changes her body has gone through since I've met her. She's much thinner now. Her ribs are visible, and her arms look like they would snap off if someone were to tug at them. She catches me staring. "What is it?" she asks.

"I just wish you could be normal again," I say.

"I was never normal. And I never will be," she slurs.

"I meant normal as in, you know, normal."

"Ugh. That word."

"What's wrong with it? I wish I was normal."

"No! *Normal* is just another word for *boring*. Don't be boring. You know what's the opposite of being normal?" she says, so passionately that she needs to catch her breath.

"No. What?"

"Being yourself."

I chew on her words, swallow them, and digest them. She's right. Orenda is not normal. There's no one like her. And that's because she is always being herself. We share a smile. I could spend the rest of my life right here, just like this, so I try to. I close my eyes and hold her, feeling her heart beat against my body.

"Life is tough," I say, not knowing why that slipped out of my mouth.

"Life is tough," she agrees, "but we're tougher."

Even now, Orenda is braver than I am. "I'm scared," I say, with my eyes closed.

"I am too ... But ... when I passed my test that night, I learned something about being scared that made me feel a lot better. I learned how to be brave. Want to hear it?"

"Yes."

"I learned that it's okay to be afraid. It's even okay to be very afraid. But it's never okay to be too afraid."

"You can be brave and scared at the same time?" I ask.

"Yes. If you're scared to fight but fight anyway, that makes you brave," she says.

I think about all the times in my life when I was so afraid that I did nothing. I was defeated before any fight began. I lost before I even started. But the one time I was afraid and stood my ground got me to where I am now. I fought back, and fighting back led me to Orenda. I decide from this day forward, I will never be too afraid of anything. I will be brave from now on, just like her.

"Orenda?" I say, but she has fallen asleep. I hope in her dreams, she's flying.

My eyes burst open! My heart pounds so hard that I actually grab my chest to make sure it didn't rip through my chest as I jolt up. Orenda is screaming. I'm not sure why. Her eyes are wide open, and she's covered in sweat.

"Where are you hurt?" I ask, but she is in too much pain to hear me.

Her screams are haunting, like there's an invisible man randomly stabbing her with a sharp, thin sword in different parts of her body. If I could see him, I'd throw him headfirst out of this tree house. But I can't.

Another pounding competes with my heart. But this time, it's her father's footsteps running up the ramp. He swings the door open, and in two long strides, he's beside us. Maybe he can see the invisible man?

Foxy scoops up his daughter and wraps the sheet around her. Before he takes her out of the tree house, he turns to me.

"Don't worry. This happens," he says, and carries Orenda through the doorway. And even though she is in a lot of pain, her hand reaches out and grabs the door frame. They stop. Orenda looks back at me, and then her eyes scan her room, searching for the invisible man. "Is that all you got?" she mumbles before her dad continues carrying her down the ramp.

Even now, feeling as horrible as she does, she's still so brave. She's still fighting. She's still challenging death. "Is that all you got?" Her words repeat in my head.

I look down and see that my hands are still shaking. I press them against my thighs to stop them, but the force pulsates my legs. I don't remember ever being this scared before. I try to remember Orenda's words. "It's okay to be afraid. It's okay to be very afraid, but it's never okay to be too afraid . . ." But it's easier said than done.

I look out the window and see that the lights to my house are on. Her screams must have woken everyone up. Before I leave her tree house to go home, I take swings at the air, just in case the invisible man is still in here. I throw as many punches as my body allows before I drop to my knees in exhaustion. I hope I hit him. I hope I shattered his nose and blackened his eyes. I hope I hit him so hard that he stumbled out of the tree house, fell off the ramp, and broke his invisible neck when he landed. Yes, I hope I killed him. Because he hurt Orenda.

I raise my head and look around. The room is still. I hit nothing. In fact, if there was a fight in here with me and him, I just lost it. Because Orenda is still hurt and I'm on my knees, sobbing.

CHAPTER TWENTY-NINE

-«◆»--«◆»-

LIFE IS BUT
A DREAM

Last night was the worst night of my life. I hardly slept. I just lay in bed and worried about her until the sun woke up. Seven didn't sleep much either. She could tell something was bothering me. She was sprawled across my chest all night, protecting me. Maybe she thought there was an invisible man with a broken nose and a twisted neck out for revenge.

One look at me from my mother this morning made her immediately tell me that I didn't have to go to school today. She and Ronnie left early to go into town for some groceries, but I have the sneaking suspicion that they just knew I needed time to myself to process everything that is going on. "Sometimes, time alone is good medicine," she said before they left.

I know I should try to get some sleep, or maybe eat something, but I can't. I need to make sure Orenda is all right. I take a quick shower to get all the dried panic-sweat off of me and get dressed.

After I feed Seven, I head out of the house and knock on Orenda's front door. I don't think I've ever used this entrance before. But somehow, going through their backyard feels invasive today. Maybe they need the time alone medicine. I can't stay away, though. I need to see her.

Foxy answers the door. Heavy sandbags line the curbs of his tired eyes. He hasn't slept a wink either.

"How is she?" I ask.

But instead of answering me, he opens the door wider, allowing me to see for myself. I enter their home and head toward her bedroom. The door is slightly open, so I push it just enough to fit through.

Her room has fully transformed to look like her tree house. It's completely white. There are no more plants, no more flowers. It is just a white cocoon. I wonder where all her things went, but the answer is obvious. She gave them all away. That's what she does.

Orenda lies in bed. Her eyes are closed. I step toward her softly, trying not to make a sound. Her chest moves up and down, but it's forced. I sit down beside her and place my hand on hers. Her eyes slowly open. The moment she sees me, she smiles.

"Hey, you," I say.

Her mouth opens, but no words fall out. She just takes a deep, quiet breath and shifts her eyes toward the window. I follow her eyes and see that there is a beautiful butterfly on the other side of the glass. It looks like the same one that landed on my nose. The same one that she called Mama.

It's flapping its brown-and-yellow wings wildly, looking directly at us. It immediately brings me back to the butterfly I saw in my room before I moved here. I remember what she wanted. She wanted the outside. She wanted freedom.

I look back at Orenda, and her eyes are hopeful that I understand what she wants.

"You want to go outside?" I ask.

Her smile stretches even further, nearly to her ears.

"Just be careful," Foxy says from behind me.

I turn to him and see the pain in his eyes. Not from a lack of sleep, but from seeing his little girl slowly withering away.

Even still, he will allow her to do whatever she wants, even go play outside with the weird neighbor dork that crashed her wheelchair into the fence not too long ago.

"We will be," I say, and walk over to her wheelchair.

It looks different. The wheels are larger and thicker again.

"I made it easier for you to push it through the forest," Foxy says.

The best dad in the entire universe prize goes to Foxy, hands down. "Forty-three. Thank you," I say, and wheel it over to her bed.

He helps me put Orenda in it and secures her with a seat belt, which he also added to it. He watches me wheel her out of their house, and as soon as the sunlight hits her skin, she lets out a sigh, like a caged bear that was just freed into the wild.

The moment we leave the road and enter the forest, Orenda smiles.

"That cloud looks like a fish," I say, and point up to the sky.

Orenda moves her head slowly and sees the cloud swim across the blue. Her eyes shift to another cloud. I stare at it. "I don't know . . . A pelican, maybe?" I say.

She nods and smiles. We wander through the forest for almost an hour, me pointing out animal clouds, and her nodding and smiling. But when I ask her if the last one looks like a turtle and her head doesn't move, I step in front of her and face her. She has fallen asleep.

I wheel her home, where Foxy is waiting patiently at the front door.

"You two have fun?" he asks.

"We did."

Foxy takes the wheelchair from me and guides her into the house. I follow them in.

"She should sleep for a bit, but she'll be in her tree house around sundown," he says to me.

"I'll see her then," I say, and kneel down to be eye level.

"I'll see you later," I whisper, and kiss her forehead.

Her eyes flicker open long enough to see my lips move off of her skin. Knowing her, she'd crack a joke or say something extremely clever right now, but instead, she gives me a grin and closes her eyes again.

I walk back to my house and find another note left on the kitchen table from my grandma. She took Seven on another adventure. That sneaky old Native ninja. I didn't even see her today, and she left with my companion. Now I'm truly all by myself.

I go to my room and plop onto my bed. What should I do? I need to keep busy or I'll drive myself insane worrying about Orenda. I can't draw any more animals, there's not a white spot left on my walls. Maybe I'll read ... But this pillow feels so nice. Maybe I'll just rest here for a bit. maybe I'll just close my eyes and ...

I am lying in a huge field of grass. I open my eyes and see the sun above me, shining down, shouting for me to get up. So, I do, but as I try to stand, I fall. I break the fall with my hands, but my hands aren't mine. Or at least they don't look like mine. My arms are covered in fur, and my hands are large paws, with sharp claws where my fingers once were. And weirdly, I feel better in this position, on all fours. I turn my head to see my body. Holy crap! I'm a wolf.

After a few failed attempts at walking, I get the hang of it. And I run. Fast.

I sprint through the field as the wind whips through my fur. I've never had this kind of energy before. I feel free and strong. Like I can do anything. I must run a mile before I enter the forest. I hear birds chirping high above me in the tall trees. I hear bugs scurry away when they realize I'm near. I hear the forest like I've never heard it before, through the ears of a wolf.

I stop before a small stream to take a drink. I bend down and see my reflection. I have a large snout, sharp teeth, thick pointed ears, and intense yellow wolf eyes . . . Suddenly, twigs crack and leaves crunch directly behind me, and the fur on my back rises. I spring around and see a large squirrel staring at me. It's as big as I am. Every instinct in me tells me to chase him, but I don't. I recognize his eyes. I know this squirrel.

"Aji?" I say in a deep wolfish voice.

"Hello, brother," he says back to me.

I rush up to him and bury my head into his neck. He wraps his little squirrel arms around me and squeezes. I finally get to see my brother. He's a lot furrier than I expected him to be, but to be fair, so am I.

"Why am I a wolf?" I ask him.

"The same reason I'm a squirrel, brother."

"This isn't real. This is a dream. What's going on?"

"What's going on? We are here to save Orenda from the invisible man," he says.

"Where is she?" I ask.

"He took her. We must go now," he says.

"Hop on my back," I say, and he does.

He points in the direction we need to go, and I run as fast as I can, deeper into the dense forest. Aji holds on tightly as we zigzag through the trees, hop over ponds, and finally enter a part of the forest that has been razed. All the trees are gone. All the green grass is gone. And the earthy ground has been covered by asphalt. There's nothing but a small cabin in the center of the deforested lot. He hops off of me and sniffs the air.

"She's in there," Aji says, and points to the cabin.

We march slowly toward it, being as quiet as we possibly can. But as we're halfway there, I hear an unpleasant familiar sound: Orenda's scream.

I burst into a full sprint and charge the cabin. Aji follows closely behind me. The front door is right in front of me, but I don't slow down. Instead, I run full speed into it just like I did with the wheel-chair into the fence. It bursts open from the impact, and splinters fly in all directions. I skid to a stop in the center of the cabin and growl, revealing my sharp teeth.

Orenda is tied to a bed, in the corner. But she looks different too. She has iridescent skin that changes colors with each step I take toward her. She has a smooth round head with two large eyes staring at me. The moment she recognizes me, she smiles.

"My rebel," she says.

But before I can approach her, she panics. "Watch out!" she shouts, and her eyes dart behind me.

I turn around, but it's too late. A thin silver sword is driven into my shoulder. I howl in pain and stumble back. The sword levitates in the air, but I don't see the—oh yeah, obviously I cannot see the invisible man holding it.

The sword points at me, challenging me to a fight. I accept the challenge with a low growl. The sword floats toward me, but from behind the invisible man, Aji charges into the cabin and jumps onto him. They both hit the ground and tumble across the cabin floor. As they fight, the invisible man slowly becomes more visible.

I can see him, but it's like he's behind a fogged-up window. He resembles a Spanish conquistador, the kind that brought diseases to the Americas way back in the day that killed millions of the Native people.

"Untie Orenda," Aji shouts to me as he tries to hold the conquistador off.

I rush over to Orenda and bite through her ropes. Once freed, she sits up and shouts, "Aji!"

I turn around and see the conquistador driving his sword into my brother's chest. The sound of a helicopter crashing into the ground and exploding fills the room. Anger fills my entire wolf being. Aji's furry squirrel body drops to the ground, dead, and slowly turns into my brother in human form. But he's not moving.

The invisible man smiles and lifts his sword. The tip of the blade red and dripping my brother's blood. I growl and slowly ready my body to attack.

I pounce. He swings his sword, but I leap over it. It grazes so close to me that it slices some of my fur off. In midair, I see the sliced off chunks of my fur float off of my body and dissolve into tiny numbers.

That was close. My body collides with the invisible man, and I immediately sink my teeth into his right shoulder. We both hit the ground, and I drag him across the floor with my powerful jaws. He screams in pain as I bite down until his bones crack between my jagged wolf teeth. Blood pours out, and I move my mouth toward his neck. I clamp down and violently shake until there's nothing left in between my teeth. The conquistador's head rolls away, and his lifeless body goes limp and lies in his growing pool of blood.

I turn to see Orenda, but the bed is empty. Where did she go? I look around but can't find her.

"I'm free," she says from above me.

I look up and see <u>O</u>renda with her giant butterfly wings fully spread out. My jaw drops. She's beautiful. Her wings are red, black, and yellow. She flutters down to me and wraps her wings around me like thick blankets enfolding a cold puppy. I immediately feel warm. She kisses me. My eyes close.

My eyes open. I'm back into my room. I fell asleep. What a strange dr<u>e</u>am. I sit up and try to hold on to the taste of her kiss before it fades away completely. This dream felt so real. I even check my hands to make sure they're not wolf paws. I think of my brother and how he died saving my l<u>i</u>fe. I think of Orenda and how I fought and killed the invisible man to save her. And then I think of what she was, a beautiful butterfly.

I look over at my window and see the night sky. Oh no, I slept all day!

I leap out of bed and rush over to Orenda's tree house. My feet move so fast that I nearly fall off the ramp as I scale it. When I enter, I see that it is completely candlelit. And I'm not the only one in here. The tree house is full of people. My mom and Ronnie stand near the wall where her paintings used to hang. My grandma and Seven are both sitting on the floor facing her bed. Her dress is now black. Foxy sits at the foot of her bed, with his hands clasped together, supporting his chin. And there's one more person in here. The old Native American man who gave me the test in the teepee. Yeah, the test I failed.

He is pacing back and forth like a wil<u>d</u> tiger, chanting <u>w</u>ords that I assume are Ojibwe. In his hands are a small drum and stick. He beats them softly, but it still somehow manages to vibrate the entire room. Everyone but the old man is looking at me.

"What's going on?" I ask to anyone who will hear me.

But no one answers. Instead it is Orenda who locks her eyes on me, luring me forward. I walk to her. My heart beats louder than the drums with every step I take. I sit down beside her. She looks exhausted but somehow still happy. I can't believe this. Everyone was up here with Orenda while I was sleeping peacefully in my room.

"Why didn't anyone come get me?" I ask the group.

The drums stop, and a very old wrinkled hand rests on my shoulder, but I don't take my eyes off of Orenda, not even for a second.

"You had to finish your dream," the old man says to me.

My eyes begin to well up. I remember Orenda's last words to me before she kissed me. *I'm free.*

"Twenty-three," I say under my breath.

I hate that my brain made me count his letters. Right now is the worst time for this. Right now is the worst time for all of this. Everyone is acting like this is goodbye. But it can't be. Not yet. I'm not ready.

"Can someone please tell me what is going on?" I ask again, louder this time. And as much as I don't want to hear the answer, I also need to.

But again, no one answers me. I turn around toward my mom to plead with her, but when I look back, everyone is gone. I'm alone in the tree house with Orenda. Even Foxy is gone. I rub my eyes, because this cannot be. But somehow, they all disappeared. The hairs on my arms rise up. The little flames from the candles all sway left, then right, and flicker.

"That's impossible," I say to myself as I check for a third time that no one is in here with us.

When I turn back around to Orenda, she sits up and smiles. Her movements are alive again. Even her skin is flushed from the sickly pale color back to the tone of fire.

"Is this real?" I ask her.

Her mischievous grin—the one I missed so much—wraps around my heart, and she reaches out her arm, placing her hand on my cheek.

"Everything is real, you dork," she says.

I grab her hand and pull it to my dorky mouth. I kiss all five of her fingers. If this isn't real, then I don't ever want to be real again. I want to stay right here, with her, in this make-believe world forever.

"I don't want you to go," I say, my voice cracking on every other word.

"I can't stay a caterpillar forever."

"I'm not asking you to stay a caterpillar. I'm asking you to stay with me," I say, and feel rivers running down my cheeks.

And like we were one, tears now fall down her cheeks to match me.

"It's time for me to spread my wings and fly," she says to me.

"No. I can't lose you. I won't lose you."

"Then don't. Keep me here, forever," she says, and reaches out, placing her hand over my heart.

I drop my head down and stare at her hand. It pulses from my heartbeat. My whole body is beating in its rhythm, and now hers is, too. I lift my head up and stare into her fiery eyes.

"I love you," I say, realizing this is the first time those three words have ever left my mouth. "From the bottom of my heart to the top of my lungs, I love you," I say again.

She closes her eyes like a door, almost slamming shut. And after a few seconds, her eyes rise, like the same door being swung back open. Her mouth opens too, and out falls the four words that make life worth living.

"I love you, too."

And the moment her sentence leaves her mouth, a pair of

butterfly wings unfold and spread out of her back. They are the exact wings from my dream. My eyes open so wide that they nearly fall out of my face. She flutters her beautiful wings and slowly lifts out of her bed. I can't believe what I am seeing. Orenda is flying. Orenda is a butterfly. All of this was real. Everything she said was the truth.

She flutters over to her open window, but before she flies out of it, she turns to me one last time.

"You know where to find me," she says, and flies out of the tree house and into the night.

I run up to the window and look outside. But Orenda is gone.

CHAPTER THIRTY

-《◆》-·-《◆》-·

THE ULTIMATE
SEASON

There is a knock on my door. I open my eyes. I'm in my room. I'm so confused right now. My face is soaking wet, and I thought I was just in the tree house looking out the window, trying to see Orenda flying away. Was this all a dream? Again?

My mom opens the door. I can see the sadness in her eyes, but she doesn't speak just yet. She doesn't quite know how to say what she has to tell me.

"What is it?" I ask.

"It's Orenda. You need to see her now," she says as Ronnie appears from behind her and puts his arms around her.

"Twenty-seven. She's still here? It was just a dream?" I say, and launch out of my bed.

"She's waiting for you, son," Ronnie says in a sad version of his voice.

"Twenty," I say, and rush past them, out of my room and toward the backyard.

I slide the glass door open and run through my yard, squeeze through the fence, and race up her tree house ramp. But inside, no one is here. Wait. Where is she? Where is everyone? I look out the window and see Ronnie and my mom looking up at me through our backyard.

"She's in her room," my mom shouts to me.

"Thirteen," I shout back, and sprint down the ramp and into her house.

I rush through her house and open her bedroom door. And just like my dream, everyone is in there. My grandma sits with Seven. Foxy sits at the foot of her bed. The old Native American man beats his drum while chanting hymns in his mother tongue. Even Ronnie and my mom enter the room behind me. And again, the bedroom is lit by candles placed throughout the room just like in my dream.

Wait! In my dream Orenda died. Is that why we are all here? Is this the time for all of us to say our goodbyes? It can't be. Dreams aren't real! Right?

"I just dreamt all of this," I say aloud for everyone to hear.

The old Native man stops his drum and turns to me, once again putting his wrinkled hand on my shoulder. "We know. The truth comes to us in dreams," he says.

"What truth? That she has ALS? That her body is shutting down? That she's dying?" I ask, barely holding in my tears.

"Is that what your dream showed you?" he asks.

"Twenty-eight. No. In my dream she became a butterfly," I reply.

Foxy lets out a huge sigh of relief. I shoot my eyes toward him. He looks at me, gets up, and hugs me. "Thank you," he says, and squeezes me so tightly I wince.

"It was just a dream. Right?" I ask him.

Foxy doesn't respond. Instead, he releases me, and I sit beside Orenda. But she isn't lively like she was in my dream. She's not moving at all, other than her forced breathing.

Her eyes are half open and half closed. I reach out and take her hand into mine. I stare at her face and remember how much she has taught me. I remember her laugh. I remember her hitting me in the head with a baseball. Our first kiss. Our last kiss. I remember everything.

Suddenly, all the lit flames from the candles begin to flicker and sway. The old Native man begins his chants in Ojibwe. I hold my breath and hope for Orenda to sit up, please sit up. Please smile. Please talk to me just like in my dream, but she doesn't. She lies there still, barely able to stare up at me. I keep waiting to see a pair of beautiful butterfly wings sprout out of her back, to witness her take flight, but it won't happen this time. I know it won't. I want to beg her to stay. I want to tell her how many more adventures we have ahead of us. I want to tell her how we can still rage against the night together. Like the brave rebels we are. But what comes out of my mouth shocks me.

"You're free," I say to her.

A small tear escapes her nearly sealed eyes. Mine, however, run down my cheeks like wild horses. And then it happens. I watch Orenda's chest rise up one last time, then it falls.

Orenda has taken her last breath. My words are true. She is now free.

I collapse and cry into her chest. I tell her I love her as many times as my mouth allows me to. I tell her that I'd trade my own life for her heart to start beating again. And through my howling, I hear my mom weeping behind me, followed by Ronnie's strong hand resting on my shoulder.

I lift my face off of her body and turn to them. My mom is

embracing Foxy. And as defeated as I feel, I can't help but think about him. All his pain. His world just ended. He lost both of his hearts. It is more than any man should bear, but for his wife and daughter, he'll force himself to survive this heartbreak. He'll live on, for them.

It is what they'd both want, and he knows it. We all know it. We all know she wants us to not be sad about death, but to be happy about life. She taught us that. Orenda was the most happy and alive person I have ever met, and she's been secretly dying this whole time. If that's not what true bravery is, then true bravery doesn't exist.

The old Native man stops his drum and approaches me. His wrinkled hand reaches out, and through my peripheral vision, I see it and grab it. His bones feel weak and brittle under his loose and stretchy skin. I look up and stare into his swollen eyes.

"Tomorrow, you will come see me," he says, and begins his drumming again.

"Twenty-four," I say under my breath, but I doubt anyone heard me.

I look back to Orenda's beautiful face, and suddenly everything around her begins spinning. I close my eyes to stop the room's rotation, but that just makes it worse. It takes every ounce of strength within me to leave her side and rise to my feet, and as I do, everything stops.

"Mama?" I call out.

The entire world stops. Everything goes black.

All I remember next is hearing a very loud thud.

CHAPTER THIRTY-ONE

- «◆» - «◆» -

MEMENGWAA

I don't exactly know who carried me to my bed last night, but I suspect it was Ronnie. He even took my shoes off and tucked me in. For a moment, I hold on to the hope that everything that happened last night was just a nightmare. That Orenda is still alive, but my hopes are shattered as I sit up and feel the pounding in my skull. By the size of this hematoma on the side of my head, I must have had quite the fall.

Seven is still asleep, and I finally have a chance to get a good look at her. Lately, I've been so preoccupied that I haven't really given Seven much attention at all. And I must say, she's put on a lot of weight. My grandma must feed her a lot during their adventures. As my feet hit the floor, Seven wakes and raises her head.

"You can keep sleeping, girl," I say to her, and she lowers her head as if she understood me perfectly.

I still feel weird as I walk. Like I've somehow been out of my body for so long that I've forgotten how to use it. I start with simple steps. One foot in front of the other. Left, right, left, right. And don't forget to breathe. I open my bedroom door and walk down the hallway.

Ronnie is in the kitchen making breakfast. He's even wearing an apron that's way too small for him. If I wasn't so down, I'd point out to him how ridiculous he looks, but instead, I approach my mom, who sits at the table and looks as <u>hurt</u> as I feel. I wrap my arms around her, and she stands up and hugs me back. We both don't break away for what feels like minutes.

"You don't have to go to school today, but you're gonna have to go back at some point," she says.

"I know. But there's somewhere I need to go first. Can you take me somewhere?"

"Of course. Where are you going?" she asks.

Even Ronnie stops what he's doing to hear my response.

"In my dream Orenda said, 'You know where to find me.' So I have to go and find out."

"Find out what?" Ronnie asks.

"If all of this is real," I say, and snatch the keys off of the counter and toss them to my mom.

I rush back to my room and put my shoes on. And even though just moments ago I wanted to curl up in a ball and wither away from sadness, I feel a newfound hope inside me. Maybe there is still a chance that everything Orenda said and did was not some fabricated fairy tale Native Americans tell themselves to make life on earth a bit better.

I need to be brave. Maybe there is just as much truth to their stories as they believe there is. I mean, if my time here with her has proven anything, it is that magic does exist. Why can't she be magic, too? Orenda was the wisest person I have ever met, and maybe I haven't even begun to scrape the surface of how deep her wisdom truly goes.

I hop into the bed of the truck. Ronnie sits passenger, and he must really want to find out too, because he hasn't even taken the apron off yet. My mom starts the truck and drives us out of the reservation. As we enter the highway, I realize I haven't told mom where to go exactly, but she is heading the right way. She must know. She must have done this drive before to see Orenda's mom.

As we turn off the road and into the forest, I take notice of all the clouds swimming above me in the deep blue sky. I smile as their shapes change from puffy clouds to animals. I shout them out so every animal in the sky can hear me. There's an albino alligator upper left. A silver-clouded potbellied pig upper right, a white-tailed deer directly above me, and in the sky's dead center, we drive under a giant white puffy turtle. If these clouds can shape-shift into animals, then maybe us people can too. Seriously. Why not? This world is full of unexplainable things.

We exit the forest and arrive to the bluff that overlooks the green field. My mom pulls over and stops.

"I'll be right back," I tell Ronnie and my mom, and I hop out of the truck.

The wind pushes against me as I walk toward the edge of the bluff. It's hard being here. The last time I was here was with Orenda, and the moment I picture her in my mind, I begin to taste her peachy kiss on my lips.

I stop at the edge and look out at the beautiful green clearing of grass and flowers before me. There's the colorful garden. It's just as breathtaking as it was when I first saw it. I feel the annoying buildup of salt water rising from the gutters of my eyes. But I don't want to cry. I just want to be here. I just want to know.

"Orenda?" I shout as loudly as my lungs will allow.

I hear her name echo off of every blade of grass below, bouncing off every rock and ricocheting off of every animal-cloud in the sky. I listen to my voice until it gets so far away and so faint that it disappears completely.

I drop to my knees. If I was a weak man, all I'd need to do is lean forward. That would end it all. I'd plummet to my death and never have to cry over Orenda again. But I'm not weak. Not anymore. Orenda made me strong. Orenda taught me how to be brave.

So I stay upright, raise my head toward the garden, and shout her name again.

As her name trails off to oblivion, something changes. There is a shift in the air, and an invisible wave of calmness rushes past me, causing all the tiny hairs on my body to stand. I look back at the truck. My mom and Ronnie must see what I feel, because they are both wide-eyed, staring past me.

I turn around to see what they see, and before my eyes, the beautiful kaleidoscope of butterflies launches up from the bed of flowers and flutters toward me. I stand perfectly still as they dance around me, circling me, greeting me.

I stretch out my arms and let the butterflies rest on my skin. Soon I am fully covered by them. They don't speak to me, but I don't need them to, I know what they are telling me. After all, it's why I am here. They are telling me Orenda is coming. I know this because I truly believe it now.

I am exactly where she said I would find her. I am here. And her butterfly family is here with me. Now all I need is her.

I've always needed her. I needed her to not fix me, but to change me. And not into a butterfly, but from a scared little boy with counting issues into a brave Native American warrior who is no longer afraid to live life to the nth degree.

In perfect unison, the butterflies covering me all lift off from my body and flutter above me. They form a circle above my head, like a swirling rainbow. I feel like I weigh nothing. Like I'm a cloud or maybe just part of the cold breeze. At this very moment, I am a part of nature, just like everything around me. I am one with this world. And it's beautiful. I see beauty. I hear beauty. I smell beauty. I even taste beauty. All around me.

From the garden rises a single butterfly. Its wings shimmer red, then black, then yellow. She dances through the air toward me. I hold my breath.

She reaches me and hovers in front of my face, staring directly into my wide human eyes. I know it's her. I know this beautiful butterfly is Orenda, the girl I love. I reach out my hand, and she floats onto it, resting on my fingertip. We stare at each other, and I can feel the love between us. It's the same feeling I had every time I was near her.

"Orenda," I say.

She flaps her wings six times. I smile. Clever girl.

And as we gaze deep into each other's eyes, I feel my broken heart slowly begin to piece itself together. Right then and there, I know everything is real. Our love. Magic. Everything she said. Everything I felt. Everything.

After my heart is fully repaired, she lifts off of my finger, dances her way up to my nose, kisses it, and flies up above me to join her butterfly family.

They circle me one more time, then the entire kaleidoscope flies back down to the garden and disappears into the colorful flowers. I stand and watch the flowers sway with the breeze for another minute or so, and when I turn back to the truck, I see Foxy standing directly behind me, watching me. In his hand is a bag full of peaches.

"You know what this placed is called?" he asks.

"Twenty-nine. No."

"Memengwaa."

I don't know how to count this word. And I'm not even going to try. He must see the strain in my eyes as I wrestle with my brain.

"Nine," he says. "It means 'butterfly' in Ojibwe."

"That makes sense," I say, which causes him to smile.

"Did you see her?" he asks.

"I did."

He smiles and walks up to me and pats me on the back. "Good," he says, and stares out toward the garden.

I look past my mom's truck, but don't see his. I don't see anything but forest in the direction he came from.

"Do you need a ride home?" I ask.

He doesn't turn to me, he just keeps his eyes forward, waiting.

"No thanks. I'm meeting my family soon," he says, and takes a bite of one of the peaches from the bag.

I'm not really sure what to say after that, so I decide to say nothing and leave him there, awaiting his family. I walk back to the truck and see my mom and Ronnie, both staring at me, smiling. I hop in the bed and give them a tap on the side of the truck. I'm ready to go home.

As the truck begins to pull back onto the road, I look back and see two butterflies rise from the bluff and land on Foxy's outstretched arms. He drops to his knees and howls up to the sky. His voice is strong and loud. He'd make a great wolf.

We enter the forest and head home. As we pass tree after tree, I can't help but realize that I once thought all these trees were the same. They were normal. They weren't special. But now I see everything differently. Maybe I stare through Native American warrior's eyes now. Everything looks different to me now. And everyone looks different to me now. Like these trees. Each one is unique. Some are thick, some are thin, some are smooth, some are rough, some are strong, some are weak, some are old, and some are young. We are just like these trees. And right now, I feel like an entire forest. I was sad, but now I'm not. I was afraid, but now I'm brave. I was alone, but now I have a family. Orenda was a human girl, and now she's a butterfly . . . But she's still Orenda.

She may look different now, but that's okay. Orenda was always different. That's why I fell in love with her.

CHAPTER THIRTY-TWO

-《◆》-·《◆》-

THE WOLF WITHIN

They say you shouldn't mourn someone's death but celebrate their life. I always thought that saying was mostly crap. But I totally get it now. The Native Americans had it right all along. Death isn't the end, it's just a graduation to the next world. Death is just a staircase. A step toward a new life, a new chapter. It's genius if you think about it. It is a truth most people have forgotten. Our family members die and return to the earth in new bodies. It should force us to treat all people and animals like family, with kindness. After all, we will be them, and they will be us.

The moment I walk into the house, the phone rings. I believe this is the first time I've heard it ring since I've arrived here. I have to follow the sound just to know where the phone is located.

"Hello?"

"Collin?" a familiar voice asks.

Whoa. It's my dad. I go speechless for a few moments, and I'm not really sure why.

"You still there?" he asks.

"Nineteen. Yeah. Hi, Dad."

"How are you?"

"Nine. I'm . . . really good."

"Really good? Wow. That's really good."

We both stay silent. The awkwardness between us floods back. We never knew how to communicate with each other.

"Twenty-eight. How are you?" I ask.

"You know me. I always fall, but I always land on my feet," he says.

"Forty-two. I like it here. A lot."

"That's great. Told ya you would," he says.

"Twenty-four. Seven's getting fat."

He laughs. "Listen, I wanted you to know that I made a lot of changes in my life. I quit drinking. And I'm trying this whole online dating thing. I guess what I'm saying is, I want to be a better person," he says, and knowing him, this was not an easy thing for him to say.

"That's awesome, Dad. Good for you."

"And to be a better person, I'd like to start with being a better dad."

"Fifty-two. Okay. That should be a lot easier for you with me being over here and you being over there."

"I'm sorry, Collin," he says. "For everything."

"Twenty-six. It's fine."

"It's not fine. I didn't know how to be a dad. I didn't know a lot of things I should have," he says.

"Sixty-four. Apology accepted. Really. Moving me here was the best thing that's ever happened to me."

"Great! So . . . I did something right?"

"Twenty-five. You did. I'm happy. I box now."

"What? You box? Like jab-jab-cross box?"

"Twenty-eight. Yep. I'm pretty good too."

"That's great, Collin. And I was hoping . . . that maybe us being farther apart, can maybe bring you and me closer. I'd love to finally get to know you."

As his letters bounce around my head and morph into numbers, something in the backyard catches my eye. It's a squirrel. Not any squirrel, but a smaller version of the squirrel from my dream. It's Aji.

I walk over to the sliding glass door, and Aji leads my eyes over toward the fence. He stops at it and stares back at me, batting his tail, telling me to follow him.

"Collin?" my dad says, snapping me back to our conversation.

"One hundred and seventeen. Dad, that sounds good. I'd love for us to get to know each other, but right now, I need to call you back," I say, and hang up the phone.

I slide open the door and walk out into the backyard. Seven is there, lying on the ground, being all fat. Aji is now on the fence, looking at me, making little squirrely noises.

"Aji?" I say, and he darts into Orenda's yard. I try to follow, but I can't. The opening I made when I first arrived has been fully repaired.

I approach it and feel the wood, just to make sure I'm not losing my mind. Nope. It's fixed. I know Orenda's dad couldn't have fixed it. I just saw him miles away at the butterfly garden. I rush back into the house and go to my mom's room. The door is shut. I now know better than to barge in, so I tap on the door.

"Mom?" I shout through the door.

"Just a minute," she says.

Ha! They were naked, I knew it.

My mom opens the door. Her hair is disheveled, and she's wearing one of Ronnie's tight shirts, which is so large on her, she could swim in it. Ronnie stands behind her, shirtless and wearing a victorious grin.

"Did you guys fix the fence?" I ask.

"No," she says, and looks at Ronnie.

"Don't look at me. I fixed one last week."

I point at her: "Two." And point at him: "Twenty-nine."

"Did Grandma?" I ask.

"It wasn't her," my mom says.

"Where is she? I'll ask her," I say.

"Oh, baby, she went home," my mom says, and touches my arm.

"What do you mean? This is her home . . . isn't it?"

"She visited us to meet you. She'd never pass on the chance to meet a grandson," she says.

"Visited us? Where does she live?" I ask.

My mom looks at Ronnie, then looks back at me.

"Collin. My mother died many years ago," she says.

What? That's impossible. I know that word doesn't mean much nowadays, especially here in Minnesota, but there's no way I've been hanging out with a spirit this whole time. I mean, she's been taking my dog out for walks!

"No. You're joking," I say.

"I would never joke about such a thing," she replies.

"But how . . . I mean . . . I saw her . . . I talked with her . . ."

My mom smiles. Ronnie sidesteps her and puts his hand on my shoulder. It's kind of his go-to move with me.

"Collin, you should have seen me when I first found out. It was over dinner. She was sitting right next to me. I tell you, our people are unpredictable. They're wild and absolutely beautiful, and sometimes beautiful things don't always need an explanation," Ronnie says.

I don't know what to believe anymore. I mean, I am fully certain that Orenda has turned into a butterfly, so I don't know why my grandma being a ghost is that far of a stretch for me.

"Are you two real?" I ask, which causes them both to burst into laughter.

"Everyone is real. But yes, Ronnie and I are both alive," my mom answers.

"So has Seven been walking by herself this whole time?"

"No. My mother's spirit walked her. You know us Native people, we love our animals," she says.

Ronnie laughs and plants a kiss on her cheek.

"You are both so strange."

"The best ones are," Ronnie says, and kisses her again.

I need to get out of here before their kissyness gets out of hand.

I turn to leave, but my mom grabs my arm. "Don't forget about your test tonight," she says.

I almost did forget. So much has happened since last night. I have a date with the old man in a teepee.

My mom, Ronnie, Seven, and I are all piled into the pickup truck on our way to my test. We drive through the pitch-black forest and enter the dirt lot. I'm nervous. I hope I don't fail the test again.

There's no crowd this time. No fire. No dancers. No rows of cars. It's just us.

As we all exit the car, Seven hops down and takes off running into the darkness.

"Seven!" I shout, but she disappears into the blackness.

"Let her go. She'll be back," my mom says, and takes my hand.

"Nineteen," I say, and walk with her.

Ronnie takes her other hand. When we get to the teepee, Ronnie and my mom wait outside of it, which is my hint to venture in. So I do. And just like last time, the old Native American man sits cross-legged before the fire. I take a seat on the other side of the flames. His eyes are open, but he doesn't look at me yet.

"I'm back for my test," I say.

He smiles, which adds twenty more wrinkles to his face.

But also, just like last time, instead of responding, he claps his hands together, once, loudly.

And within seconds, the same four robed people enter the teepee, each holding a pair of tongs. I now can't help but wonder if these four people are ghosts. Am I surrounded by spirits? And just like before, gripped in each tong is a different color stone. I remember all of this perfectly. They kneel down beside the fire and place each stone into the fire. The stones sizzle and send clouds of smoke into the teepee. The heat engulfs my body. It feels hotter this time.

Then, the four spirit people leave us without saying a word. Silence ensues.

"There is still a battle within you," he says.

"Twenty-eight. It's really hot in here. But I bet you're just gonna tell me to become the heat again, right?

"Yes," he says.

"Three. And that still doesn't make sense."

And like clockwork, he waves his arms in front of me, mixing his hands with the orange flames. I still haven't figured out how he is not burning right now.

"Close your eyes," he says to me.

"Thirteen," I say, and close my eyes.

"Do you see the battle inside you?" he asks.

"Twenty-six. I see nothing. Just . . ."

As I look through the familiar blackness, I find myself standing inside my mind again. This time, I know what to do. I'll repeat my steps from last time and go find that wolf waiting for me somewhere deep in my mind. I take a step forward.

"Hello?" I shout, and hear my own voice echo through my mind.

As I walk forward, I hear the same faint whimper. So I break into a run. And as I get closer, it gets louder—and louder. And then I see it. The wolf. It still looks just as large and just as angry. It growls and drools when it sees me approaching, locking its black eyes onto mine. Its fangs, coated with saliva, shine white through the darkness, revealing how sharp each tooth is.

I stop and feel my heart beating through my chest. I was hoping I wouldn't be as scared this time around, but I am. I try to breathe slowly, but fear keeps my breaths uneven. The thick heavy rope is still tied to the wolf's back leg.

This is where I'm supposed to look down and see that Orenda's knife is in my hand. So I do, and so it is. The wolf growls and steps toward me. As it moves, black numbers and letters shimmer in its fur. Last time I failed this test. I need to think differently this time.

"Fear ceases to exist once you confront it," I say to myself.

I study the wolf closely. Am I afraid of this wolf? Yes. But that's okay. I remember what Orenda told me. It's okay to be afraid; it's even okay to be very afraid, but it's never okay to be too afraid. I need to be brave. I need to focus more on my courage and less on my fear. That's it. I will not be afraid of this wolf . . . Then it hits me. Maybe it's not actually the wolf I'm afraid of, but the numbers it's covered in? I've been afraid of those numbers my entire life. And in my dream, where I saved Orenda . . . I was the wolf . . . In fact, I was this wolf! The wolf covered in numbers. That's it! It all starts to make sense to me. The battle within me. I am the wolf.

"I am the wolf," I shout as loudly as I can.

My voice drifts far out into the sea of black. And as soon as I say it, the fear inside of me is gone. I know what to do. I need to free myself from this prison in my mind. I'm not supposed to fight the wolf. Being brave doesn't always mean fighting. I'm supposed to help this wolf. I need to free it, to let it go. I take a step toward the wolf. It snaps its jaws.

"I'm not afraid—that means you're not afraid," I say to the wolf. It growls.

"As brave as a brave," I tell myself, and take another step forward.

I approach the wolf. It could easily kill me if it wanted to. But it won't, because it is me, and I don't want to die. It growls as I grab the rope attached to its leg. I raise the knife and pull the rope against the blade as hard as I can. The rope untethers and snaps. The wolf looks deep into my eyes, then howls to an unseen moon and runs off into the wild black forest of my mind.

The wolf is free. I am free.

CHAPTER THIRTY-THREE

-《◆》-·-《◆》-

I AM THE BRAVE

Everything is black. I can't feel the difference between down and up. I feel like I am floating through space. Then I feel a hard slap across my face. My eyes burst open. It jolts me back into the teepee. I'm lying down, with the old Native American man standing over me.

"Did you just slap me?" I ask, and sit up.

"I did," he says. "And quit thinking of me as the old Native American man. My name is Henry."

"That would have probably been my last guess at your name," I say, and rise to my feet.

I still feel a bit dizzy, but it wears off as I take a few steps out of the teepee. As I open the flap, I see my mom and Ronnie standing there, waiting for me. I can see the anticipation in their eyes.

"He passed," Henry says as he joins us outside.

My mom jumps up in pure joy and charges me. Her arms wrap around and squeeze me tightly. Ronnie watches us, smiling.

"How do you feel?" my mom asks me.

"I feel ... free," I say.

Her jaw drops. Even Ronnie is speechless. "What?" I ask.

Why are they looking at me like that? What did I do?

"Hello?" I ask.

"You didn't count my letters," she says.

I didn't? Holy crap. I didn't even notice. But she's right. I didn't count them. I didn't even feel the urge to. Oh my God! I wish Orenda were here. She'd be so proud of me.

"I'm free!" I shout up to the sky.

I can't wait to go back to school and not be afraid to make eye contact with anyone. I can't wait to talk to people. I can't wait to tell my dad. I need to tell Seven. Where's Seven? "Seven!" I cup my mouth with both hands and shout.

But I don't see her yet.

"There's another little surprise for you," Henry says, and snaps his fingers into the air.

And right on cue, two dogs run up to him. One is Seven, and one is a golden colored dog a bit smaller than she is.

"Who's this?" I say, and point to the golden dog.

"This is Papillon. He's a forest hound," Henry says.

Papillon walks up to me. I kneel down and let him lick my fingers. "Hey, Papillon. Were you taking care of Seven?"

"You can say that," Henry says, which makes Ronnie and my mom snicker.

"I don't get it. What's so funny?" I ask.

My mom kneels down and pets both dogs. "Seven and Papillon fell in love. And you see ... when two people fall in love—" she begins.

"Are you really giving him the birds and the bees talk right now?" Ronnie asks.

"Technically, it's the birds and the bees and the dogs talk now," Henry adds.

I stand up as the truth hits me. Oh my . . .

"That's why Seven is so fat now!" I say.

Ronnie laughs and looks at Seven. "No offense, girl."

"So, this is where Seven has been when my ghost grandma said she was taking Seven on an adventure. She took her to see Papillon."

"Yep. And there's no better adventure than motherhood," my mom says.

I wrap my arms around Seven, knowing exactly what she feels. Love.

"This family just got a whole lot bigger," Ronnie says, and extends his hand to Henry.

They shake hands. Staring deep into each other's eyes. There's a history between them, I can tell. "Thanks for everything, Henry," Ronnie says.

"Take care of them."

"I will," Ronnie replies.

"I was talking to him," Henry says, and points to me.

"Me?" I ask.

"Yes, you. Take care of Seven and Papillon. Take care of Ronnie and your mom. You're a brave now. And braves take care of their families."

"I will."

And as my family walks back to the truck, I can't stop thinking of the person I owe everything to. The person who believed in me, loved me, and showed me what it means to truly be alive. The bravest person I've ever met. The girl who fluttered into my life and changed everything.

CHAPTER THIRTY-FOUR

- «◆» - «◆» -

A DEAL IS A DEAL

One week later, I am in Orenda's tree house feeding her butterflies. It's something I plan on doing for the rest of my life, and it's actually gotten me pretty addicted to peaches.

Ronnie and Foxy came up with an amazing plan for this place. They are going to repaint this tree house and turn it into a playground for all the neighborhood kids. Ronnie is going to build a slide, and Foxy is going to add a jungle gym to it. It's pretty cool seeing how excited they both are about starting a new project. My job, well, since I'm so good at it, is to knock down the fence so all the kids can come play anytime they like.

I still think of her every day. I still draw her face at night, when I can't sleep. But sadness isn't what I feel when she enters my mind. I'm grateful. I was one of the lucky ones. I got to know Orenda.

When they removed her bed, Foxy found something under her pillow. A letter addressed to me. I haven't read it yet. I've been carrying it around in my pocket for days now, waiting for the right moment.

There's a full moon out, and we are supposed to get our first night of snow tonight. And even though that doesn't really mean much to me, I know it would be something incredibly special and magical to her. So, I'm going to read the letter now, with you.

I sit in the center of the empty room and pull it out of my pocket. My fingers are shaking. *THE BRAVE* is written across it in puffy letters, resembling our friends, the clouds. I unfold it.

Dear Collin,

If you are reading this letter, then my transformation from human to butterfly was a success. And your transformation from dork to brave was also a success. So, congrats to us, we did it.

There are a couple things I need you to know about being a true brave.

1. Keep reading! This is very important. I want every book in that garage to be read. It's the second best way to get to know people and understand people who are different from you. Also, it's an invitation into a world you never knew existed, and trust me, entering new worlds is super cool!

2. Talk! Even though you still know the exact number from everyone's words, you have now realized you no longer need to blurt it out. If you do it, it's because you want to, not need to. This achievement allows you to speak to anyone you choose to. So use this gift. Talk. Laugh. Ask questions. Give your opinion. Say hello to everyone you meet. This is the first best way to get to know people and understand people who are different from you.

3. Keep punching! Because let's be real, bullies suck, and even though you won't be the one being picked on anymore, someone else will be. And if you see some kid being bullied, intervene. And if the bully doesn't stop, make him stop. Sometimes, a good punch in the face is exactly what a bully needs.

4. Last but not least, don't mourn me. When you think of me, I don't want you to ever be sad. I want you to remember how much fun we had and how much we taught each other in our short but very special time together. Do not cry, but laugh. Laughing is food for the heart . . . that and peaches! Eat up!

If you live by these four rules, every day, then your training is over, and I have done my job. I promised you I'd help you win this fight, and like I told you on the day we met, I never lose. I will be watching over you, literally, to make sure you don't ever lose sight of your mission in life: to be a good human.

And being a good human is simple. All you have to do is treat everyone and everything like they were me. I will be in every butterfly, in every bird, dog, cat, cow, pig, fish, flower, tree, and stranger you meet. I will look different, talk differently, and believe differently than you remember, but it is still me.

So do not think you will never see me again. You will see me a million more times in a million different faces, because even though I have changed my body, I am still here. I will always be here. Your brother will always be here. We will be on the sidelines, cheering you on as you run this race we call life.

Never give up. Keep going. But keep your head up and eyes open. Because the beauty isn't reaching the finish line; it's seeing everything, everywhere, and everyone along the way. And when the day comes for your run to finally be over, I'll be right there waiting for you, ready to teach you how to fly.

Thank you for believing in me. But most of all, thank you for being you. I got to go now, my ride is here. ☺ I love you.

Your flutterby girl,
Orenda

P.S. Your grandma says hi.

A breeze shoots in through the open window and grabs the letter from my hands. I reach for it, but the wind is too quick, and I watch the letter dance around the room before riding out of the window on another strong gust. She was right. Her ride is here.

I watch the letter float across the windy sky and out of view. Tears begin to escape my eyes. They're not sad tears, not mournful tears, but tears of absolute excitement. For the first time in my life, I am excited about the future. I am excited for her to see me become the best version of myself I can be. I know being a good person won't always be easy. It may sometimes be painful and difficult, and it may take a whole lot of patience . . . But I'm a brave now, so I can do it.

And I know exactly what to do. I will tell the world about Orenda. I will write a book about our adventure together. I will show people that magic does exist. In all of us.

And that's exactly what I've done. I wrote her story.

Now you know her the way I know her. And you will never forget her. How could you? She's everywher<u>e</u>.

So, reader, remember in chapter three when we made each other a deal? Well, it's time for you to live up to your end. You ready? Here is what you have to do.

In every chapter of this book, there are certain letters underlined. When you collect each underlined letter, you'll find a hidden message I left for you. Once you reveal this message, you will be on your way to becoming as brave as me.

Your training begins now. Good luck.

Love,
Collin (THE BRAVE)

PS. Wanna know something cool? I have NO IDEA how many letters are in this book . . . Because I didn't count them. ☺

ACKNOWLEDGMENTS

Thank you to my brave kaleidoscope of butterflies that made this book what it is. My agent, Rosemary Stimola, who took a chance on me and never stopped believing in me. You are a precious gem I will forever treasure.

My wonderful editor, Liz Szabla, who not only made this a better book, but also made me a better author.

Thank you to everyone at Macmillan: Mallory Grigg, Madison Furr, Elizabeth Baer, and Foyinsi Adegbonmire, as well as Jean Feiwel and everyone at Feiwel & Friends for inviting me to be part of your family.

Muchas gracias a la maravillosa Beatriz (@Naranjalidad) por crear la preciosa portada de nuestro libro.

Thank you to my wonderfully wild family: Adriana Mather, Wolf, Anya, Mama, Sasa, Penny, Crimson, Amy, Dan, Peter, and all my Ojibwe fam across America.

My beautiful fur fam: Smeagle, Banana, Princess, Von, and Sheldon. We miss you, Noonoo.

Everyone at FAMB, and all the amazing authors who continue to inspire me, especially Anya Remi and Bridget Hodder. You all make the world a better place to write in. I will forever be grateful.

I also want to thank all the readers—without you our stories have no homes. Thank you for letting my characters live inside of you. Thank you for buying books. Thank you for keeping reading alive.

Thank you Los Angeles for raising me. Thank you Minnesota for teaching me. Thank you Massachusetts for welcoming me.

And lastly, thank you to all the Native American authors out there who continue to tell the stories of our blood. We were here yesterday. We are here today. We will be here tomorrow. Be brave. Fight on. Write on.